MARY ROBINETTE KOWAL is an author, professional puppeteer and voice actor. Mary currently lives in Chicago, Illinois. Visit www.maryrobinettekowal.com for more information about her fiction and her puppetry.

The Glamourist Histories

*Shades of Milk and Honey*
*Glamour in Glass*
*Without a Summer*
*Valour and Vanity*

# WITHOUT
*a*
# SUMMER

MARY ROBINETTE KOWAL

corsair

*For Rob*
*My Muse*

Constable & Robinson Ltd.
55–56 Russell Square
London WC1B 4HP
www.constablerobinson.com

First published in the US by Tor ®,
a registered trademark of Tom Doherty Associates, LLC, 2013

First published in the UK by Corsair,
an imprint of Constable & Robinson Ltd., 2014

A copy of the British Library Cataloguing in
Publication Data is available from the British Library

ISBN: 978-1-47211-017-6 (paperback)
ISBN: 978-1-47211-039-8 (ebook)

Printed and bound by CPI Group (UK) Ltd, Croydon CR0 4YY

1 3 5 7 9 10 8 6 4 2

# ONE

## *Birds and Snow*

Jane, Lady Vincent, could never be considered a beauty, but possessed of a loving husband and admirable talent, had lived thirty years in the world with only a few events to cause her any true distress or vexation. She was the eldest of two daughters of a gentleman in the neighbourhood of Dorchester. In consequence of her mother's nerves, Jane had spent the better part of her youth acting as mother to her younger sister, Melody. Her sister had received nature's full bounty of beauty, with all the charms of an amiable temper. At the age of twenty, it was therefore surprising to find Melody not only unmarried, but without any prospects.

Since Jane's marriage, she had rarely been to visit her parents, but finding herself there for an extended holiday visit, she had ample opportunity to observe her sister. While Melody still possessed the natural grace she always had, the bloom upon her cheeks seemed dimmed. Jane suspected that the unseasonable March snows, which kept so many families indoors, had limited the opportunities for the society that her sister so delighted in. If she could leave the house to take walks, perhaps that might have restored her humour, but in want of occupation, Melody had become afflicted with severe melancholy.

Jane knew all too well how the want of purpose could oppress even the brightest spirit.

And so Jane had taken it upon herself to host a card party, inviting all those neighbours who were willing to make the trip to Long Parkmead.

She expected this would delight Melody, but was surprised to find, upon glancing up from a game of whist, that her sister stood by the window, looking out at the snow. Her golden curls seemed to cry for sunlight quite as much as the daffodils, which peeked above the layer of snow outside.

Jane reached the end of her game and waited while she and her partner, her mother's friend Mrs Marchand, counted their tricks. Mrs Marchand was only too delighted to discover that they had nearly twice as many points as their rivals. Leaving her to triumph in their victory, Jane excused herself from the table upon the pretext of wishing to cool her temples by the window and went to her sister.

'Have you had much luck this evening?'

'Hm? Oh . . . some.' Melody pulled her shawl up around her shoulders. 'I won a round of lottery.'

She seemed disinclined to say more, where once she would have soliloquised about how many fish tokens she had won at the card game.

'And you are satisfied with that?'

Melody shrugged. 'My head aches.'

Knowing that the headache was a fancy of her sister's to explain away her lowness, Jane sighed. Her breath frosted the window for a moment. Struck by an idea, she leaned forward and blew on the glass. She drew a bird on the fogged pane. 'Do you remember when we tried to draw snowflakes in all the windows for Christmas?'

Melody shook her head, a single line appearing between her brows. Forcing a smile, Jane tried not to let the disappointment show on her face. It had been one of the treasured memories of her childhood. 'I suppose it is not surprising. I was thirteen, so you could have been no older than three, I think. You wanted to learn glamour but were too young to hold the folds. I showed you how to fog the glass and you went around ornamenting all the windows.'

'Little has changed then, since I still cannot work glamour.' Melody glanced over her shoulder. 'How is Vincent enduring the party?'

'Tolerably, though I had to rescue him from Mrs Marchand once, who tried to insist on his being the fourth for a hand of whist.' Jane wrinkled her nose at the thought of her taciturn husband being forced to sit next to their sociable neighbour. He now stood engaged in conversation with her father. Though he held her father in high esteem, Vincent still had an edge of tension to his stance, simply from being in a room with so many people.

'La! He is patience embodied.'

'I promised him that as soon as we perform the *tableau vivant* Mama requested, he can retreat under the pretence of fatigue.' An illusion such as a *tableau vivant* would not ordinarily be enough to tax the strength of a professional glamourist, but Jane was quite willing to take advantage of her mother's sometimes excessive imagination to offer her husband an escape.

'I declare, I do not know how you managed to attach such a hermit, but sometimes I am exceedingly jealous.' The shadow came back to Melody's countenance as she leaned forward to blow on the window. With a finger, she drew a simple snowflake. 'I almost remember, I think.'

'I look forward to wishing you joy.'

'You may hold that wish for a long time.'

'With your beauty? My dear sister, you were made to attach gentlemen.' Jane tried to tease her sister back into something like her natural spirits.

'Really?' Melody dropped her finger and turned to face Jane fully. 'Who should I attach?' She glanced toward the room filled with their friends and neighbours.

Standing with her sister made the room change in aspect, as though a glamour had been drawn over it. Where before Jane had noted the merriment and general air of pleasant conversation, she now attended to the individuals. The room seemed composed almost entirely of women, young and old. There were men, to be certain: Mr Prater, the old vicar; their father, Mr Ellsworth; Mr Marchand and his assembly of daughters . . . but there was not a single young bachelor. Once their neighbourhood had held several eligible gentlemen, but many of them had gone away to fight Napoleon and never returned. Others had left for different reasons.

Jane had thought that Melody's depression was due to being confined indoors, but her loneliness was of a far deeper nature than that.

The morning after the card party, Jane made her way down the hall to her father's comfortable study at the back of the house. He had always been a source of steady counsel for her, and she had hopes that he might have some thoughts on what to do for Melody.

Voices met her in the hall. She hesitated on the threshold of the study.

Mr Ellsworth looked up from a sheet of paper that he was

bent over with Mr Maulsby, the estate manager for Long Parkmead. 'Come in, Jane. We will be but a moment longer.'

She slipped into the leather wingback chair by the fire and made herself comfortable. She had known Mr Maulsby all her life and he had long been a good steward for her father's estate. Before him, Mr Maulsby's father had attended to the running of the fields and harvests and all the other things, which good English culture required. He was a tall man with a perpetual stoop to his shoulders, which Jane thought must come from spending so much time hunched over his papers or looking at the ground. His hair had silvered in time, like her father's, but remained as thick on his head as always. He nodded to her as she settled in her chair, but did not break his conference with his employer.

'I'll tell you true, Mr Ellsworth, I think we have to replant the south and east fields. The sprouts were just coming up when this hit and now they're black in the ground.' The manager tapped the paper with one nail-bitten finger. 'Perhaps the north-west one too, but that gets more sun because of the elevation, so it might be all right if the snow passes soon.'

'You are certain? No—no, I know that you are, or you would not come to me.' Mr Ellsworth sighed heavily and scratched his thinning pate. 'Well. Well. You had best order the seed, then, before the prices go up any further.'

'Yes, sir. That I'll do.' Mr Maulsby rolled up the paper. 'It's worse up north, I hear. The ground's not thawing at all. If this keeps up, we'll see food riots.'

'Let us hope, then, that the weather warms soon.'

'Aye, or we'll have troubles in the autumn bringing in the harvest.'

'We shall fret about that when it happens.' Mr Ellsworth

clapped the estate manager on the shoulder and saw him out. After the man had gone, her father stood in the door for a moment before sighing heavily. When he turned back to Jane, he had a smile on his face, which she was certain he wore solely for her benefit. 'What can I do for you, my dear?'

'I feel that I should ask the same of you.'

Mr Ellsworth grimaced. He glanced down the hall and shut the door. 'You will not tell your mother?'

She shook her head. Mrs Ellsworth was a good woman and not without understanding, but her worries sometimes carried her far beyond reason. Jane was well used to guarding her mother from things that would upset her without need.

Settling into the chair opposite her, Mr Ellsworth crossed his legs and stared into the fire. He was silent for some minutes, fingers moving across the arm of the chair as though he were plotting on the leather what to tell her. 'Well. Well . . . as you might have heard, the cold has killed our barley shoots. We can replant, but it is an expense I had not looked for.' He offered her a sorrowful smile. 'It will not ruin us. Others will not be so lucky. But there is still a cost, and I worry, as always, about making sure that my daughters are provided for.'

Jane reached over and took his hand. 'You know that I am provided for, at least.'

He chuckled. 'I am your father. One never ceases to worry.' He patted her hand. 'But—but you are correct. Melody is my chief concern. I will not need to touch her portion, or anything so severe, but in spite of my steward's brave words, I must plan as though this harvest might fail.'

'Do you think that likely?'

'No. But then, I have never seen it snow so late in the year. A flurry, perhaps, but we are very nearly in April and there are eight inches of snow upon the ground. I would be a fool not to consider how we might retrench if the harvest were to fail.' He shook his head and patted her hand again. 'Do not let your mother hear the word "retrench".'

Jane could well imagine the terrors her mother would create at any talk of practising economy. 'I promise I shall not.'

He released her hand to tend the fire. 'I had hoped to send Melody to London for the Season. She is . . .'

'Depressed.'

'Yes.'

Jane had the uncomfortable sense that her father was waiting for her to offer a cure for her sister's depression. She had none. 'Perhaps Bath? It is not so expensive, and might offer her some prospects.'

'Do you think? The last trip went so poorly that I fear a trip to Bath might revive her wounded sensibilities.'

Jane bit the inside of her lip. She had not considered that at all. The road to Bath was where Melody had lost all hope for the man she had loved. 'We are both resolved, though, that a change of scene would do her good?'

'Indeed.' Mr Ellsworth shifted his chair closer to the fire. 'But perhaps we are showing unnecessary alarm, and London will be possible after all.'

Outside the window, the snow continued to fall. Jane could not allow herself to hope that her father's optimism was correct.

# TWO

## *Weaving Invitations*

Jane entered the parlour carrying the morning mail, eager to show her husband the letter that they had received from London. She stopped in surprise in the doorway. The snow had ceased during the night, and the morning sun made a dazzling wave across the parlour. It cast Vincent's form into severe relief as he stood next to the fireplace, scratching his back against the corner of the mantelpiece. His eyes were closed and his brow furrowed in concentration. In spite of his blue coat of superfine wool, tan trousers and tall boots, Vincent looked like nothing so much as a bear come in for the winter. Jane half expected him to produce a honeycomb and begin eating it. She laughed, covering her mouth in delight at the image.

Vincent opened his eyes in alarm, springing away from the mantelpiece. He blushed charmingly. In an instant, his aspect changed from that of a bear to that of a schoolboy caught out. 'My back itches.'

'So I see.' Jane crossed the room and set the letters on the side table. 'If you remove your coat, I can scratch it for you.'

She helped Vincent shrug out of his coat, admiring once again her husband's fine form. How had a woman as plain as she attached such a figure of a man? She did not understand it, but any doubt she might have held of her husband's deep love for her had long since vanished. It was the source of her greatest happiness.

Jane curled her fingers and applied them to Vincent's back. Even through his waistcoat, she could feel the knots and ridges of scars where he had been flogged by Napoleon's men. They had healed without infection, thank heavens, but the cold weather often caused the new skin to itch.

He heaved a sigh of relief, leaning into her hand. 'Thank you, Muse.'

'Shall I fetch some liniment from Mother?' Jane managed to keep the smile out of her voice and offer the question with sincerity.

'No!' Vincent straightened, shuddering. 'I mean, thank you, but—' He turned to regard her and broke off as he saw the smile she had been unable to keep from her countenance. 'Muse. You are wicked at times.'

'Me? I thought you were the one who was not a nice boy.'

'But I am a nice man, whereas you are cruel and heartless.' Vincent rubbed his hair, mashing it against his head. 'Can you imagine what your mother would do if I were to actually admit of an infirmity? Even one so small as dry skin?'

Laughing, Jane wrapped her arms around her husband and pulled him close. Her mother was peculiarly good in a real crisis, but, in the absence of difficulties, tended to create them. A sliver could promote thoughts of gangrene. 'I promise that I will protect you from her remedies. When I go to town next, I shall pick up some liniment, though. Until then . . . turn around and let me continue.'

He complied, letting his head hang forward with a grunt of

contentment. Her bear had a sweetness beneath his grumbling exterior. 'You are very good to me. Even if you are wicked.'

'Hush.' Jane slipped her hand around his chest to brace him as she dug her fingernails into his back. He relaxed into her embrace, the warmth of his chest serving as a balm against the chill. Outside, the snow sparkled in the sunlight. With luck it would begin to melt soon, though that would leave the roads dirty and unpleasant for a while yet. 'Oh. I nearly forgot why I came in. We had a letter in the morning mail.'

'Is it Major Curry? I am wanting his answer to more than a few questions about percussion glamours.' The military glam-ourist had been assigned to tend to them while they recovered from the Battle of Quatre Bras, and had become a great friend due to his kind and attentive care. Afterwards, Vincent contin-ued to trade letters with him, comparing techniques that could be shared between ornamental and military glamours.

'It is a request to commission us.'

Vincent's head rose with curiosity. 'Anything of interest?'

After they had created the glamural for the Prince Regent's New Year's fête for the second year running, the Vincents had received scores of commission requests, but most had been from parties who could not afford them, or who lived in parts of the country they had no wish to visit, or were simply banal. Now, though, Jane was restless and wanted to be doing some-thing. 'I think so. It is from the Baron of Stratton – sent by Sir Lumley – which gives me hope that he has some taste. It is on the table if you want to read it yourself.'

Vincent lifted Jane's hand from his chest and kissed it, before pulling away to fetch the letter. He carried it to the window for better light and stood reading it, a shade against the snow. 'He offers excellent terms. I suspect Skiffy informed them.'

Jane still could not bring herself to call Sir Lumley St George Skeffington by his college appellation, but then he and Vincent had known each other through their connections at Eton so could be allowed that familiarity. 'Do you think he is trying to draw you to London?'

'Doubtless.' Vincent pointed to a line near the top of the paper. 'I must say that their notion of hiding a musicians' gallery behind a glamural of songbirds is appealing. I wonder . . . we might scatter birds throughout the room to carry out the theme.'

'Perhaps we could experiment with a variation on the *lointaine vision* to transfer the sound to other parts of the room so that the music comes from the various birds.'

Vincent canted his head to the side and stared into the middle distance with a look that Jane recognised, and she knew they were going to London. Vincent had already begun drawing plans in his head. Jane, too, had plans that she had begun sketching, but they did not involve glamurals – or, at least, not directly. Her plan involved her sister.

'Vincent . . . do you think we might take Melody with us?'

He straightened his head and regarded her. 'Would she enjoy it?'

'I think the change of scenery can only do her good, and her marriage prospects would be brighter with London's social season.'

'I suppose. But would she not prefer a husband who could keep her close to your family?'

'Who?' Jane waited for Vincent to see that there was no one in their neighbourhood with eligible sons.

He nodded slowly. 'Then, by all means, she should come.'

'Thank you, my love.' Jane traced a hand along his arm. 'Would you issue the invitation?'

Under Vincent's sleeve, the muscles of his arm tightened. 'Me? Would she not rather have it from her sister?'

'It would be natural coming from me, but I think it would mean more if it came from you.'

A minute whine of protest escaped him, as though he had imperfectly held his breath. He was, to the best of her knowledge, unaware that he made this sound when afflicted with contrariety. Jane had not enlightened him, as it proved useful to know with what he struggled. She waited as he thought, watching until the lines between his brow smoothed. He nodded. 'Of course. Though I shake at the thought of your mother's answer to our departure.'

'Particularly for a glamural.' Taking pity on her husband, Jane said, 'Well, I will relate that much, at least.'

'Thank you, Muse.'

With that settled, she helped him back into his coat and led him down the hall to the breakfast room, where the rest of the family still sat at table.

Mrs Ellsworth had a volume of correspondence before her from acquaintances likewise afflicted with nerves. Mr Ellsworth kept his newspaper up as a shield, making the occasional noise in answer to his wife's exclamations.

Melody had his discarded pages. As Jane and Vincent entered, she clipped an item from the paper – likely a description of London fashion. She alone glanced up. 'You look as though you have news.'

Mr Ellsworth folded his paper with interest. 'I suspect so, the way you hurried out with that letter.'

Smiling at her father's discernment, Jane nodded. 'Indeed. We have received a commission from the Baron of Stratton for his London house.'

'London?' Her father raised his brow. His gaze darted towards Melody, demonstrating a wish that she might accompany them.

Before Jane could reply, Mrs Ellsworth exclaimed, 'Oh! Oh, I do hope that you will decline it. I hardly see how it is possible, with your troubles. Sir David, say that you will not accept.'

Vincent shrank at the sound of his title. He had been simply Mr Vincent when he and Jane met, and seemed more comfortable that way, but he had become Sir David Vincent when he was raised to the honour of knighthood last year. He felt it was ostentatious and would have avoided the title altogether if he could, but one did not say 'no' to the Prince Regent. Jane had attempted to explain his preference to her mother, but he would always be Sir David to her.

Jane stepped in to save her husband. 'Mama, you must see that we have already been performing glamours.'

'But you should not try your strength so soon after your troubles. Indeed you should not. Why, last night, you were exhausted after a *tableau vivant*. What might a glamural do?' Mrs Ellsworth shook her head, the lace of her cap fluttering. 'I am shocked that you would attempt to work glamour at all. Who knows what could happen? Why, the house might explode!'

Vincent coughed and covered his mouth. Though she was used to her mother's hysterics, even Jane found it difficult to not laugh outright at this notion. 'That is hardly possible, as glamour is largely ornamental. If it could make something explode, then that technique would be used in the military.'

'But it does! What of Major Curry? And I do not see why, if coldmongers can make things cold, you could not make something explode.'

'Coldmongers may only chill things a few degrees, and it is

an—' Jane stopped herself from saying 'unstable', which her mother would misconstrue, '—a purely temporary effect.'

'No, no! *They* are what is making the weather so unseasonably cold. I have a letter here from Lady Worrick, who explains it all. She got it from a lecture in London by a Professor Van Reed. If that is the case, then I see no reason why glamour could not explode.'

'I am afraid the lady misunderstood what she heard. The thermal transference alone—' Jane broke off again, recognising the impossibility of Mrs Ellsworth comprehending the full scientific reasons that her fears were unfounded. The notion that coldmongers could affect the weather was so far from truth as to be ridiculous, and glamour causing explosions was even more so. While it was *possible* to warm things with glamour, the effort was so great as to be impracticable. Moreover, that form of glamour took an unhealthy toll on its practitioners, and resulted more often than not in death. No one used heat glamours for that very reason. But knowing her mother, invoking the mere hint of death would only serve to heighten her fears. 'You may trust me that coldmongers cannot affect the weather.'

Melody slid the paper she had cut out closer to Jane. 'I read something of that! Here it is: 'Though it is too much to state that the Worshipful Company of Coldmongers is the cause of the current weather, many educated gentlemen of our city have raised the question of whether they might be, at least unintentionally, the cause of the alteration in our climate.' She squinted at the page. 'Oh, but wait . . . the writer goes on to say that it is not possible.'

'There. You see, Mama?'

'What can a writer know?' Unrelieved, Mrs Ellsworth sank back in her chair. 'Oh! It is too much. And in your state!'

'My state is one of general health.' Jane glanced at Vincent, who shifted anxiously, as if he were about to quit the room. She had no wish to revisit the subject of her miscarriage. Vincent still felt it was his fault, when he had been as much a victim as she. Though it had happened eight months previous, it seemed as though her mother would fix on nothing else whenever Jane or Vincent picked up a thread of glamour. As they were professional glamourists, this presented a few challenges. 'Truly, I have been quite well for some time now.'

'But you are so pale. I cannot believe that you are in good health if you are so pale, especially with such an unhealthy flush to your cheeks.'

Melody laughed and set her paper down. 'La! She cannot be both pale and flushed.'

'But of course she can! Look at her, poor dear. I fear Jane's health will never be the same if she continues on in this manner.'

Jane said firmly, 'There will be no difficulty in going at once, as we are both quite well. Indeed, Mama, to decline a connection such as this would be to our detriment. Being in London during the Season has every advantage.'

Vincent cleared his throat. 'In fact, with the Season approaching, we were hoping that Miss Ellsworth might accompany us.'

'Oh.' Melody's blue eyes widened with astonishment. 'Oh!'

'Unless you do not wish to, of course.' Vincent offered her a bow.

'Not wish to? I should adore going to London above all else.' The anticipation already restored some of the bloom to her features.

The prospect of London appeared to affect the sensibility of more than one person in the room. Mrs Ellsworth clapped her hands together and bounced in her chair like a girl a quarter of her age. 'Oh! London in the Season! We shall have such a merry time.'

Beside Jane, Vincent emitted his trifling whine, audible only to her ears. Jane raised her hand to stop her mother's effusions. 'We had thought only to take Melody with us. You would not wish to leave Papa all alone, and he can hardly leave, with all the work to be done around the estate.'

'It is true, my dear. I would be intolerably lonely if you were to go as well.' Mr Ellsworth caught his wife's hand. 'It has been too long since we had the house to ourselves.'

'But she must have a chaperon! How can Melody go if I do not accompany her and protect her from improprieties?'

Jane smiled, more than ready with an answer for that objection. 'That is no trouble at all. As I am a married woman now, I am more than able to act as Melody's chaperon.'

She had the satisfaction of seeing her mother unable to protest. More to the point, Vincent stopped holding his breath.

It was nearly another month before they were able to make the move to London. There were terms to negotiate with the Baron, a house to rent, trunks to ship and finally their own travel arrangements to make. Though the snow had abated, the roads remained clogged with mud and would be slow going for a hired carriage. Even as the calendar had turned to April, the weather remained tenaciously chill. Snow still capped the hills as though it were January. It was a great relief when they clattered onto the London pavement and saw the great buildings crowd around them. Everywhere they looked, people thronged the streets, wrapped up against the cold.

Glass-front shops lined the roads and displayed their

merchandise to tempt passers-by inside. The more garish establishments had façades smothered in glamour to draw shoppers' attention. Grocers set out winter greens and squashes under awnings that dripped on the unguarded. Carriages, hacks and swells on horseback crowded the streets. Melody pressed her face against the glass and exclaimed at it all.

Jane leaned against Vincent with some satisfaction that the novelty had already begun to revive Melody's spirits. She had been to London before, but there is a distinction between coming as a child with one's parents, and arriving as a young lady who was Out for the Season. A very great distinction indeed. Jane's father had given her some banknotes before they left with instructions that she was to buy Melody some new dresses and any other fripperies she desired. This was a task that Jane would undertake with pleasure.

Their carriage slowed. Outside, Jane could hear a clamour of voices. After a moment, the driver turned the horses and drove them onto a side street. Through the window, she glimpsed the road they had been on. A mob of people clogged it, shouting and dragging a large wooden frame out of a building. A man raised a sledgehammer over his head and dashed it into the side of the frame.

'What is happening?' Melody changed sides of the carriage and gave the street her attention.

'From the looms, I would guess they are Luddites.' Vincent lowered the window and the unintelligible rumble became a roar. He leaned out to address the driver, but his words were lost among the voices of the crowd. After a moment, he pulled his head back in and fastened the window. 'Just so. He has another route that will take us around the disturbance.'

When they had been in London last, working on His Royal

17

Highness's commission, Jane could not recall this sort of disorder in the city, though she would grant that they had been busy the entire time. 'Is this common?'

'Not in the City. I have read of disturbances in the North, but did not know that they had been felt in London.'

Jane cocked her head. 'What are Luddites?'

'The followers of an imaginary man.' Melody leaned closer to the window. 'They claim to follow Ned Ludd, but there is no evidence that there is such a man. They are largely weavers who have lost their place to the new weaving machines, but others who oppose progress support them.'

Jane could not help but be astonished. 'How do you know that?'

'La! It was in the papers.'

As the carriage went over a bump, Jane swayed against Vincent's side. 'Those were looms, then?'

He nodded. 'I cannot be entirely unfeeling towards their complaint, but at the same time, we do live in the modern age.'

'I do not care for modern times, then.' Melody settled back in her seat with a decided flounce. 'If they make people act like madmen.'

'More than mere modernity can induce madness.' Vincent glanced out the window as the carriage turned onto a smoother street. 'Ah . . . this is ours. Look—'

Anything further he might have said was lost as Jane and Melody crowded to the windows to look out. The carriage filled with cries of 'That shall be our baker!' and 'What cunning hats!' and 'Is that a bookseller?'

'That is not just a bookseller; that is our home.' As the carriage pulled up in front of a handsome red brick building, Vincent opened the door and stepped out.

The façade was striking, with a total of five bays, three that projected slightly towards the street while the two end bays jutted forth almost like towers framing the building. The whole structure rose four stories above the foundation, with a multitude of narrow windows. The house had been divided into three addresses at some point, with the one in the centre being taken up by Beatts and Co., Booksellers, and the one to the right being occupied by McGean's Cloth, Laces and Ribbons. They were to occupy No. 80, on the left.

Jane and Melody followed Vincent out of the carriage as a footman came out to help the driver with the trunks they had brought with them from Long Parkmead. The housekeeper who came with the establishment met them at the door.

Mrs Brackett was an older woman with iron-grey hair pinned up severely.

'Welcome, Sir David, Lady Vincent.' Her gaze landed on Melody and she gave an approving nod, as though glad to have a young lady under her care. 'And Miss Ellsworth. It is a pleasure to welcome you to Schomberg House.'

Mrs Brackett led them through the front door into a wide marble hall. Even divided as the house was, it still opened on to parlours to either side and had a stair going up further. The small staff that had come with their terms for taking Schomberg House gathered in the foyer, at attention. With the house, they had acquired a cook, two housemaids and the added luxury of a footman who could double as a valet.

It was a smaller staff than they had at Long Parkmead, but more than Jane had managed when they last lived in London. Then, they had been so consumed by work that they had one small apartment and only kept a maid-of-all-work. Here, though, Jane planned to entertain when they were not working, in the hopes of finding a suitable match for Melody.

Her sister was alight with wonder, sighing over all the accoutrements of the foyer as though she had never been indoors before. In truth, the furniture the house came with was clean but a little shabby, as though the previous occupant had used it harshly in spite of Mrs Brackett's efforts. Still, the side tables had arrangements of evergreens in the absence of flowers, and the paintings on the walls were of very good quality.

'Thank you, Mrs Brackett. Would you see that our trunks are settled?' Vincent pulled off his greatcoat and handed it to one of the maids.

'Certainly, Sir David.' Mrs Brackett nodded to the staff, dispersing them back to work. 'Shall I show you to your rooms?'

'If you would do that kindness for Miss Ellsworth.'

The sound of her name called Melody out of her raptures over a folding screen in the corner. 'But what are you going to do?'

'I want to show Ja—' He paused and corrected his address in front of the staff. 'I have something to show Lady Vincent. You do not mind?'

Jane supposed that she would have to become used to calling him Sir David as well. If they were to use their position to make a good connection for Melody, then they could not continue to act as simple artisans. The staff would talk, and that news would circulate through society as gossip, even if no one admitted to gossiping with their valet or maid.

Melody shook her head and turned in place. 'I shall have quite enough to do with settling in. Oh, what a delight!'

With a short bow of thanks, Vincent motioned Jane to the next flight of stairs. She paused only long enough to make certain that Melody truly was comfortable before following him up to the first story and again to the second. They went up again to the third floor. Vincent paused outside a wide door. 'I hope you like this.'

Jane raised her brow in question.

In answer, he threw the door open. The whole of the top story was taken up with a wide room bright with skylights and surrounded by windows. The effect made it seem open and airy, as though they were outside. The broad wood beams of the floor were stained here and there with paint, but it did nothing to mar the sense of wonder that the room provoked.

'What . . . how? What is this? Vincent, why did you not tell me?'

He laughed and spun her around in a circle. 'When I was a pupil at the Royal Academy, a picture dealer had his establishment here. I visited many times.'

'You told me as much when we saw it on the list of properties to let. But the studio?'

'I wanted to surprise you. And look.' He led her over to a corner, where a tube projected up out of the floor. Atop it was a bell, with a string that ran down into the tube. 'Do you know what this is?'

Jane had only seen engravings, and never been in a house that still had a *bouclé torsadée* installed. 'A speaking tube? Truly?' In the 1740s, these had been all the rage in wealthy homes and allowed near instant communication within the household through the use of glamour. A long thread of glamour ran through the tube and could be set to spin, carrying sound from one point to another. Since the sound ran continually, a glamourist would have been stationed in an operator's booth in the servants' quarters to start and stop the *bouclé torsadée*.

Bells like this one signalled the glamourist. They had gradually fallen out of favour as the fashionable set realised that it was just as easy for the servants to eavesdrop as for them to send orders to the kitchen. Between that and the maintenance the glamour required to continue working, people had returned to using servants. The only vestige that remained in most of those homes was a system of bell pulls. Jane bent over the tube to peer down it. It had been filled in at some point, no doubt to prevent drafts. 'Did it still work in your college days?'

He shook his head. 'The glamour frayed long before the picture dealer took over the house. We toyed with trying to get it to work again, but most of the tubes were blocked, and the *bouclé torsadée* requires a clear line of sight to function. The operator's station is a linen closet now, but this artefact . . . It makes me think of what glamour *could* do, if we could but think of new methods to try.' He slipped behind her and wrapped his arms around her waist. 'Do you see the possibilities here, Muse? A place to practise our art uninterrupted. We might continue to explore glamour in glass.'

'Without fear of explosions?'

He chuckled and spun her in his arms. 'Well . . . perhaps none of glamour.' Vincent reached back with his foot and kicked the door shut.

# THREE

## *At the Crossroads*

The Baron of Stratton lived in an impressive house facing Whitehall. Rising four stories above the street, it had elegant Corinthian columns supporting the façade of the building. The good proportions continued on the interior, with a broad stair hall that rose to the first story. As they were led through the halls, the art and furniture gave every indication of a patron with excellent taste. This gave Jane significant relief, because it increased the likelihood that they would not be asked to create an insipid glamural.

Lord Stratton met them in a formal library and proved to be an older gentleman with thinning hair who ran to stout, though no more than might be expected of a man in his fifth decade. He smiled and greeted them with hearty enthusiasm, coming around his large desk to shake hands with Vincent.

'Well, you certainly waste no time. I appreciate that, so I will try not to waste yours either. Lady Vincent, would you prefer to wait here while I show your husband the ballroom?'

Jane was beginning to suspect that they would have this conversation with every client who commissioned them. 'Thank you, but no. It will be easier to do my work if I see the location as well.'

'Ah. Of course. Sir Lumley had mentioned that you assisted Sir David.'

Vincent, bless him, cleared his throat and corrected the Baron. 'My wife is my creative partner, not my assistant. We work in full concert on all of our designs.'

If this surprised Lord Stratton, he did not betray that beyond a slight rise to his brow. Instead, he bowed quite properly to Jane. 'You have my apology, madam, for the presumption. I should have known better, truly, as you will see when you meet my wife. She is also my partner in all things, and I commend you for what must be a happy marriage.'

Jane liked him better at once.

The ballroom to which they were led had been decorated with glamour in an older style. It had a profusion of poorly rendered cherubs in the corners, and fairly dripped with flowers growing in the most unlikely of arrangements. As was the fate of glamours, the various threads had frayed and degraded over time, leaving the illusions faded and thin like ghosts on the walls. This made the artifice of the glamour conspicuous, and seemed to be a postscript to the room, rather than an enhancement of its natural qualities. The modern vogue in glamour was one that endeavoured to present an authentic representation of nature, seen through an artist's romantic eye. As daily life kept people indoors, the practice of bringing the natural world inside, even in an illusion, gained popularity.

In the centre of the room, looking up at a musicians' gallery, stood an unprepossessing woman of middle years. She was above average height, with a figure grown thick, but still quite proud. Her hair was a cream colour that looked as if it had once been red. Upon hearing them enter, she turned, her face lit with a smile, blue eyes glimmering merrily. She came forward as their employer introduced them to Lady Stratton.

'So good of you to come. We have heard nothing but raves about you since we arrived in town and are so honoured that you are willing to work on our ballroom.' Lady Stratton tucked her hand under her husband's arm. 'Our son Alastar will be coming down for the Season, and we hope to have a number of balls when he docs.'

'This is a very agreeable room.' It was not a grand affair, and would hold no more than twenty couples plus any who chose to watch, but the proportions were pleasing and the floor was a fine polished hardwood. Beneath the faded glamour, large windows lined one wall to let in light, while the opposite wall had mirrors facing them. At the far end of the room, a little raised gallery waited for musicians to play from it. Two large crystal chandeliers hung from the ceiling.

They would have to design the work with care to avoid having their illusions refracted by the crystals.

Jane paced the length of the dance floor, making notes in her drawing book. They would sketch the design in paint first, then do a few small, rough renderings in glamour before beginning work on the final. She became aware of Lord and Lady Stratton watching her and made an effort at conversation. 'From where is your son coming?'

'Cambridge. Studying law. A fine boy. Very proud,' Lord Stratton said.

Lady Stratton beamed. 'I think you would be hard-pressed to find a more upright figure, though I must allow that I am partial. Alastar has a sturdy character and a quickness of understanding that I sometimes wonder at.'

Jane's curiosity was piqued by the mention of an eligible son.

If he was at Cambridge, then he could not be too much older than Melody. Perhaps she could contrive to bring Melody with them and make an introduction. *If* he were unmarried. 'Will he be bringing his family with him?'

'Ha! He is not yet married, more is the pity. That is why my lady wants to hold these balls.'

Insensible to anything save the details of their commission, Vincent walked to the balcony and looked up at it. 'How does one access the gallery?'

'There are stairs through . . . they are here somewhere.' Lord Stratton led the way to a florid shrubbery under the balcony and waved his hands through the illusion until he patted the wall. He made quite the strange picture, half in and half out of the glamour. It looked as though the bush had sprouted a head. 'Ah. Here it is.' He disappeared entirely as he stepped further into the shrubbery.

Jane followed him through the shrub, into a steep staircase. Tempting though it was to undo the glamour masking it immediately, she merely marked the stair on the plan of the room she was drawing. They would have to confirm that decision with their patrons before taking any action.

'Is there any other access?' She could hardly imagine a musician carrying a harp up that narrow flight, but perhaps they only used violin and flute.

'None that we can find.' Lady Stratton eyed the stairs doubtfully. 'I think I shall have to speak to our housekeeper. That is rather more dust than I would like.'

'All in good time, my dear. All in good time.' Lord Stratton led them up the stairs to the gallery. 'We only took the house at the new year, and there is much to be done yet.'

The gallery was a small, enclosed space with a good view

of the ballroom. Folding chairs leaned against the walls, half-disappearing into tangles of glamour. Like the rest of the ballroom, the decorations were somewhat gaudy. The illusion of thousands of candles played on the wall, but did little more to dispel the shadows of the space than a painting of flames would have. Too often amateur glamourists would try to flood an area with the illusion of light, not understanding that it would make the space seem darker by contrast, as the eye and the mind disagreed on what they saw. Only in a completely dark space, such as a cave, could one perceive the feeble light provided by glamour. The *illusion*, however, seemed bright, which caused the pupil to close and thus make the entire room appear darker. Of all the threads of glamour, representations of light required the most delicacy – delicacy that this glamourist had sorely lacked.

It did not help that, even with snow upon the ground outside, the balcony was stifling. Frowning, Vincent reached into the ether and twitched a thread. At once, a breeze circulated through the tight space.

'Someone had bound the cooling breeze into the candles, no doubt during a repair.' Vincent shook his head, the corners of his mouth turned down in disdain at the mistake. 'We shall have to pull all of these out. Unless there is something you wish to keep?'

The tone of his voice left no doubt that he assumed that good taste would not allow them to keep *any* of the current glamour. Lord and Lady Stratton hastened to assure him that they wanted the room completely refashioned.

Jane studied the balcony and made notes as they went. In the course of their examination, they discovered that there was a door leading off the back of the balcony onto a servants' hall.

The challenge with such things was to mask them in a manner that allowed one to find them again – a trick that the previous glamourist had also not employed.

For the next quarter hour, they talked over the broader points of the design, defining the ideas that they had put forth in their correspondence. The glamural was to create the illusion of a forest creeping into the ballroom. Rather than attempting to fully mask the room, this would cause it to appear that the wood panelling on the walls was reverting to its natural state. Branches would spring forth from between panels. The frames of the windows would resemble twisted vines, and tremble with verdant greenery, even in winter. Throughout the whole, songbirds would perch and flit, and in some cases fly in arcs across the ceiling.

After agreeing upon the general plan, Jane and Vincent left the Stratton household. As soon as they were in the carriage, Jane said, 'Do you know what I was thinking?'

'That the previous glamourist should be drawn and quartered? Using *nœuds de vache* for tying off? No wonder everything was unravelling.' Vincent drew the curtains and put his arm around her shoulders.

'I agree with you there, but I was thinking of a different matter.' Jane could not expect his thoughts to always run in the same vein as hers. She snuggled into his warmth, tucking her hands inside his coat front. 'I was thinking that we should introduce Melody to their son when he arrives.'

'Eh? Why?'

'He might be a good match.'

'I am surprised that you think so.'

'It is true that I have yet to meet the young man, but with his age and situation, it is at least a possibility.'

Vincent peered down at her. 'The fact that they are Irish Catholics does not trouble you?'

Jane pushed away from him, all astonishment. 'What can you mean? Irish Catholic? They have no accents, no brogue. Nothing aside from Lady Stratton's red hair could mark them so.'

'Beyond the crucifix in the library and their name, you mean?' Vincent peeked through the curtains, which showed a glimpse of Whitehall. 'As for the accent, the sons of Irish nobility that I went to school with had the brogue beaten out of them.'

'But what about their name? Stratton is not a particularly Irish name, I think.'

'He is Baron Conall O'Brien of Stratton.'

Doubtful, Jane tried again. 'I do not recall a crucifix.'

'It hung on the right wall of the library, near the door. It is possible that only I saw it because you were on my right, so I faced that direction, while you faced the windows.' Vincent shrugged. 'You may look when we return.'

'No . . . no, I believe you.' She frowned, considering. 'Do we need to ask them for payment in advance?'

'What? Why?'

'Well . . . you said they were Irish. I thought there might be concern about payment.'

Vincent laughed. 'No more so than with any other nobleman. In my experience, Irishmen are more prompt with payment than others, because they are aware of their reputation.' He kissed the top of her head. 'Do not fret about that.'

In spite of Vincent's assurances, Jane was hesitant to recommend an Irishman and a Catholic to her sister's attention. Even if she were not concerned that a Papist would place loyalty to Rome over England, the Irish reputation for being dissipated was too well known to be entirely unfounded. Still, she would have ample opportunity to observe the family while they were employed at Stratton House. Perhaps Mr O'Brien might yet prove to be suitable.

The carriage rocked to a halt. With London's traffic, this was not entirely unusual, but a moment later, she became aware of shouting. 'Another riot?'

'Let me see.' Vincent disengaged himself from her, and looked out the window. He shook his head. 'It is in front of us. A moment.'

Before Jane could protest, he had stepped out of the carriage. Cold air gusted in, stirring Vincent's hair as he stood on the step of the carriage, peering over the crowd. With the door open, Jane could now make out some phrases coming from the mob, like 'coldmonger' and 'weather fiend' and 'stop the snow'.

Jane leaned out to look down the street. She had expected to see more Luddites pulling a frame out of a building, but instead a crowd had gathered in front of a grocer's. Their anger was affixed upon a clear spot in their midst. One protester held a sign on a stout stick demanding 'God's wrath for weather meddlers'. Another read, 'Coldmongers are the Devil's servants.'

Jane stared in disbelief. 'They cannot think that coldmongers are responsible for the weather. It flies in the face of science'.

'Superstition rarely troubles with facts.'

The crowd rushed around that same clear area. A man in a ragged muffler lifted a cobble from the street and threw it into the middle. For a moment, Jane had a clear view of the centre.

In the middle was a young man of colour wearing the blue armband of the coldmongers' guild. He was bleeding.

# FOUR

## Relations

As the mob heaved around the young man, Vincent's jaw tightened. 'Jane. Stay in the carriage.'

She did not. Jane ran behind her husband as he raced towards the crowd. She snatched her gloves from her hands so that she would be better able to seize glamour. At the back of the crowd, Vincent came to a sudden halt. He drew a mass of glamour out of the ether and knotted it quickly.

It sounded as though an enormous detonation went off in the middle of the street accompanied by blinding light. Neither was true, but the illusion so confounded the crowd's senses that they backed away from the perceived blast. Jane darted through the gap in the throng.

Vincent shouted at her, but she paid him no mind, intent on the young coldmonger. Behind Jane, her husband caused another concussion, employing military tactics from the Battle of Quatre Bras.

When Jane reached the coldmonger, she seized glamour. As Vincent's next explosion caused the crowd to cry out and cower, Jane twisted light into a ball, which she expanded quickly into a *Sphère Obscurcie*. This invention of Vincent's would hide them from the eyes of the crowd. It was too difficult to maintain the folds while walking, but it would guide the sunlight around them and leave them masked for the time being.

She turned to the lad, who had blood trickling from a cut over his eye. 'They cannot see us.'

Indeed, someone in the crowd shouted, 'He got away!'

Jane wove again, using a variation on the percussion glamour to create the sound of horses galloping closer. It would not pass as real were it not for the discord around them. As it was, the syncopated beats gave the crowd an alarm. She left that to loop around and used a separate thread to sound a whistle, as though the Bow Street Runners were on their way. Crying in dismay, the crowd separated and fled.

One man ran through the apparently empty space where Jane stood with the coldmonger. He collided with her, knocking Jane back and out of the *Sphère*. She fell hard against the cobbles and he tripped, landing heavily atop her. His elbow came down on her ribs and forced all the air out of her lungs. Stars and dark spots swam in front of her eyes as though she had done too much glamour.

A moment later, the man seemed to fly up and away from her. Vincent had seized him by the collar and flung him down the street. After making certain the ruffian was gone, Vincent stood over Jane, wanting only a flaming sword to be a modern interpretation of the angel Gabriel.

He knelt to help her sit. 'Are you all right?'

Jane nodded, not entirely trusting her voice. Her breath sounded too loud in her own ears, but she stoutly pretended that she was fine and that her ribs did not ache where the man had landed on her. With Vincent's help, she clambered back to her feet. The crowd had vanished and even the usual foot traffic had thinned due to the fracas. They stood, nearly alone, on the street.

'Where is the lad?'

'I wove a *Sphère Obscurcie.*' She had become so turned around that she was not entirely certain where she had woven it. The benefit – and trouble – of this particular fold was that the glamour was stretched to such thinness as to be almost impossible to discern even with second sight, unless one peered so deeply into the ether as to obliterate all view of the mundane world. Vincent steadied her as she looked for the *Sphère* and marked the spot when she pointed to it. They walked forward to the seemingly empty patch of pavement. The lad appeared suddenly as they passed within the *Sphère's* influence.

With some of the urgency gone, Jane had time to examine him more closely. That the coldmonger was a young man of colour came as no surprise given that they were in London. In the country, it was more common to see coldmongers of British stock, but in the City all those coldmongers who had come to London as slaves had stayed and settled. They intermarried among this community, and now a London coldmonger was as likely to have some touch of the tawny as not.

What did surprise her was how young he was – likely no more than fourteen. Blood flowed from a cut over his eye, but he appeared otherwise free from injury.

'They have gone,' Jane said, though the boy could surely see that on his own.

'I know. I wasn't sure how far I could move.' His vowels marked him as being a Londoner born and bred. 'This is a clever thing you've done. Thank you.'

Vincent nodded absently, still watching the street. 'I will bring the carriage over. Jane, will you unstitch the *Sphère*?'

She agreed, and they were shortly in the carriage with the young coldmonger only visible for a brief moment. Once settled, with Jane and Vincent on one bench and the young man on the other, the carriage pulled away from the greengrocer.

'Before we go too far, I have two questions.' Jane offered him a handkerchief to wipe the blood from his temple. 'First, do you have a safe place to go? Second, what happened?'

'Thank you ma'am, I do: the Worshipful Company of Coldmongers.' He dabbed at his temple. His hands had the characteristic rough, chapped skin of a coldmonger and his knuckles looked as though they had cracked many times over, leaving pink scars on his fawn-brown skin. 'I oughtn't to have left, but I saw the snow and I was hoping for work.'

Vincent opened the window and leaned out to direct the carriage driver. He had a shouted conversation and was very red in the face when he pulled his head back in. Jane raised her eyebrows in question. He compressed his lips and shook his head slightly, which she took to mean that the carriage driver had objected to the destination but that Vincent had convinced him otherwise.

She patted his knee in thanks, then turned back to the cold-monger. 'I confess some confusion: I thought snow would mean *less* work?'

'Oh, it does and all. Most of what I do is keep food cool or help get groceries home without them wilting in the heat. Days like this, though, are the only time I can make things freeze. Can't drop the temperature far enough otherwise.' He shrugged and looked bewildered. His lower lip trembled a little. 'I ain't never seen nothing like it. Not in all my days.' – which, as he continued to speak, Jane considered amending to about twelve years old. 'I was just asking these grocers if they needed ice, same as I always do in winter, and people just started yelling. And then there were a lot of them. And the

fellers with the signs . . . I don't know where they came from.'
He lowered the handkerchief and twisted it in his grasp. 'I'd
heard other 'mongers talking about it, but . . . I thought they
were having me on.'

Vincent stirred and spoke to the lad for the first time since
they got into the carriage. 'Other coldmongers have been
beaten? Or other riots have sprung up?'

'Both, I should say.' He huddled into his coat, miserably.

'What is your name, dear?'

'William.' He half-laughed and knuckled his ear. 'My friends
call me Chill Will, but I reckon I shouldn't use that right now.'

Jane hid her smile at the ridiculous name. 'Likely not, nor
wear your armband outside the Company for a time.' She put
her hand on Vincent's arm. 'To complete our introductions,
this is my husband, Sir David, and I am Lady Vincent.'

The boy's eyes widened. 'Not the Prince Regent's glamourists? Cor! The lads'll never believe it when I tell them. And
here I was telling you that you were clever.' He dropped back
against the cushions of the carriage in astonishment. 'I ain't
never thought, in a million years—it beats all, it does.'

His astonishment could not be greater than Jane's at being
called the Prince Regent's glamourists. It was true that they
had done a number of commissions for him, but they had
no title to show for it. It was not as though they were the
Principal Painter in Ordinary like Sir Thomas Lawrence or
the Master of the King's Music like Sir William Parsons. Jane
paused, wondering if preparing Vincent for a formal position
as Court Glamourist had been part of why His Royal Highness
had raised her husband to a knighthood last year. While the
Prince Regent had said nothing about making such an offer,
he had also made his preference for Vincent's work quite clear.

It did not bear thinking on. She smiled at William. 'I am glad we were able to be of service.'

The carriage took them through a less reputable part of London, and finally stopped in front of the tall iron gates of the Worshipful Company of Coldmongers.

Vincent climbed out of the carriage with young William and saw him safely to the porter at the Company's gate. When he returned to the carriage, he was shaking his head with amusement. 'You have an admirer, I think.'

'Me? You were the one who frightened off the mob.'

Vincent put his arm around her and pulled her close. He kissed the top of her head. 'But you were the one who charged into the middle and kept him safe. I could hear him telling the porter about it all the way into the building. I believe you are seven feet tall and carry a bow.'

Laughing at the image, Jane burrowed closer. They occupied the rest of their ride home ascertaining that neither had been hurt. This required much of their attention, and many tender kisses to scrapes that another might have deemed too small to notice.

When they arrived home, Mrs Brackett met them in the foyer before they even had their coats off. 'You have callers. Miss Ellsworth is entertaining them now in the front parlour.' Her mouth turned down as she spoke.

Jane pulled off her pelisse, thankful that most of the dirt from their encounter was on that long, sturdy coat. 'Callers?' She looked to Vincent, who frowned. They had not yet paid any calls to let their few London acquaintances know they were in town.

'Yes, my lady.' Mrs Brackett lifted a silver tray from a side table and displayed the abundance of cards upon it. It looked as though half a dozen people had called during the course of the day. 'The two gentlemen whose cards are on top are with her presently. I have sent Betsey in to keep things proper.'

'Thank you, Mrs Brackett.'

Their cards proclaimed them to be a Mr Robert Colgrove and a Sir Prescott Worrick. The latter name sounded somewhat familiar, though she could not place it immediately, but the quality of the cards proclaimed them both to be gentlemen. Still, she had trouble applying that honour to them if they were paying a social call to a young woman to whom they had not yet been introduced. It would be quite a different thing if they were known to the family.

Beneath their cards was one Jane was glad to see. 'Oh, we have missed Major Curry. Did he have the opportunity to meet Miss Ellsworth?'

'No, madam. I told him the family was out, as was proper, with the young lady at home alone.'

'Quite right . . .' Although if she were to trust anyone with her sister's honour, it would be the Major. In fact, it might be worth making an introduction for other reasons. Though not a great match in terms of his situation, in terms of his person, Melody could do far worse than attach the Major. It was something to consider. For the moment, however, Jane needed to turn her attention to the gentlemen now in their home. She handed the cards to Vincent. 'Do you know them, my love?'

'No.' He chewed on his lower lip, frowning.

'Well, I suppose we should go in. Perhaps they are our neighbours?' Jane examined her reflection in the mirror, as she removed her bonnet, to make certain her mobcap was still straight after the riot. With the cap in place, it was difficult to tell that her mouse-brown hair was cropped like a gentleman's. She had cut it short the previous summer and kept it so because it had more life that way and was frankly cooler when they were working glamour. It also amused her to see fashionable ladies turn their heads and stare.

Vincent made a strange grunt. She turned from the mirror to see that he had turned quite pale, with a deep crease between his brows. He held an elegant card of simple cream. The corner of the card had been bent down to indicate that the individual had called, not simply sent a footman.

'Who is it?'

'My sister.' He stared at the card, then tossed it on the side table. The cream card slipped along the marble surface, coming to rest against a vase.

In a clean script, it read LADY PENELOPE ESSEX.

Jane had known he had sisters, of course, though Vincent had called her Penny on the few occasions when he had spoken of her. 'The youngest?'

'Yes.'

She put a hand on his back, feeling the tension there. 'What is it?'

Vincent sighed, pressing his lips together. 'Penny was always my father's favourite.'

'Is this a reason for concern?'

'She would not—without his . . . I have not heard from her since I left.' He ran his hands through his hair. 'I had not looked for her card.'

Vincent had been born Vincent Hamilton, the third son of the Earl of Verbury. His father had not made his early life anything like easy, and Vincent had been estranged from his family since he had decided to become a professional glamourist. Jane was uncertain which offence his father considered greater: that he worked for a living, or that he worked at glamour, a womanly art. 'Do you think your father knows?'

He shook his head, then shrugged as though he did not even have the resources to hazard a guess. 'Shall we go in?' Without waiting for her reply, he strode into the parlour. The lines of Vincent's back were tight and his carriage stiff.

Jane followed, wishing she understood fully what about this familial visit upset him.

In the parlour, Melody sat in one of the straight-backed chairs by the sofa. She wore a celestial blue day dress that set off her eyes to advantage. A heavy cream wool shawl warded her from some of the chill. Behind her, Betsey presided over the tea tray, but spent most of her time glancing at the two gentlemen who shared the room with them. Jane dismissed her with a nod and the girl bustled out of the room.

The sofa was occupied by a gentleman of advanced years who had maintained his fighting trim. With a hawk nose and a full head of grey hair, he reminded her a little of the Duke of Wellington, but without his quickness of gaze. The other gentleman was the same age as Melody, and saw them first. He rose, making a pretty figure in his buckskin trousers and blue jacket. His hair was a fashionable brunet, but his eyes were shockingly pale, almost without colour.

The older gentleman stood and introduced himself to Vincent, as was proper. 'Sir Prescott Worrick, sir. I am the first cousin of Miss Ellsworth's mother, and I thought I would welcome you to town. This is my nephew, Mr Colgrove.'

Of course! Her mother often corresponded with Lady

Worrick, as they were prone to the same nervous complaints and were first cousins.

Vincent bowed gravely and returned the courtesy, introducing Jane as 'My wife, Lady Vincent.'

Then he was silent, leaving Jane to make an effort at pleasantries. More than his usual discomfort with strangers, Vincent wore a brooding expression as he stood by the fire. Jane sat in the chair opposite Melody, so the other gentlemen would feel at their ease again. She smiled at Mr Colgrove. 'Then we must be second cousins.'

'Indeed.' Mr Colgrove bowed from his seat but seemed to feel that some additional explanation was owed by their presence in the parlour. 'Miss Ellsworth was passing through the foyer when we arrived to leave our cards, and was kind enough to invite us to take tea with her.'

'It was so cold outside, and they were quite covered with snow.' Melody shivered becomingly. 'The tea was already laid, and it seemed silly to send our cousins out again.'

By which Jane took her to mean that the day had been tedious and that Mr Colgrove cut a handsome figure. 'Quite understandable. And it gives us the pleasure of making your acquaintance.' A second cousin was not so closely related as to be considered ineligible. No doubt that was why her mother had written to Sir Prescott of their presence in town. 'I am delighted that Melody was able to act as hostess in our absence. Have you been in London long?'

'Oh bless me, no.' Sir Prescott chuckled and patted his knee. 'I always come up for the Season, and I brought Robert with me this time. The weather has played us quite the trick, though.'

Mr Colgrove inclined his head towards Melody. 'I cannot mind it, since the day has been so fair in other ways.'

'As we are cousins, you need not wait for snow to bring you next time.' Melody touched the sofa, next to his arm.

Sir Prescott turned to Vincent and Jane. 'Which brings us to one of the purposes of our visit. We are having a party for Robert's birthday on the thirteenth of May. He will have achieved his majority. We do hope you can join us. A formal invitation will be coming, of course, but from what your mother says about how hard you work, I thought it best to extend the invitation early so as to save a spot on your calendar.'

'That is very kind.' Jane glanced at Vincent, but he was even more inscrutable than usual. Although her husband disdained most company, the party would nevertheless be a good opportunity to introduce Melody to more young people. 'We would be delighted.'

Melody pulled her small appointment book out of her work-basket. 'Here, I shall mark it down in my diary. Such a joy to look forward to.' She smiled at Mr Colgrove as she wrote in the little book.

Jane raised a brow at this obvious display. It appeared her mother was quite correct to send this young man their way.

'Excellent.' Sir Prescott beat his knee with pleasure.

'I only hope the weather improves by then.' Mr Colgrove chuckled drily. 'I do wish you could make it warm, Sir David.'

Vincent turned from his place by the mantel. 'You are welcome to stand by the fire.'

'Surely a glamourist of your calibre does not need a fire.'

A muscle clenched in Vincent's jaw. His temper showed the effects of more strain than a sister's visit ought to cause. Jane stepped in before her husband could reply to the ignorance, and poured a cup of tea for him so that he would have something to do with his hands, which were currently clenched. 'Heatmongering is deadly, I am afraid.'

'But I have done warming charms for my brandy when hunting,' Mr Colgrove protested.

'I should advise you not to do so.' Vincent took a sip of tea as though to calm himself. When he spoke again, his voice was tolerably indifferent. 'The folds outside the visible spectrum are injurious, though one might not notice when warming a thing so small as a flask once a year. To start a fire or heat a room would kill a man before the day's end.'

A look of horror crossed Mr Colgrove's face. Likely he used the warming charm more than once a year and was wondering about the effects on his life. Still, he had enough quickness of intellect to exhibit an understanding of the larger implications. 'This is why there are no heatmongers, then?'

'Correct. Although coldmongering is also dangerous if done too often.'

Melody turned her gaze upon Vincent. 'I did not know that. But the coldmonger our grocer uses is a boy.'

'Most coldmongers die young.'

Jane shivered, thinking of young William. His hands had already shown the signs of his trade. She had known of the difficulty in managing cold, but had never connected that with the general youth of coldmongers. As she thought on it, she could not recollect seeing any coldmonger much past his thirtieth year.

Mr Colgrove remarked, 'Then my coldmonger should have been grateful that I did not require his services in this blasted cold! He should have thanked me for saving his life when I let him go.'

'Quite so! I had not thought that I was doing a social good

by not yet engaging a coldmonger.' Sir Prescott laughed, pounding his knee again.

Jane could not find amusement in the misfortune of others. Melody had a moment of shock on her face as well, but masked it behind her teacup. Sir Prescott set a poor example for his nephew by encouraging such ill-judged humour. The young gentleman she could excuse, from nerves and youth, but Sir Prescott should surely know better. He displayed remarkably poor taste, but continued to expand on the subject until even his nephew looked conscious of the way his uncle exposed himself.

Biting the inside of her lip, Jane poured a fresh cup of tea for herself, though she was far from thirsty. She was thankful when the talk moved to trivial things.

Though Jane faced her cousin, the edge of her vision was occupied with her husband. After a day of working, what he most needed was solitude, particularly as his equilibrium had clearly been upset by the surprise of his sister's call.

Jane sipped her tea and tried to be attentive, but she could not help wondering what would happen when they met Lady Penelope.

# FIVE

# A Duet for Glamourists

It took Jane and Vincent much of a week to pull the old glamour out of the ballroom. It seemed as though the previous glamourist had taken pains to tie the most obscure knots possible. Jane was inclined to conclude that he had been experimenting with new techniques, but Vincent seemed convinced that the glamourist had been the worst sort of amateur. He muttered constantly while removing the old work. Jane shared his sentiment, but was hard-pressed not to laugh at her husband's inventive turns of phrase – her favourite was 'goat-licking amateur', followed closely by 'mongrel's handmaiden'.

While there was no perfect metaphor for glamour, in this regard it was most like needlework. Each thread or fold of light which had been pulled from the ether had to be tied off to remain in place. To undo it, they had needed to unpick each knot. Indeed, even tearing the building down would do nothing to remove the glamour, which would remain in place until it gradually faded back into the ether. Jane had seen follies in which the remnants of glamurals still haunted the air where the original walls had once been. Nothing save a direct lightning strike would speed the process. It would be lovely if someone would invent a pair of scissors that worked on glamour, but as it stood, everything had to be removed by hand. Now that the room was clear, Jane could finally anticipate the coming day's work with pleasure. It would be their first opportunity to lay in new glamour, and the start of a project always excited her with its possibilities.

As they prepared to leave home, Jane had to restrain herself from skipping with the basket of their nuncheon to the front door, where Vincent waited for her.

On the way out, she observed Melody sitting by the window in the parlour, staring out at the snow. She had a book in her lap, but it lay neglected against the fabric of her dress.

Vincent tilted his head, studying Jane's sister as though he were going to draw her. Flexing his hands, he said, 'We are not in such a hurry.'

'Thank you.' Jane entered the parlour as though to ascertain the weather. Pausing by her sister, she looked out at the snow drifting down. 'What are you reading?'

Melody jumped, only now seeming conscious that Jane had approached. She picked up the book as though she did not know it. '*St. Irvyne*, by . . . oh. By a "Gentleman of the University of Oxford". How odd. At any rate, it is quite engrossing.'

'I have not had the pleasure yet. What is it about?'

'Oh . . .' Melody turned the pages, frowning. 'A young woman. No. A man. Well, it starts with a violent storm and . . . la! I can barely do it justice. Perhaps you should read it when I am through.'

'On your recommendation, certainly.' Jane stared out at the snow, though she really watched Melody's reflection in the window. 'Are you well? Your eyes seem a bit reddened.'

'They are only tired.' Melody glanced across the room to where Vincent waited in the doorway. 'You should go.'

Jane hesitated until Melody lifted her book again and began to read. Across the room, Vincent raised his eyebrows in question, clearly asking if she had any success with Melody. Jane shook her head, thankful that her husband could read her silent moods so well. He compressed his lips and nodded with understanding. With the snow, Melody had been cooped up, and any plans to go exploring had come to nothing. Perhaps Jane should have brought her mother to London after all, so that Melody would have some company while they worked. It seemed clear that they had left her too long alone.

Vincent tucked his chin in as he did when he was thinking. She tilted her head towards Melody, asking if it were all right to invite her, and he gave a bare nod. Jane suspected that if he were closer she might hear his little whine of protest, but he had not raised an objection.

'Would you like to come with us today?'

'Oh!' Melody sat up, almost dropping her book. 'Truly? I will not be in the way, I promise, and if you need me to do anything or to run any errands, you have only to ask.'

'Yes, truly. It might be dull, but it will at least be a different sort of dull.'

'Let me get my pelisse and bonnet, then.' Melody bounded to her feet. She glanced again at Vincent standing in the door. Lowering her voice, she leaned closer to Jane. 'Are you certain that Vincent will not mind? I know he prefers not to have spectators when he works.'

'It was his idea.' Or close to it, at any rate. This half-truth was enough to set Melody's mind at ease, though she needed little persuasion.

In a matter of minutes Melody returned, pulling her warm pelisse over her dress to ward off the cold outside. Somehow she managed to make the long outer coat seem fluid and grace-ful as she skipped down the stairs and to the waiting hack that they had hired.

Jane would rather have walked to the Baron's, but the snow formed a slushy blanket on the footpaths. The streets had turned into grey quagmires of melted snow and other, less agreeable, liquids. Even with the carriage, the passage through the streets was slow and unpleasant as the horse started and stopped frequently to accommodate the uncertain foot traffic. Most of the walkers picked their way through the streets on tall metal pattens that clinked against the pavement. Those less for-tunate had their mouths squeezed with distaste as they walked through the slush. Even the tradesmen looked annoyed by the weather. She kept an eye out for William, but saw no signs of him or any other coldmonger.

The walk in front of Stratton House had, thankfully, been swept clear of the ice and snow, but Jane still had to hold up the hem of her dress to keep it from dragging on the damp pavement as they went inside. Even the stout brown wool of her work dress would show this amount of dirt.

The butler only raised his eyebrows a fraction at the addi-tion of a third member to their party, but that did not slow the readiness with which they were greeted and shown to the ballroom.

Vincent paused only long enough to remove his greatcoat and hat before setting to work. He strode to the far end of the ballroom, where the musicians' gallery now stood fully revealed, and vanished up the stairs.

Jane set her basket on the floor by the entry and pulled off her gloves. She would leave her pelisse on until she had warmed up a bit with activity. 'We shall spend most of our time neglecting you, I am afraid.' Jane pulled her apron on over the pelisse.

'Oh, I am not afraid of that.' Melody looked around the room and frowned. 'Where shall I sit?'

Discomfited, Jane could only stare at the room. They had removed all the furniture so that it did not interfere with their work. Quite a few random pieces of glamour had been obscured by chairs, making Vincent's mutterings change to swears every time they found another loose thread. She had forgotten that there was nowhere to sit in the ballroom. 'I will ask if they can bring you a chair.'

Before she could do more than turn towards the door, Vincent reappeared from the stairs. He had a folding chair from the musicians' gallery under one arm. 'Will this do?'

'Thank you, yes.' Melody skipped down the length of the ballroom to meet him. 'Where shall I sit so that I am not in the way?'

'Anywhere.' Vincent set the chair in the middle of the floor. 'So long as you do not mind moving if we require it.'

'Not at all.' Melody sat in the chair and pulled a book from her reticule. Studiously, she opened it and began to read, as if to show that she intended to be no trouble.

Smiling to herself, Jane joined Vincent as he climbed the stairs to the musicians' gallery. 'That was very nice of you, love.'

He grunted in answer and Jane laughed outright at him. Vincent stopped on the stairs and turned in the narrow space. Even in the dim light filtering from the door, his eyes twinkled. 'Muse, you must know that I would do anything to make you happy.'

'Anything?' She ran her finger along the ribbon of his pocket watch, coming dangerously close to other delicate areas.

He caught her hand and raised it to his lips. 'Anything – after our work is finished.'

'Then let us work swiftly.'

When Melody sighed for the third time in as many minutes, Jane carefully tied off the fold of glamour that she was stretching along the wall. It would serve as an undercoat of pale gold to brighten the darker weaves she would place over it later.

'Is something the matter?'

'Oh, no.' Melody shifted in her seat. 'I was merely thinking.'

She had long since laid her book aside, saying that it made her head ache. It was becoming clear that she regretted her decision to accompany them. At least at home, she could move from room to room when a sense of ennui struck her. Here, she was limited to the ballroom while the Vincents worked, and Jane had run out of activities for Melody.

'Would you like to draw?'

Melody rolled her eyes. 'I am not a child that you need to amuse. I merely sighed.'

'All right.' Jane held up her hands in surrender and returned to work. Melody could suffer ennui if she liked. It was the affliction of the fashionable, after all.

At the other end of the room, Vincent had his feet spread wide in his operating stance. He had greater stamina and reach than she did, so he was placing the glamour along the ceiling. To someone whose eyes were only adjusted to the visible world, Vincent appeared to be waving his hands at random while washes of colour came into view overhead. When Jane let her vision expand to include the ether, his real work became apparent. Vincent pulled skeins of pure glamour and folded their light to his whims. Almost like a puppet showman working a marionette upside down, he wove a pattern on the ceiling with the folds.

Scholars of glamour found that it had properties resembling textile, water and light. The nature of glamour caused it to want to sink towards the earth once it was brought out of the ether. A glamourist who wanted to work at a distance had to think of it as a jet of water, diffusing and curling towards the earth. This made distance work doubly hard, due to the effort of supporting it while attempting to work with any degree of precision.

Though the room had the bite of winter still, Vincent had removed his coat and worked only in his waistcoat and shirt sleeves so he did not overheat with the effort of working across so great a distance. Jane paused to make certain that he was not breathing over-quickly. Like any activity, glamour required energy to manage, and Vincent had been known to work past his limits.

Satisfied that he was not straining himself, Jane began to work again. Scarcely had she pulled a new fold from the ether when the door to the ballroom opened. Lord Stratton entered with a footman bearing a small tray of comestibles.

'I thought you might need some refreshments.'

Jane released her fold without troubling to tie it off. 'Thank you, my lord.'

Likewise, Vincent stepped back from the work he was doing and rolled his shirt sleeves down. 'That is very kind, sir.'

The Baron glanced at Melody and raised a brow in question. Jane stepped forward beckoning Melody, who rose. 'May I present my sister, Miss Ellsworth.'

'Ah, they had mentioned you had a companion, but not how lovely.' He bowed very correctly over Melody's hand. 'Are you also a glamourist?'

Melody shook her head. 'No, alas. I confess that I came to escape our house. The weather, you know.'

'Quite understandable.' He hesitated, then said, 'If you would like to use our music room, you are more than welcome.'

'That would be very—' Melody broke off and glanced to Jane, seeming to recognise that this was not a social call. 'That is, if it would not be any bother, I should be grateful.'

'None at all.' He bowed to Jane. 'If it will not deprive Lady Vincent of your company, that is.'

Jane managed to reassure him that Melody was welcome to go, without making it sound like she was eager for her sister's absence. But in truth, once Melody left the room with Lord Stratton, Jane was significantly more comfortable concentrating on her work.

It astonished her how distracting a sigh could be.

At the end of the day, Jane's arms ached as she pulled her pelisse back on. They had managed to place much of the underlayer of the glamour, but they still needed to tackle the musicians' gallery before they were ready to begin sketching the broad strokes of the forms they wanted to add. Vincent often added an underlayer of paint, but they did not want to disturb the ballroom's panelled walls, so they had decided to create the whole of the glamural with illusion.

With Lord Stratton's offering, they had not needed to eat the bread and cheese that Cook had packed for them. Vincent stooped to pick up their basket from where Jane had left it by the door. He groaned softly as he stood. Placing a hand behind his hips, Vincent leaned backwards and cracked his spine. 'I am getting old, Muse.'

'You are younger than I am by a full year.' She took his arm, feeling every one of *her* thirty years, as they left the ballroom. 'What must Melody think of us if you think yourself old?'

'We are ancient, infirm creatures on the edge of our graves.'

As they walked towards the front of the house, the sound of a pianoforte led them to the music room. The tune was a simple one, adequately played but without the authority of a true musician. Melody's voice rose above it in a clear, sweet accompaniment.

Jane tilted her head, listening. 'It sounds as though she has been practising.'

'She may not have had anything else to do this week.' Vincent grimaced and buttoned his coat. 'I dislike neglecting her so much after inviting her to come to London, and yet . . .'

'And yet, we have our work to do.' Jane squeezed his arm. 'She is my responsibility, not yours.'

Vincent stopped her in the hall and looked down with a serious cast to his features. 'Do not think that I consider her less of a sister than if she were my own.'

'Like the one you were afraid to see?' Jane teased him, but regretted her words the moment they were out of her mouth, as Vincent winced, turning his face to the wall. 'I am sorry, my love.'

He shook his head, staring at the bust of a cupid sculpted into a nook and traced a line down its nose with his finger. The muscles in his jaw bunched. Letting his breath out in a huff, Vincent said, 'It is not Penny that I am afraid of. Or rather . . . not precisely her. I am afraid that my father sent her, and I do not know why.' He laughed rather desperately, gripping the cherub's wing.

Jane stood on her toes to kiss Vincent on the cheek. 'He has no hold over you.'

'No.' He let go of the statue. 'So, shall we rescue your sister from ennui?'

A burst of laughter came out of the music room. Jane raised a brow. It was not only Melody, but a gentleman laughing. 'I wonder if we need to.'

They walked down the hall and entered a sunny room, which contained not only a pianoforte, but also a harp and a cello. Melody sat at the keys with the sun shining behind her, making her hair fairly glow.

A young gentleman leaned against the pianoforte, resting his elbows upon the cloth thrown over it. He was a tall, slender man, with a riot of red hair, which sparkled in the sunlight like ruby to Melody's gold. His blue eyes were a match for Lady Stratton's, though a pair of wire-rimmed spectacles framed them. His clothes, which showed all the signs of an excellent tailor, were splashed with mud. There could be little doubt that this was Alastar O'Brien, eldest son of Lord Stratton.

As the Vincents entered, he straightened, the casual nature of his posture altering to something more formal, but none the less attractive for that. 'Good afternoon?'

Vincent offered him a short bow and made the appropriate introductions. Jane could never get used to being introduced as Lady Vincent, but she smiled and curtsied. 'I see you have already met my sister.'

'I was drawn to the music. It was quite improper, but when one hears a muse, one must follow.' He was quite the gallant.

Looking up through her eyelashes becomingly, Melody said, 'I should say that the one who inspires the music is the muse, rather than the one who merely plays it.'

'It depends, I suppose, on where one finds inspiration,' Mr O'Brien said.

'I have often felt the same way, sir.' Vincent suppressed a smile and almost winked at Jane.

Mr O'Brien gestured at the dirt on his trousers. 'Forgive my attire. I have only just arrived in town, and my parents did not tell me that we had guests.'

'Ah. That is because we are not guests.' Jane paused, seeing that he did not understand. 'Your parents have hired us to adorn the ballroom. We are glamourists.'

'Oh.' He looked back at Melody, the open expression fading from his face. 'I did not know. Forgive me for presuming on your time.'

'Not at all.' Melody rose from her place behind the pianoforte. 'I was very glad to make your acquaintance.'

'Likewise.' He bowed to her and to the Vincents. 'Now, if you will excuse me, I need to find my parents and let them know that I am here.'

As he left, Jane stifled the urge to call him back and tell him that Melody was the daughter of a gentleman, and not merely the sister of an artisan. Regardless of the Irish reputation for being wastrels, Jane could not stand to see her sister slighted.

# SIX

## *Hades and Persephone*

The following day, Melody stayed at home, which Jane could not help but think had something to do with Mr O'Brien. Now that Melody had the use of the music room, Stratton House should have offered more diversion than their own. She complained of a headache, so Jane did not press her, but left Melody to recline in the relative darkness of her bedchamber with a damp rag over her eyes.

Though concerned about her sister, Melody's absence left Jane and Vincent free to attend to the glamural. The work absorbed them to such an extent that, when they finally left Stratton House, Jane was surprised by the lateness of the hour. Dusk had fallen over the streets and painted deep shadows at the corners. It had begun to snow while they were inside and the walk home, while beautiful, was cold and damp.

When they arrived home, Melody met them in the foyer. She had a heavy cream envelope in her hands and was fairly dancing with excitement. Any sign of her prior affliction had vanished.

'Look! Oh, look! I never thought to see this.' Melody held it out so that the Prince Regent's seal was visible on the paper. 'Is it real? Is it really him?'

'It is.' Vincent exchanged a look of perplexity with Jane as he shed his coat, which made it clear that he had no more notion as to why the Prince Regent was writing to them than she did. 'May I?' Melody passed him the envelope, but continued to describe an orbit about them, glowing as though she were lit by glamour. If Mr O'Brien could see her now, he would not mind that she was the sister of an artisan.

Jane did not attempt to look over Vincent's shoulder as he read the sheet inside the envelope. He would let her know soon enough what it contained, and at the moment, she was more interested in finding her way to her rooms and getting out of her wet clothes. 'I am going up to dress for dinner.'

'Are you not curious, Jane?' Melody hugged herself. 'La! I have been staring at it for most of the day. What Miss Baker at home will say when I tell her that we had a letter from His Royal Highness.'

'I am more damp than curious.' Jane displayed her dirty hem. 'Mrs Brackett will not approve of me dripping on her foyer, I think.'

Lifting his head, Vincent passed Melody the letter. 'Allow me to relieve the curiosity, nevertheless. In light of the weather, we have been invited to a skating party on Monday.'

A squeak escaped from Melody as she regarded the letter. 'All of us?'

'Yes.' Vincent tucked his chin in and compressed his lips. A faint whine escaped him as he stared at Melody. Taking a deeper breath, Vincent squeezed his eyes shut for a moment as though to brace himself. When he opened them, he said, 'I shall write to accept.'

Her dear had never been one who enjoyed a press of people. Jane had thought she would have to convince him to accept for

Melody's sake. To voluntarily submit himself to an afternoon in the company of the peerage was a great sacrifice, which she doubted her sister fully understood.

Melody threw her hands in the air with a cheer of delight that would have been more suited to a schoolgirl than a young lady. 'I must write to Miss Baker and Miss Downing. Oh! What shall I wear? I have never skated. What if I fall? La! Where does one even get skates? Oh! This is the most exciting thing that has ever happened to me.' Her exuberance overran her sense, and she embraced Vincent and then Jane in turn. 'Thank you for bringing me to London. I must enter this in my appointment book. How grand that will look. Skating with the Prince Regent! Oh, and I must write to Mama and Aunt Genevieve. Oh. And Miss Marchand.' Clutching the letter, Melody hurried into the drawing room, still listing those whom she must apprise of the coming event.

Vincent stood in the centre of the hall with his mouth a little agape. Jane slipped her arms around him and nodded to where her sister had vanished. 'You have made her very happy.'

'So it appears.' He hesitated. 'It seemed necessary.'

She leaned her head against his broad chest. 'And that is but one example of why I love you.'

The day of the skating party dawned bright and clear. It had snowed all day on Easter Sunday and drifts were piled around the city. Melody and Jane were wrapped in their warmest dresses with extra petticoats and shawls to guard against the chill. They carried new skates, procured by the efficient Mrs Brackett, as the carriage dropped them off in the broad circular drive of Carlton House.

Jane could not help but notice the picture her sister made

as they were escorted through the palace interior and to the grounds behind it. Over her dress, she wore her celestial-blue Hessian pelisse, which fastened with broad ornamental frogs up to her throat in the manner of an officer's uniform. The regularity of the braids cast the swell of her bosom into graceful contrast. Her gold curls were piled onto her head and peeked becomingly from beneath a high-crowned hat that had been trimmed with blue and white ostrich feathers. She carried before her a muff as white as a cloud against the sky.

The grounds at Carlton House had been transformed into a wonderland of winter, with nods to the vanished spring. Snow sculptures of deer and fawns shared the pristine white grounds with frozen swans and flowers made of frost. A shallow reflecting pond already featured gentlemen and ladies gliding over the ice. Their habits, in mulberry, pomona green and primrose yellow, stood out against the severe landscape like flowers on a banquet table.

The Prince Regent stood in a cluster of men by the pond. His figure, restrained by corsets, had yet another layer of bulk added to it by the heavy fur coat he wore. He noticed them come out of the house and motioned Vincent over.

'Well, Melody,' Vincent sighed and waved back, 'you had wanted to meet His Royal Highness.'

Melody's eyes got very round, but she kept her composure admirably. Jane had not seen the Prince Regent since they had removed to Long Parkmead. She recognised a few of his companions. The gentlemen from his set stood in various poses, as if a fashion plate illustrator might wander by and engrave their image at any moment.

As they walked up, Sir Lumley waved an aromatic handkerchief and beamed with delight upon catching sight of her. His greatcoat hung open to show off his usual dark blue coat with gold buttons and a yellow waistcoat. The white ribbons of his breeches peeked out of his top boots as though he had puffs of snow clinging to his knees. 'My dear Lady Vincent. Such a pleasure. You have kept too much away from us. How are you, my dear?'

'Quite well, thank you.' Jane offered him a curtsy and turned to introduce her sister.

Before she could begin, the Prince Regent clapped Vincent on the back. 'Skiffy is quite right. Who has hired you away from me?'

'I am always at your Royal Highness's service.' Vincent bowed as though they did not have an entire ballroom to finish for Lord Stratton.

'Good. You are lying, but I may hold you to it later in any event. My daughter is getting married in May, you know.'

Vincent cleared his throat. 'I am not in the habit of performing for weddings.'

The Prince Regent laughed and beat Vincent's back again. 'Ah, you are always a treat. Meanwhile, I need a diversion. These gentlemen have come for an afternoon of pleasure and talk of nothing but uprisings.'

'Oh, Prinny. You do exaggerate. We also discussed the high food prices.' Sir Lumley waved a handkerchief at him, briefly perfuming the air with lavender.

'And soldiers,' another gentleman teased. 'You must not forget those.'

Lord Chesterford, who clearly did not understand a jest, shook his finger and his moustache quivered. 'Our good men fought for our country and have returned to a thankless home. We serve them ill if they cannot find useful employment. Mark me! The Luddite riots in the north are just the beginning.'

The Prince Regent held his hands out in mock despair. 'Always, you return to riots.'

'We saw a riot on our wa—' Melody broke off, face colouring with the realisation that she had spoken without being introduced to His Royal Highness.

'Gracious me.' The Prince Regent peered around Vincent with an expression of some surprise. 'Sir David! Ah . . . I see that you have brought your most worthy wife, and a vision of loveliness.'

Once, such a comparison between them would have nettled Jane, who had long felt the shadow of her younger and more beautiful sister. The fact that she had found contentment with her situation and Melody was as yet unattached, if not a happy thought, at least relieved her of any symptoms of jealousy. So she was able to receive the Prince Regent's words with a smile and say, 'Your Royal Highness, may I present my sister, Miss Ellsworth.'

She was less able to overlook the surprise on that gentleman's countenance or the way his gaze darted from one face to the other, seeking a resemblance. They shared only the shape of their eyes, which they had from their mother.

The Prince Regent, ever the gallant, took Melody's hand and bent over it. 'A pleasure, madam.'

'The pleasure is entirely mine, I assure you, sir.' Melody lowered her eyes so she looked through her eyelashes at the Prince.

'But of course you are required to say that.'

'Not required, no.' Melody tilted her head towards him as though she were sharing a joke. 'I am required to say that I am grateful to be invited – which I am – and that you are most kind to invite me – which would be true, had you known that I was coming – but I am not required to tell you that it is a pleasure to meet you. By that, you may know that I am sincere.'

Throwing his head back, the Prince Regent laughed. Jane envied her sister the ease with which she made even the most excessive statements charming. She had the Prince Regent firmly in her grasp, along with the rest of his set.

'Now then, my dear, you had begun to say something when overwhelmed by my Most August Presence. Would you be so kind as to repeat it?'

'Only . . . it is about riots again, sir.' Melody dipped her head becomingly. 'We saw a riot of Luddites upon our arrival in London, so it is not only in the north.'

'Well, do not fret. We shall have no riots *here*.' He looked around at the other gentlemen and said more firmly, as though his word could cause it to be so. 'No riots.'

'My sister has come with us to experience the Season.' Jane pitched her voice so that the other men in their circle could hear, though not so loudly as to be indecorous. She wanted them to know that Melody was Out. 'This is her first event in London.'

'Then we shall direct our attention to pleasure, and leave these topics of unrest for another day. Sir David, Lady Vincent . . . would you be so kind as to offer us a diversion?'

Vincent inclined his head coolly, as if a request from a member of the royal family were part of everyday life. His colour mounted, though. From the sudden warmth that Jane felt in her cheeks, she suspected that she had flushed at the attention rather more than her husband had. Offering his arm, Vincent led her a little away from the group.

Jane lowered her voice to ask, 'Would you really decline the royal wedding?'

Vincent shuddered. 'Any wedding. I do not do weddings, which His Royal Highness knows. He is merely teasing me.'

'Ah.' Her mind drifted back to their own wedding, which had been a small affair, to her mother's eternal regret. If Melody—when Melody was married, Mrs Ellsworth would want more pomp than Jane and Vincent had obliged her with. Thinking of pomp . . . 'Would a *tableau vivant* serve, do you think?' Jane pulled her gloves off and the wind found her newly bare skin, chilling it.

'Admirably.' Vincent tucked in his chin and considered the lake. 'Would you feel up to a Jack Frost?'

'Of course, though it feels rather obvious.' More than that, she wanted some colour to relieve the ice and snow. 'What about Persephone?'

His eyes narrowed with thought. 'Her return, or when Hades seizes her? Ah . . . her return, of course. The spring.'

'My thoughts as well.'

With a grunt of assent, Vincent cast a *Sphère Obscurcie* around them, making them vanish from view within the ball of glamour. Outside the *Sphère*, several of the Prince Regent's guests gaped in astonishment. The technique that Vincent had developed was faster and more thorough a method for masking than any other Jane had seen. He took a single fold of glamour and twisted it to create a path for the sunlight to follow, guiding it around whatever lay in the *Sphère*'s midst. Other glamourists masked objects by creating a *trompe-l'œil* and deceiving the eye with a fully rendered illusion of the space without the object. That technique took scrupulous care and sometimes weeks to complete.

The speed of Vincent's technique had allowed the Duke of Wellington to defeat Napoleon the previous year at the Battle of Quatre Bras. Her husband employed it more regularly, as he did now, to create a private space in which to prepare a *tableau vivant*.

With haste, Jane sketched a Persephone around herself, looking back at Vincent's Hades. Working so quickly meant that their glamours were less completely rendered than the ones that they were creating for Lord Stratton. Jane likened it to creating a watercolour instead of an oil painting. Still, it took effort. By the time they had drawn the rugged cave from which Persephone was emerging, Jane's heart beat rapidly. A crowd had gathered around the Prince Regent in anticipation of their display.

'Ready?' Vincent's breath puffed in white plumes from Hades's mouth, as though the lord of the underworld were breathing fire.

Jane marked her hold on the slipknot she had ready. If Vincent's forte was his strength and speed, Jane's was her cleverness with knots. 'Yes.'

With a simple twist, Vincent dropped the *Sphère Obscurcie* that masked them. An audible gasp went up from a number of those assembled as the tableau appeared. Using his formidable stamina, Vincent managed all of the threads and folds surrounding him to make Hades's arm reach for Jane's Persephone. Jane answered by having Persephone step away from him. She would not have been able to do this before she had begun to work with Vincent. Her constitution had improved since then, though her heart raced as she held the threads, and her breath came rapidly. She had been cold before, but the exertion vanquished that.

Jane released the threads she had bound into a slipknot and the ground around her seemed to bloom into a patch of green dotted with purple crocuses. For this brief moment, spring had come. Led by the Prince Regent, the crowd burst into applause.

Jane and Vincent held the tableau for a moment longer, then released the folds masking themselves. They could, if the situation had warranted it, tie off the threads and step out of the illusion, but part of the charm of a *tableau vivant* was its transient nature. If their audiences were allowed close scrutiny, they would see the broad strokes and coarse stitches that went into creating so fast a glamour.

As they reappeared, the audience granted them another polite burst of applause, then went back to mingling, talking about what they had seen and what the weather was likely to be on the morrow.

Vincent wiped the sweat from his brow. 'I fear that the time spent resting at your parents' house, for all that it was comfortable, has left me without the endurance I once had.'

'I know.' Jane was all too aware of her breath as each exhalation hung steaming in the air. 'A week back at work is not enough, it seems.'

'We should have practised more at your . . .' Vincent raised his head, looking out at the lake. 'Is that Mr O'Brien with your sister?'

So involved had she been in creating the *tableau vivant* that Jane had not seen Melody depart from the Prince Regent's set, but now Melody hung on the arm of a young gentleman, not far from the edge of the lake. Both wore skates, and, though Mr O'Brien seemed uncertain on the ice, he supported Melody as they skated. His red hair flamed like a torch in the light. 'It is.'

Jane could not feel sanguine about seeing Mr O'Brien in

such intimacy with her sister. It was impossible to disregard the way that his interest had faded upon understanding that Melody was the sister of artisans. Entirely separate from his heritage, she wondered if his interest were sincere. Had the Prince Regent not so recently condescended to notice Melody, Jane would feel fewer doubts about the attention Mr O'Brien paid her now.

'Muse . . . what is wrong?'

'Nothing. Why?'

Vincent tilted his head and regarded her with incredulity. 'Perhaps I am misled, then. I thought I heard you snort.'

'That would not be ladylike.'

'Hm.' Vincent offered his arm. 'And yet . . .'

Sighing, Jane walked with him along the edge of the pond. 'If you will press me, then yes. I am disturbed that Mr O'Brien is attending Melody.'

'And?'

'He did not consider her so worth his while before the Prince Regent noticed her. I worry that he thinks to use her for her perceived consequence.'

Vincent peered past her to where the pair glided laughing across the ice. 'This seems unlikely.'

'No? Did you not see the way he cut short his visit when he realised who her relations were?'

'I thought he was simply being polite. We had finished work and were ready to depart. He, very properly, did not detain us.'

Jane opened her mouth to object, breath steaming out, and closed it again to think. When had Mr O'Brien made his excuses? 'Perhaps . . .'

A gust of wind caught laughter from the pond and carried it to them. Melody held Mr O'Brien's hands as he guided her across the ice. Even at a distance, the delight on her countenance was plain.

'She is happy. Is that not why we brought her to London? Where is the—' Vincent went rigid beside Jane, coming to a halt in the path. He turned and almost let go of her hand. Catching himself, Vincent made a studied effort to regain his composure.

Alarmed, Jane put a hand on his chest. 'Vincent?'

He caught her hand and bent down to whisper in her ear. 'My father. With his back to us.'

His father. Here? On the path ahead of them stood a tall well-built older gentleman with an elegantly cut coat. His hair had once been a dark brown, but was now brushed with silver where it fell over his collar. He rested one hand on a walking stick in a posture of casual disregard.

Facing him was an older gentleman with hair that matched the snow. His cheeks were reddened, though it was difficult to say if it was from the cold or anger. 'Sir. I may promise you that the extreme cold of the season is in no way caused by coldmongers. You may have my assurance on that.'

'Of a certainty, Lord Eldon. Your assurance is worthy of much consideration. I can think of no reason why you should have any partiality to the coldmongers.'

That Lord Verbury was here should cause no great wonder. He was, after all, an Earl, and as a peer he was likely to be in town for the Season. And yet it was beyond anything she had looked for to come upon him unawares in this manner. At Almack's Assembly, or in a salon, perhaps that might have been expected; but outside in the snow seemed an ill-fitted place for such an encounter.

In spite of her deep astonishment, Jane could not help but

study Lord Verbury, seeing Vincent in his height and the lines of his back. Jane had met none of Vincent's family in the time since their marriage, and, until Lady Penelope called, had assumed that she would not. Frederick Hamilton, the Earl of Verbury, had cast Vincent off when he decided to pursue a career in glamour. Jane's one attempt to contact the man, when Vincent's life had been in danger, had met with silence. She had had no desire to meet him since.

Lord Eldon's nostrils widened. 'Do you insinuate something, sir?'

'Should I?' Lord Verbury's inquiry chilled in the air.

'You seem to. I would rather you said it than hide behind a façade of seeming politeness.'

With a shrug, Lord Verbury drew his walking stick across the snow, marking a line between them. 'I have no need to insinuate anything. If you tell me that the coldmongers are not creating this unnatural cold, why would any right-thinking man dispute you? Your heritage is a matter of common knowledge. "Common" is perhaps the best word for a man who was born a coldmonger's son.'

With that, Lord Verbury gave Lord Eldon his shoulder and turned on his heel. He was now facing Jane and Vincent, though his countenance betrayed nothing.

Vincent's arm tightened under her hand. He murmured, 'In all likelihood, he will not even condescend to notice us.'

'There you are.' Lord Verbury crossed the snow and stopped in front of them, planting his walking stick. 'I was told you would be here.'

'I did not have the same intelligence, alas.' Vincent's voice was steady and easy, but his hand pressed Jane's so firmly against his arm that her bones ached.

'You might have, if you had spoken with Penelope.' Inclining his head, Lord Verbury seemed to see Jane for the first time. 'This is your wife?'

'Lady Vincent.' Jane could almost hear his teeth grate. 'Allow me to present the Earl of Verbury.'

'How do you do?' Jane dropped a curtsy, as was owed to mere filial duty.

'Very well, thank you.' He bowed with a surprising degree of charm. 'My son spoke so highly of you that I was disappointed when he did not bring you to our home.'

'I—we have been quite busy.' Jane had not looked for anything like interest from all she had heard of Vincent's father. She had rather expected a dismissal.

'Perhaps we might remedy that, since we are all in London.' That courtesy was all the attention the Earl paid her, fixing again on Vincent. 'I had heard the Prince Regent honoured you with a knighthood. The Royal Guelphic Order, I understand. I congratulate you.' He tucked his chin in, the same way that Vincent did when thinking. Jane shivered. 'It seems that your chosen profession is turning out to be a benefit rather than the stigma I expected.'

'Do I hear an admission of a mistake?' Vincent's voice was admirably level.

Lord Verbury pursed his lips. After a moment, he looked at the ground. 'You hear a wish to repair the relations with my son.'

'I must admit this comes as something of a surprise.' Through his coat, Jane could feel Vincent trembling, but he gave no visible sign of how deeply affected his sensibility was. Had she not known him, she might have thought he was indifferent.

'A surprise that I should have an interest in my son?'

'You have not shown one thus far.'

'What do you expect? You came to me a year and a half ago, asking to return so you could marry, and then threw me over again.' He glanced at Jane. Here was the sneer she had expected. 'To be a *glamourist*.'

She lifted her chin and matched his gaze. 'You have a peculiar way of mending bridges, sir. Have you really so little understanding of your son as that? His art is his life.'

'Glamour.' He snorted. 'I should advise you to give up glamour as a profession. Have you considered having children?'

Jane stiffened, shocked into silence by the bluntness of his attack. She had made every effort to put her miscarriage behind her, but all the horror returned. She could lay the blame for the unhappy event on no one but herself, and yet, had this man replied to her letter when she needed his aid to save Vincent's life in Binche, she would never have been forced to the exertions that she had faced.

'That is quite enough.' Vincent turned Jane from Lord Verbury. 'Good day, sir.'

'Wait! If you will not treat with me as your father, then treat with me as a client.'

Jane laughed openly. 'Why on earth should we consider such a request? You have established that you have no use for me, Vincent or our skills.'

'I spoke poorly.' Lord Verbury ground his teeth and stared away from them, watching Melody skate on the pond. Jane could not but imagine that he was aware of who she was. 'I need to commission you.'

'Your dining room needs to be redecorated?' Vincent raised a brow.

'No . . . no, I refer to your other talents. The ones that earned you the knighthood.'

Vincent glanced at Jane. They had told no one of his reasons for being in Binche in the days before the Battle of Quatre Bras. The Prince and the Duke of Wellington had asked them to keep the matter private. The one person to whom Jane had laid the situation bare had been Lord Verbury, when she had written begging for aid. In this moment, Jane knew that Lord Verbury had received her letter and had *chosen* not to answer. He had chosen to let his son die.

'It is a matter of some discretion.' Lowering his voice, Lord Verbury stepped closer. 'You have access now to people of quality who would not suspect you. The Prince employs you often, I think?'

Jane shivered. Though he had not stated it, there could be no doubt that Lord Verbury wished them to spy on a peer – likely a member of the cabinet.

Bowing, Vincent said, 'I will work for the good of the Crown, but spying on my fellow Englishmen is not to my taste.'

'Will you—'

Without waiting to hear what his father had to propose, Vincent led Jane away. They left the Earl of Verbury standing in the snowy path, quite alone.

# SEVEN

# Disordered Senses

At home that evening, Jane attempted to carry on the whole of the dinner conversation by herself. Vincent stared into his soup and made the occasional requisite reply, but she had no real sense that he heard her. Twice, he drew breath as though to speak, but, upon seeing Melody, exhaled and asked Jane to pass the salt. The second time, she was obliged to point out that he already had it.

Melody pensively drew flowers with the sauce for her lamb and said little beyond noting that the day had been lovely. Her every look at Jane, though, spoke expressively of a desire for conversation, if only they were alone. It was with some relief, then, that Vincent pushed back his chair and announced that he was 'going to the studio to work' and Melody declared an intention 'to go to the parlour to practise the pianoforte'.

Jane sat for a moment after they left, trying to decide which to approach first. Her immediate desire was to go to Vincent, whose disturbed sensibilities had been more freely displayed than was his usual habit. It spoke to the disorder of his mind that he could so little govern his countenance. She suspected, though, that he required some time alone to organise his thoughts. His natural reserve had come up like a shield around him. Working glamour would relieve some of his tension.

She went, therefore, to Melody.

Her sister sat at the pianoforte, turning through the sheet music on the instrument. Occasionally, she would lift a page and hold it at arms' end, squinting at it. Jane shut the parlour door. 'You appeared to enjoy yourself today.'

'Yes . . .' Melody picked out a scale on the piano. Sighing, she closed the keyboard. 'It was very kind of Mr O'Brien to assist me on the pond.'

Cautiously, Jane leaned against the instrument as she felt her path forward in the conversation. 'He paid you a great deal of attention.'

'I am conscious of that. La! When he rescued me from the Prince Regent I was beyond grateful.'

'Rescued you?'

'Oh—oh, well. You were occupied with the *tableau vivant,* and the Prince Regent—he is very gallant. But. But he is . . . well.'

He was fat and given to drink. His excesses could cause him to take gallantry beyond mere approbation and into indecorum. 'I see. I am sorry that I left you to his attentions.'

Melody coloured and Jane wondered how far the Prince might have gone in her absence. Thoughtless. Truly thoughtless of her to have left Melody to her own devices amidst that group. Worse – no, far worse – was that she had willingly pushed Melody among them without regard for how their attention might be displayed. The Prince Regent's set had a well-known reputation for licentiousness.

'Do not feel bad. It was only a few moments, truly. Mr O'Brien saw my . . . my confusion and asked me to skate. It was over quickly.'

Jane closed her eyes. With any other man, she might have hope of some consequences to such an affront, but not the Prince Regent. Even in their own home, his rank was such that she and Melody were assiduously avoiding any details, lest they be overheard. The difference in their stations alone left them with little recourse, no matter how objectionable his attentions might become. 'I will not leave you in that circumstance again.'

'Thank you.' Melody smoothed her skirts. 'Honestly, there are days when I am tempted to stomp about in boots and cut my hair.'

'Like me?' Jane touched her cropped hair where it peeked out from under her mobcap. Even if Melody's head were shaved, she would still be of surpassing loveliness.

'Well, yes. If I had accomplishments, then perhaps . . . at any rate, Mr O'Brien was very kind. He reminded me, at times, of someone else, though they are nothing alike. But the way he looked at me, as though . . .' She broke off, sighing heavily, and stood. She paced around the pianoforte, stopping to square the small vase on a side table. 'I know that I should not feel sorry for myself because I am pretty, but sometimes it is nice to have someone speak to me as though I am not.'

'Was he impertinent?'

'Oh no.' Melody continued her turn around the room. 'Not at all, but . . . I suppose it is only his spectacles, but it did feel as though he looked at *me*.'

'Are you certain you were not simply grateful to have been rescued?' No matter what service he performed for her at the skating party, Jane hoped that Mr O'Brien's interest in Melody was not simply because of her perceived connection to His Royal Highness.

'I do not know.' Melody straightened a shawl hanging over the back of the sofa, smoothing the lace edges with a frown. 'That is my trouble, I think. I do not trust my feelings in this.'

'You have met him only twice. This is too soon to have a sense of how you feel.'

'How many times had you met Vincent before you knew? You disliked him violently at first – do not pretend that you did not.' Melody turned to her with earnest confusion lifting her brows. 'That is what frightens me so. If I am to judge by my history, then I should distrust any man for whom I felt an instant regard.'

'Do you . . . am I to understand that you hold Mr O'Brien in high regard?'

'I don't know. Oh, Jane. I do not know. Do I hold him in regard, or am I merely lonely?'

The pain in her voice led Jane to cross the room and put her arms around her sister. 'I am so sorry that I have neglected you.'

Melody clung to her as she had done when a child. After a long moment, she said, 'You are busy, with your work and with Vincent.' Lifting her head, she wiped her eyes, which were quite red. 'La! I am simply spent from the excitement. Do not fret on my account. It is nothing that a good night's sleep will not cure, which is where I shall take myself now.'

'Are you certain? Is there nothing more that you want to discuss?'

Firmly, Melody shook her head. 'Thank you. No.'

They said their good nights, but Jane was left feeling that she had failed her sister. She had thought that as a married woman she could be Melody's chaperon, but her work seemed to prevent it. Who had the strongest claim to her time? Her sister or her husband?

For some time, Jane remained in the drawing room, thinking through everything that Melody had said and what she had implied. She stared into the fire, but found no answers among the embers. So she roused herself and climbed the stairs to the studio and Vincent.

When she opened the door, Vincent stood in the middle of a whirling mass of glamour. He had fashioned a *thing* that had no distinct shape, no defined illusion, only an abstract accretion of colour and light. Folds of crimson and black roiled like a confusion of storm clouds. It filled the space, obscuring even the walls.

The disorder of the glamour struck a raw nerve in Jane. The deep reds and charcoals spoke of fear and anger. It almost obscured Vincent, who stood in its midst, directing enormous folds in swirling patterns. The amount of energy it must take to maintain so large a structure astonished Jane. More, it alarmed her. She had seen Vincent distressed, but never so undone.

On the ground near the door, Vincent's coat lay in a crumpled heap. Not far from that, his cravat nestled atop his waistcoat. She half expected to see his shirt abandoned as well. In the silence of the top floor, his breath sounded loud and ragged.

If the nature of art was to convey emotion, this glamour might be applauded for the sense of panic it caused her. Jane took a few steps into the illusion. 'Vincent?'

The structure stopped its revolution, a few pieces at the outer edges drifting to a halt after the rest. In a moment, it began moving again. 'Yes?'

'Do you have anything you wish to discuss?'

With a sigh that sounded like the ether tearing, Vincent released the glamour masking him. The heavy crimson folds faded first, taking the yellows and deep ash with them until the studio was bare of glamour. Jane shivered, recognising that Vincent had held *all* of that glamour at once. Nothing had been tied off. The amount of effort it must have taken was all too visible in his appearance.

His cheeks had a high colour to them. His shirt was soaked with sweat and the fabric clung to his broad chest. He gasped for breath as though he had been running for hours. Vincent wiped his hand across his face, smearing the perspiration on his brow. 'I dislike burdening you with my troubles.'

'It is not a burden. Truly. And if you need further justification, consider that I will feel guilty when I burden you with mine.' She paused, shifting from one foot to the other. 'Or would you rather I not confide in you?'

He grunted and almost laughed. 'I will grant you the point.' He slid his hand across his hair, matting it down. 'There is little to tell. My father and I do not get along.'

At least he made no pretence of misunderstanding what she inquired about. Jane wet her lips and tried again. 'Is it that he— you said that he disciplined you when you were a child?' Some things she knew, but Vincent had always been guarded with his past. He was willing to discuss everything that had happened since he became Mr David Vincent, but said little about his life as the Right Honourable Vincent Hamilton, third son of the Earl of Verbury. From few things he had told her, his father possessed strict ideas of propriety and exacting standards for what comprised the masculine ideal. He had thought Vincent's interest in the 'womanly' art of glamour beneath him, and made every effort to break him of it. Even knowing that, she was unprepared for the severe disorder of senses that Vincent now displayed.

'You mean the beatings?' Vincent shrugged, lacing his fingers behind his neck. 'It is not that. My father made sure I was well trained in all things masculine, and I feel certain that I should win any corporal confrontation since I am younger than he. To be honest . . . to be honest, the strength of my feelings surprised me.'

'You were shocked to see him. Naturally so.' Jane went to her husband, stopping just short of touching him. His resemblance to a wild bear was so strong that she was not certain touch would be welcome.

'I will own that I was. More so that he would acknowledge me.'

'It is no wonder that when he spoke to us your sensibility should be affected.'

Vincent stared at the wall, brow knit in thought. In a very low voice, full of feeling, he said, 'But it was when he spoke to *you* that I—' Groaning, he tilted his head back and stared at the skylights and the dark sky beyond. 'I could not think. I could not draw breath. I could only hold myself still and not hit him. I had forgotten what it was to be angry all the time.'

'It did me no harm.'

He dropped his gaze back down to her. 'Not yet. That . . . you see, that is the genius of my father. The punishment always comes, but you never know when.'

Jane could only stare in appalled fascination at Vincent. His childhood was so foreign from the convivial household in which she grew up that she could scarcely comprehend it.

'The only question I have is—I keep thinking that I should not have turned down his commission so I could at least know where the battle is to be played.'

'Why must there be a battle? Is there a reason we must engage?'

'I—perhaps not.' Vincent groaned again and turned in a great circle, as though he were still managing the glamour. 'It is hard to think not. He controlled every minute of my life until I went to university.'

'But he no longer has any hold on you.'

Vincent was silent, but pulled a fold of glamour out of the ether. He sketched a rough tree in the air, passing his hand through the branches. He was so focused Jane thought he might have forgotten her, but Vincent unstitched the tree and stared at where it had been. 'He has always found a way to make me do what he wants.'

Jane laid a hand gently on his arm. 'Not always, I think.'

Recalling himself, Vincent looked at her. He lifted the tips of her fingers to his lips. 'No. I suppose not always.'

In spite of the dampness of his shirt, Jane snuggled in and lifted her head to kiss him on the cheek. His skin tasted of salt. 'Come to bed?'

He squeezed her close. 'Ah, Muse. I shall not be good company tonight. You go, and I will be down shortly.'

She wanted to protest, but recognised his urge to exhaust himself and drive thought from his mind. She could not do that for him, so she kissed him again and went to bed, leaving Vincent to weave webs of glamour alone.

# EIGHT

# Feeble Protestations

Vincent did not come to bed until sometime long after Jane had fallen asleep. When she awoke, he was in his nightshirt on the window seat, with one leg drawn up and his elbow propped upon his knee. His head rested against the glass as he stared outside. She doubted he saw anything beyond the window.

When she stirred, he abandoned this pensive stance and greeted her with admirable aplomb. By mutual agreement they did not speak of his upset of the day previous. Still, she saw it in his silence on the way to Stratton House, and in the way in which he applied himself to their work.

Vincent often threw himself into glamour when he was troubled. She could not complain about this tendency since it was one she shared. The urge to have something which one could control, to fold light and have it answer, gave her a satisfaction that no other art did.

They worked through the morning. When Jane stepped back from the birdcage she was rendering for a better view, her fingers ached from the fine work. She rubbed her hands together, trying to ease some of the stiffness.

Vincent was still at work, pulling clouds into being in the sky he had fashioned overhead. Jane wondered anew at her husband's ability to work delicate glamour from such a distance. She would have needed a scaffold in order to get close enough to manage the folds.

She waited until he tied off the thread he was working before addressing him. 'Shall we pause for a nuncheon? I brought apples and cheese with me.' Lord Stratton had been providing them a regular tea, but a bite at midday served as a useful break.

'Hm?' Vincent spun, as though he had forgotten anyone else was in the room.

His face paled and he staggered, knees buckling. He dropped heavily. Catching himself before he pitched forward, Vincent knelt on the floor, braced on his right hand, his left pressed to his brow.

Jane was by his side in an instant. She should have been paying more attention. He always worked himself too hard, and she had known he had exerted himself to a great degree last night. Jane steadied him with a hand on his back. Through his waistcoat, she could feel his heart pounding against his ribs.

'I am all right.' His voice suggested anything but good health.

She brushed his hair back from his brow, taking his temperature. He was overheated. Jane wove a cooling breeze with her free hand. 'Did you sleep at all last night?'

'I was only unsteady for a moment.' Vincent straightened, gathering himself to rise.

Jane pressed her hands to his shoulders. 'Pray be still for a moment longer.'

'Truly, Jane. It was only because I turned too fast.' His voice sounded steadier, and his breath was somewhat more regular. 'This is not unusual. You have fainted on more than one occasion.'

'Yes, but you have a history of working nearly to death and I do not.' She glanced at the door, wishing that they had brought Melody with them today. Jane would have liked to send someone for a cold compress.

'This is not the same.'

'And I would like that to remain true.' She should take him home. Though she did not think he was in serious danger, she did not trust him to govern his own health today. Jane gathered her gown about her and rose. 'If you will wait here, I will ask to borrow the Strattons' carriage.'

'No. Absolutely not.' Sitting back on his heels, but thankfully not rising beyond that, Vincent looked at her with an aghast expression. 'We have work to do.'

'The delay of half a day will not set us behind time as much as if you work yourself into an illness.'

'I am fine.' His voice was sharp, but he still did not rise. 'When I became ill, I had been working till dawn for a fortnight.'

'Can you tell me that you did not work glamour until nearly dawn?'

Vincent opened his mouth and closed it again without speaking. He scrubbed his hair and grimaced. 'I begin to see why other couples keep separate bedchambers.'

Jane pressed her advantage. 'Can you tell me that you slept last night? At all?'

'I tell you that I only lost my balance for a moment.' Vincent pushed himself to his feet, not entirely holding back a groan. He straightened and brushed his waistcoat off. 'It has passed. You see? I am fine.'

'And I am getting a carriage.' Jane took his hand, squeezing it. 'Please. Do not let him do this to you. You will make yourself ill, and for no cause.'

Her husband stared at the floor, lips tight. A drop of sweat trickled from his brow unheeded and followed the line of his cheek. He gave a single nod. 'Very well.'

Relieved, Jane squeezed his hand again and left the ballroom. Lord Stratton could usually be found in the library at this hour, so she sought him there. As she neared the open door, she caught the edges of a heated conversation. One of the participants spoke with a strong Irish accent. Through the door Jane could make out words such as, 'Cannot allow—' and 'Luddites' and 'learn from history.'

Then, Mr O'Brien's voice carried clearly out of the library in a full sentence. 'If we must, we will march on Parliament itself.'

Startled, Jane stopped on the threshold. Mr O'Brien was addressing a young man with dull brown hair and spotted cheeks. He wore the clothes of a servant, complete with deep green knee breeches and coat. Only the want of a wig kept his habit from being full livery, although even then it would not have been from the Stratton household.

Both men started at her appearance in the library doorway. Mr O'Brien's countenance showed his alarm with a flush of deep red. He removed his spectacles and polished them with a handkerchief. 'Lady Vincent. To what do I owe the pleasure?'

Affecting not to have overheard anything, Jane came further into the room. 'I was hoping to speak to your father and arrange for the use of the carriage. I am afraid that Sir David has taken a turn, and I should like to see him home with a minimum of fuss.'

Settling the spectacles once more upon his nose, he made no acknowledgement of the other man in the room, as though he were nothing but a servant. 'He is not ill, I hope?'

'Oh, no. Nothing so severe. It is not unusual for glamourists to sometimes overheat when working. It will pass, but with the weather so cool, I do not want to chance him catching a chill.' She smiled with what she hoped was a demure expression. 'He will not admit to it, of course.'

'I understand, quite well. We men are as prone to infirmity as any lady, but are trained from an early age to deny it. I envy your husband for having you to watch over him.' His colour had almost returned to normal, although his cheeks might have been a trifle pinker than before. 'Of course, you may have the use of the carriage.'

The other man stood in silent attention, as though he were awaiting orders. He looked past them both to the wall.

'Thank you, that is very kind.' Jane glanced to where the man looked, and saw that his gaze was fixed upon the crucifix hanging there.

'I will have the carriage waiting at the front door for you.' Mr O'Brien crossed the room to her side. 'Your *tableau vivant* at the Prince Regent's skating party yesterday was quite wonderful.'

'Thank you.' Jane let him lead her towards the door.

'I must admit that I have been so intent on my studies for the past few months that I did not recognise your name when we met, though I have come to understand that I should have. My friends are beside themselves with envy that we have engaged the Prince Regent's glamourists.'

'That is very kind.'

'How is Miss Ellsworth?'

'She is well, thank you.'

'And is she with you today? I had looked in the music room, but did not see her.'

83

'She stayed home today.' Interesting that he appeared to have sought Melody out, though it was *possible* that the inquiry was simple courtesy. Still, Jane could not help but note that his interest seemed to coincide with learning that they were 'the Prince Regent's glamourists'. She smiled at him. 'I am grateful to you for your kindness to her yesterday.'

'Ah . . . well, she seemed not entirely comfortable. I thought she might appreciate the opportunity to skate.'

'I believe she enjoyed it.'

'Did she?' He stopped by the door, a smile brightening his face. 'I am glad to hear it. Well. I shall call that carriage for you right away.' He stepped out of the library with her and closed the door behind them. The nameless servant stayed in the room.

As Jane went back to the ballroom to retrieve Vincent, her thoughts were in a tumult. What had Mr O'Brien been discussing when she entered?

Vincent protested again when Jane came to fetch him, but the waiting carriage served as better persuasion than any of her words. It would be thoughtless to call for the carriage and then send it away unused. Jane waited until they were at home and in the privacy of their bedchamber before she felt comfortable speaking to Vincent about her concerns.

Thankfully, Melody was out shopping when they came home. Jane shut the door, reminded uncomfortably of Mr O'Brien closing the library door on the nameless servant. 'Are you feeling any better?'

'I felt fine there.' Vincent eased off his coat and hung it over a chair by the fireplace. The fire had been laid but not yet lit. They were home during the day so rarely that they had no doubt caught the servants off guard. 'I would feel better if we were still working.'

She had no wish to review that question, and so changed the subject as she walked to the hearth to light the fire. 'I overheard something odd at the Strattons'.'

'Mm?' He crossed to her and took the matches off the mantelpiece. 'Let me. You will dirty your dress.'

'Thank you.' They could call for someone to light the fire, but Jane wanted Vincent to herself for a while. 'Mr O'Brien was talking to a serving man who was not in Stratton livery. He said, "If we must, we will march on Parliament itself."'

Vincent raised his eyebrows. 'In what circumstance?'

'I hardly know. I heard him mention Luddites, but he does not seem the type.' Jane leaned against the mantelpiece as he struck a match. 'They had been having a conversation with some heat before I arrived, but I only heard a few words. I did not mean to hear even that much.'

He held the match to the kindling and a twist of smoke rose into the air. 'But it was unavoidable?'

She struck his shoulder playfully. 'Stop. It was not as though I were eavesdropping. The door was open, so I could hardly help it.'

'Then it must not be anything terribly diabolical, or the door would have been shut.' The thin piece of wood caught and Vincent sat back on his heels with a grunt of satisfaction.

'But they seemed so surprised when I entered. I think they thought it *was* shut.'

Vincent pushed himself to his feet and grasped the mantelpiece. His hand clenched the marble and he stared straight ahead with the half-vacant expression that Jane recognised as another dizzy spell.

'Are you all right?'

He let go of the mantelpiece and turned away from her. 'I was thinking of what plays might have lines such as this. They were, perhaps, practising for amateur theatricals.'

Jane frowned, considering. 'But the serving man was not in livery from the Strattons. He was in green, and had left his wig off.'

'No wig!' Vincent dropped into a chair in front of the fire and stretched his legs out in front of him. 'I am shocked. Shocked.'

Jane glared at him. 'You are not taking me seriously.'

Vincent pulled at the ends of his cravat as though wishing to shed it. 'Do you want to change out of your work dress?'

'Yes, thank you.' Jane sat on the arm of his chair. 'But I can fend for myself quite well.'

'I am not actually ill. I am fully capable of untying laces. There is no need to coddle me.'

Jane held up her hands in conciliation. 'I know you are not, but I want to keep you healthy. Having almost lost you once, I am perhaps overcautious, but I would rather ask you to humour me than . . . than any alternatives.'

Vincent let his head fall back against the chair and scowled at the ceiling. 'I confess that I am not certain what you fear. About Mr O'Brien, that is. You have made your fears abundantly clear with regards to me.'

She let his ill temper pass as the sign of fatigue that it was. Her husband could be the very definition of a curmudgeon. 'My fear is that Mr O'Brien might have meant that he is planning a march on Parliament.'

'Why?'

Very slowly, Jane enunciated, 'Because that is what he said.'

'No, I meant, why would he march on Parliament?' Vincent rolled his head to regard her. 'Do you want help with your dress?'

'Thank you, yes.' Jane sighed at his continued attempts to change the subject, but turned so that he could undo her laces. Resolutely, she returned to her purpose. 'I do not know why he would march, but consider: his loyalties might lie in Ireland or with the Pope.'

'It seems unlikely. Who tied this knot?' He tugged at the back of her dress.

'You did.'

He snorted and tugged again. 'I might have to cut it. Muse, I did not think I was fatigued, but this knot . . . I must have been half-asleep.'

'More than half, I think.' Jane turned her head to look at him over her shoulder, favouring him with a smile.

He humphed in reply, but she did not regret pulling him away from the Strattons. Deep circles lined his eyes, and his lids were half lowered. 'Did our Mr O'Brien say anything else of import?'

'He asked after Melody.' Her dress loosened suddenly as Vincent released the knot with a cry of triumph. 'I worry, Vincent. Recall how he began to flirt with Melody at the skating party? What if he is interested in her because of your connection to the Prince Regent?'

'Again, I say this is unlikely.' Vincent pulled on her sleeve, sliding it off her shoulder, and sat up to kiss the skin exposed there.

Jane shivered. 'But you saw . . . you saw how his manner to her changed both at the house, and again at the Prince Regent's.'

'Yes, but, Muse . . .' He kissed higher on her shoulder,

moving to her neck. 'You are proposing that Mr O'Brien is plotting to overthrow the government using your younger sister. How?'

Jane opened her mouth and stared at the wall. Said aloud, it made no sense. Yet she could not discount Mr O'Brien's very real alarm at being overheard. Vincent had not seen him. Jane did not know what was happening, but she felt quite assured that something untoward was afoot.

# NINE

# A Fair Exchange

Over the next weeks, Vincent's spirits regained something of their usual steadiness. If he did not sleep well, neither did he stay up deliberately late. Jane did her best to distract him, but only met with limited success. Melody continued to come with them to Stratton House, professing that it was because of the weather and as an escape from ennui, but it was clear to Jane that the attraction was due to Mr O'Brien.

More than once she found him in the Strattons' music room with Melody, their heads bent over a book or engaging in some other pretext for closeness. While she never found them behind closed doors, and there was always a servant in attendance, she could not feel entirely comfortable with his attentions. It was not a possible match. Jane could only imagine the hysterics her mother would indulge in if she knew that Melody was attaching an Irish Catholic man, no matter that his father was a Baron. And so Jane was relieved when their cousin's birthday fête finally came around, as it gave her an opportunity to introduce Melody to some other gentlemen.

On the day of the party, nature saw fit to deliver yet more snow, though it melted almost as soon as it touched the pavement, leaving only slush on the ground. A line of footmen stood outside Sir Prescott's residence with umbrellas to convey guests into the house.

Once the Vincents and Melody had shed their wraps, they joined the throng and looked for their host in order to offer their felicitations to Mr Colgrove for reaching his majority. The parlour had been entirely done over with a glamural portraying the Battle of Quatre Bras with the Duke of Wellington astride his horse, Copenhagen, and his sword held over his head. The work was quite good, with some interesting uses of colour to direct the eye.

Vincent made a noise of approbation and bent his head to Melody and Jane. 'This is Moyer's work, unless I miss my guess. See how he forms faces in the clouds? It is a peculiarity of his.'

Melody tapped his arm with her fan. 'Do you never stop working? La! I declare, I have never known someone so possessed. It is one of the things which appeals about you, I suppose.'

To Jane's surprise, Vincent blushed. 'He is an associate. We were in school together.'

'Do you think he is here?' Melody looked around with interest.

Jane said, 'We can inquire of our host. It might depend on how recently the glamural was created, and if there are additional effects for the party.'

The crowd stirred and revealed Mr Colgrove, chatting amiably with a mixed selection of young men and women. He showed to advantage in the abundance of candlelight. It lent his pale eyes some warmth, and the animation with which he attended his companions spoke well of him. He noticed Melody and his face lit further. Stepping forward, he greeted her with some warmth. 'Miss Ellsworth, this is a pleasure.'

Introductions were quickly made to the others in his set.

To Jane's surprise, one of the young ladies was a woman with dark skin and features which suggested that she was from India, though she was introduced as Miss Godwin. Dressed in the height of fashion, she offered Vincent a curtsy. 'Sir David, I had the pleasure of seeing your work in the ballroom at Carlton House. Having heard so much about you, it is a great pleasure to make your acquaintance.' Her voice was beautifully modulated, without a hint of her foreign origin.

'Thank you, but I cannot claim the credit for my own.' Vincent indicated Jane. 'My wife is my equal partner.'

'How fortunate . . . ' she murmured. The men in the circle leaned forward to hang upon her words. She had a decided beauty and a quickness to her expression that held one's attention.

Mr Colgrove pulled his eyes away from Miss Godwin to bow to Jane. 'Of course, any man would be happy to have a helpmate as accomplished as my cousin. I think, above all, that one should strive to find a partner with whom one is well matched.'

The young ladies surrounding Mr Colgrove seemed to take note. Jane could almost see them stationing themselves in the hunt for his inheritance. Her mother's letters had it that, upon achieving his majority, Mr Colgrove was now worth some twenty thousand pounds.

'I have often had the same conversation with my sister,' Jane replied, attempting to bring Melody forth. Her sister's bright hair shone in the candlelight as if it had been gilded. Though she did not often think much of her mother's attempts at matchmaking, Mr Colgrove would indeed be a good match, and there were several other gentlemen in his set who might also be appropriate.

'Speaking of glamurals, might I inquire who did yours, Mr Colgrove?' Vincent broke in, studying a detail on the wall nearest them.

'Hm? Some chap from the Royal Academy.' He frowned, looking about as if just noticing it. 'Do you like it? We should have asked you, of course, but thought such a simple thing beneath your notice.' To the rest of the group, he said, 'I trust you will forgive my pride in my relations. Sir David and Lady Vincent have received several commissions from the Prince Regent.'

Vincent gave a brief smile of acknowledgement with his lips pressed firmly together. The poor dear did so dislike praise, especially when he thought it unfounded. 'Is Mr Moyer here, by chance?'

'The glamourist? He is in one of the rooms belowstairs until we are ready for—well, I do not want to spoil it, but we do have a *tableau vivant* planned for later.'

Jane once again reflected on how different their lives would be if Vincent did not have the favour of the Prince Regent. The notice that they received here had nothing to do with their abilities, or their relation to Mr Colgrove, or anything save His Royal Highness. Even being a highly proficient glamourist would have left them in the servants' quarters. Mr Moyer was not as good as Vincent, but Jane doubted that anyone who was not adept in glamour could have told the difference in their abilities. She would have accepted that life – and willingly – to be with Vincent, but it made her all the more conscious of how much he had chosen to give up when he abandoned his family name.

'Then perhaps this is a good time for me to pay my respects, as he is not presently engaged.'

Jane repressed a smile, recognising her husband's need to flee the press of people. Though she wished him to be comfortable in groups, she knew him too well to insist that he stay when so clear an opportunity to escape presented itself.

'Good of you to offer encouragement to the lesser talents.' Mr Colgrove turned to look for a footman and motioned him forward. 'Will you show Sir David where we put that glamourist chap?'

Jane was tempted to go with him, but her duty to Melody was quite clear, so she stayed by her sister's side. Turning to Mr Allsbrook – a young dandy with dark hair of the 'frightened owl' variety and a suit so snug that he surely could not sit – Jane opened with the usual conversation about the weather.

He replied with, 'I shall be grateful when the snow has departed. Snow in May is absurd! Do you know, I have not been out to my country house once?'

'Not at all?' Melody raised her eyebrows with curiosity. 'What a pity. I have always loved the way snow clings to trees. It is so picturesque.'

Jane need not have any concerns about bringing Melody to anyone's attention. As she spoke, every gentleman in their group leaned unconsciously towards her. The only woman who possessed even a tenth of her grace was Miss Godwin. Once, Jane had despaired of ever escaping the shadow cast by her sister, but now she rejoiced to see her shine so.

'You would not love snow if you were depending on fine weather to do your hunting,' Mr Allsbrook replied.

'The weather truly has been wretched.' Mr Colgrove vied for Melody's attention. 'I was telling Lady Vincent that we had dismissed our coldmongers because they were an unnecessary expense.'

Another gentleman tucked his hands behind his back with a complacent look. 'As did we. They demand high wages for the little they do.'

Miss Godwin tilted her head, ostrich feathers waving gracefully above her hair, and pointed her fan at Mr Colgrove. 'If the weather changes, what will you do then?'

'Why, ask Mr Moyer to cool the room. What is a coldmonger, but a glamourist who can do only one thing? Why retain one when you can hire someone who can do both?'

Melody spread her fan and waved it slowly to stir the air. 'But a coldmonger's work is treacherous. One can hardly deny them a reward for that.'

'Spoken like a gentle soul, Miss Ellsworth,' Mr Colgrove said. 'But would you have me pay for work that I do not require?'

'La! From what I understand, their wages are set to take into account that a coldmonger works only part of the year.' Melody folded her fan and rested it in her open hand, in a challenge. 'What of the bill that Lord Eldon has proposed to offer relief to the working poor? Coldmongers would not be in that class if the great houses retained them as they used to do.'

Jane could hardly contain her astonishment. Where had this sudden political consciousness come from? Melody had never shown an interest in anything beyond the dictates of fashion, and in Jane's memory read nothing but novels.

Mr Allsbrook shook his head. 'It is more likely to cause social unrest than not, if people begin to think they deserve care without holding a job. Look at what is happening with the Luddites, if you need proof of that. They seem to think that they are entitled to weave, when there are better and less expensive ways of making cloth now.'

'Exactly,' Mr Colgrove said. 'Let them find other work, and

help them in that. But wages for doing nothing? That I cannot support, no matter how much I admire the worthiness of your good intentions.'

'So long as you admire something, I can hope to convince you of more.' Melody flirted her fan open and peered at him over the top.

From behind Jane, a scrap of conversation pulled her attention away. A gentleman with the hoarse tones of an older man said, 'Lord Verbury, a pleasure to see you this evening.'

Jane sent thanks that Vincent had already left the vicinity. What in heaven's name was his father doing at her cousin's birthday? She could not help but think of Vincent's statement that they would have to engage. Bracing herself, Jane stepped away from Melody, confident that her sister was in her element, and turned to address the Earl of Verbury.

He was in conversation with another gentleman, who wore the braids of an Admiral and a hoary moustache in the older style. The Admiral was shaking Lord Verbury's hand, heartily. 'Devil of a good speech about the coldmongers the other day. I might wish you could do something about the Catholic situation as well.'

'That is likely to take care of itself. So long as His Royal Highness does not give in to the temptation to allow them to take a seat in Parliament, I think we shall have no trouble.'

'Quite so, quite so . . .' The Admiral shook his head. 'I still remember all that business when the Prince Regent's illegal marriage to the Fitzherbert woman came out. I think half the kingdom was afraid he would convert to marry her, and the other half wished he would so he could not inherit the throne. Still, it is a bloody good thing they cannot marry outside their faith, or we would be a Papist state for certain by now.'

Jane glanced back at Melody. Catholics could not marry outside their faith? She had never known a Catholic to do so, but had not realised that it was actually forbidden. And yet, hearing them speak, she remembered the uproar when the Prince Regent's attempt to marry Mrs Fitzherbert came to light. She had been too young at the time to pay much attention to it, but the memory made her heart sink. What did it say of Mr O'Brien's intentions if he could not even offer his hand to Melody?

Much as she might wish to hear more of this conversation, it was but a matter of moments before the Earl noticed her, and she would rather have the benefit of approaching him first. Hardening her resolve, Jane stepped forward and offered the Earl a curtsy of greeting.

'Lord Verbury, it is a surprise to see you.'

Her surprise increased when he appropriated her hand and lifted it to his lips with a bow. 'I trust you did not take a chill at the skating party?'

'Not at all.' She arranged her face into a placid expression to hide the disquiet she felt.

Lord Verbury turned to the Admiral and presented Jane. 'This is my youngest son's wife. May I present Admiral Brightmore?'

'A pleasure, madam.' The Admiral beamed at her. 'Verbury has been telling me all about the glamours that you have been working. Remarkable accomplishments. I saw the one at Carlton House myself. Truly a work of art.'

'Thank you.' Jane spread her fan, trying to cool herself. She had been given to understand that Lord Verbury did not approve of Vincent's work with glamour. To have him not only present her as a relation, but to also boast about their work for the Prince Regent confounded her beyond reason. 'We are presently working on a commission for the Baron of Stratton.'

The Admiral frowned. 'Stratton? I do not know Stratton. Do you, Verbury?'

'I have not had the pleasure of his acquaintance, nor seen him in the House of Lords.' As a Catholic, Lord Stratton could not take his seat in Parliament without forswearing his allegiance to the Pope.

'He is Irish Catholic.' Jane paused to see what, if anything, either gentleman would say.

The Admiral laughed. 'Well, make sure he pays you in advance, then. That is all I have to say on the matter.'

'I am certain Vincent will have no difficulties in that regard. Perhaps I might visit sometime to see your work in progress?' Lord Verbury's question was posed with an openness of interest that Jane could not trust in the least, and yet . . . and yet, she recognised his smile as the one that Vincent offered her in private. Might he have been sincere in his desire to repair his relationship with Vincent?

'In general, we prefer not to show our work until it is completed.' Which he must surely know about Vincent – or perhaps not, given their history. To turn the gentlemen's attention from their work, she indicated Miss Godwin. 'I wonder if either of you know the lady over there?'

'Oh, yes.' Admiral Brightmore chuckled and crossed his hands upon his stomach. 'I had the pleasure of serving with her father before he began working for the East India Company. Made his fortune in Calcutta with silks.'

'She is valued at thirty thousand pounds, I understand.' Lord Verbury conveyed the information about Miss Godwin's dowry as though he were discussing a horse.

Admiral Brightmore concurred. 'Her complexion is no impediment with that, believe you me. And her father comes from one of the best families.'

'She seems to be elegance embodied.' It was true that the young woman was a model of good breeding in her carriage and deportment, but Jane had expected her dark skin to limit her eligibility. Apparently, a single woman in possession of a good fortune would find herself with no shortage of suitors.

'You need not look so astonished at our approbation,' Lord Verbury chuckled. 'She comes from good British stock on her *father's* side. It is not as though she were Irish.'

The look he gave Jane was so pointed, she wondered how she could have mistaken his manners for anything like charming. He could only be referring to the day that Melody skated with Mr O'Brien.

'Oh, bless me, no.' Admiral Brightmore chuckled, with his belly shaking in delight. 'Her father's as honest a man as ever was born. Miss Godwin takes after him in every regard save one.'

'She will have no trouble finding a husband.' Lord Verbury tilted his head and looked at Jane, as though an idea were just occurring to him. 'If you should like my help with making introductions for your sister, you have only to let me know.'

'Have you a sister?'

Before Jane could answer, Lord Verbury said, 'Oh yes. Her sister is quite pretty.'

His implication that Jane was not went unnoticed by Admiral Brightmore. 'I should be delighted to meet her, Lady Hamilton.'

Jane stared at the Admiral for a moment before understanding that he was addressing her. 'Pardon, sir, but I am Lady Vincent. My husband no longer uses the Hamilton surname.'

Smoothly, Lord Verbury said, 'Vincent has the Hamilton pride, I am afraid. He wanted to succeed on his own merits. Stubborn fellow has been calling himself David Vincent these last few years. The Prince Regent raised him to a knighthood that way, so I suppose we are stuck with it now.'

'Bless me. It sounds as though he is just like you.'

Jane's cheeks burned with anger at the way the Earl perverted the past. She tilted her chin up to address Lord Verbury. 'My understanding, sir, is that you were embarrassed by him and requested that he not use your name. Perhaps that is my mistake?'

'Yes.' Lord Verbury's tone was cool and gave away nothing of his emotions. 'Perhaps it is.'

The Admiral's laughter died away. His gaze darted between the two, seeming to recognise slowly that they were somewhat less than fond of each other.

'Good evening, gentlemen.' Jane turned and made her way through the crowd, feeling as though she had attempted to manage a fold of glamour too large for her. What she longed for most was to find Vincent and depart, but she would not let that man chase her away. Even if her pride would allow it, her duty would not. Jane had brought Melody to London hoping to find a match for her, and she would do that without the Right Honourable the Earl of Verbury's help.

She also felt that she should warn Vincent that his father was in attendance, though what that would do to his spirits she did not like to contemplate. He should at least have an opportunity to prepare himself. She knew that he was belowstairs, so she went in search of a footman who might be able to take her to him.

As she crossed the room, her attention was arrested by the welcome sight of a friend. 'Major Curry? Is that you?'

The good gentleman, in his smart red uniform, turned and regarded her with pleasure. 'Mrs—no, it is Lady Vincent now. Forgive me.'

Jane blushed. 'I have difficulty becoming accustomed to it, myself. My mother is beyond pleased, you may be certain.'

'As well she should be.' Major Curry glanced around the room and lowered his voice. 'And your health?'

Jane smiled at his concern. After the Battle of Quatre Bras, he had been charged with conveying her and Vincent to Brussels. Lord Wellington had assigned him to guard them for the months they resided there, until their health permitted them to make the Channel crossing. He had proven himself to be a worthy friend. 'I am quite well. We both are.'

He sighed with relief. 'I must say that it is fortunate Sir David taught me about the—you know. The Duke of Wellington has kept me in service thanks to that. I owe him a debt. So many soldiers returned that there is not work for us all, and a military glamourist . . . well, I would have had few prospects, were it not for that. As it is, he has quite made my career.'

'I would not think there was much use for it, with Napoleon defeated.'

'Sadly, the troubles in the north of England have kept us busy. The Luddites . . . the coldmongers. . . Everyone is unhappy, it seems.'

'You do not . . . have you had to fire upon them?'

He looked pained. 'I dislike it.' Hanging his head, Major Curry tugged at the trimming at his cuff. 'I know that it is for the good of England, but I do not like firing upon my fellow countrymen, no matter what their offence.'

'You are a good man.' He was. And he had a promising career in the military, as well as a passion for the arts. She had thought before that he would be well matched in nature to Melody. 'Are you occupied at the moment? I should like to introduce you to my sister.'

'I am at your service, madam.' Major Curry offered his arm, which Jane accepted.

She led him through the throng to Melody, who was engaged in conversation with a flock of young men. Jane had not often had a chance to see her sister in full form. She wondered at how Melody could give each gentleman enough attention that it seemed she wished to speak to him alone if only the others would leave them, without at any point making the other men feel slighted. It was a miracle of charm more intricate than any glamour Jane could weave.

'Melody, may I present Major Curry?'

Her sister's face lit with delight as though she had been waiting to meet him for years. 'Of course! My sister has spoken of you with such high regard.' She touched his sleeve with her fan. 'I cannot thank you enough for your service to her.'

Major Curry coloured and cleared his throat. 'It was nothing, Miss. Merely my duty.'

'Your duty, sir, would have been to take her to Brussels and stand outside her door with your rifle, but it was more than mere duty that kept you there reading to her during her recovery.' Melody tilted her head up to look at him. 'She said she could not do without you.'

'I—ah. You are most kind.'

'It is one of Melody's best features.' Jane raised a brow at her sister. 'She also has a lovely singing voice. I only wish we had the opportunity to show it off to you.'

'And I share that wish.' Major Curry bowed his head to Melody.

Jane offered, as though she had just thought of it, 'Perhaps you could come for tea sometime this week? I know that Vincent will be sorry to have missed you.'

'Will I? Ah, Major Curry! I will indeed.' Vincent appeared beside her and shook Major Curry's hand with enthusiasm.

As they completed their addresses and general inquiries about each other's health, Melody leaned over to Jane. Raising her fan, she masked her lips and said in a low voice, 'Is it necessary for you to throw me at every young man who appears?'

Of a sudden, the room felt overwarm as Jane blushed deeply. 'I did not know that my efforts were so transparent.'

'La! I dare say half the room knows that I am for sale.' Melody closed her fan and laughed at something that Major Curry said, as though she had not cut Jane to the quick. With ease, she entered into the conversation, chatting amiably with the Major and Vincent.

Jane did not hear that or the subsequent comments, being involved in rebuking herself. After a moment, Vincent touched her arm. 'Muse? Are you all right?'

'Yes. Only distracted for a moment.' She lifted her head, suddenly remembering why she had sought him earlier. 'Oh! My love, your father is here.'

'I know.' Vincent grimaced. 'We spoke.'

The conversation could not have been a pleasant one, but he offered nothing beyond the fact of their speaking. Jane took his hand and squeezed it, offering the only comfort that she could in a crowded room. Privately, she resolved to do better by her sister and by her husband.

## TEN

# *The Catholic Problem*

Rather than eating her breakfast, Jane stirred her baked beans with her toast. Sighing, she looked across the table to Vincent. 'Would you be all right without me today?'

He looked up from the paper he was sketching upon. 'Hm? Is anything the matter?'

'I thought to take Melody shopping today. I have given her no real attention, and I felt that want, last week at Mr Colgrove's party.' In truth, she felt that about Vincent as well, but while at work they did not speak of anything beyond glamour, and he had been strikingly guarded after the party. Of the two, she felt that Melody would benefit most immediately from an excursion.

He settled back in his chair. 'She has seemed happier of late.'

'I worry that Mr O'Brien is attaching her.'

'I thought that was desirable. He stands to inherit a Barony, after all.' Vincent sipped his coffee, watching her over the rim of the cup.

'Yes. A Barony in Ireland.' Jane set down her toast and pushed her plate away. 'Vincent . . . can a Catholic marry outside his faith? I have heard that it is illegal.'

Vincent frowned and lowered his cup. 'My study of law was

animals. 'Oh! Jane, are these not cunning? Would Vincent like one, do you think?'

The window display had a variety of stuffed birds in various poses as well as fossils of improbable creatures. 'For reference, do you mean? He might.'

Melody wrinkled her nose. 'I was thinking of Vincent's birthday. Is that not why we are shopping? I thought I was just a pretext.'

'Oh. No.' The weather had been so odd of late that she had forgotten it was almost summer and that Vincent's birthday was rapidly approaching. They had not marked it the year prior because of the aftermath of the Battle of Quatre Bras, and it had slipped her mind completely. 'He might, though he tends to not want anything. A book might be more to his taste.'

'Then I shall have to ask Mr Beatts for a suggestion.' Melody straightened and continued down the street.

'Who?' The name sounded familiar, but Jane could not place it. Perhaps one of the gentlemen at Mr Colgrove's party.

'La, Jane. The booksellers that share our building. Do not tell me you have failed to notice them. No, no, say nothing. You are like Vincent in this regard. Always thinking of work.' Melody linked her arm through her sister's. 'I know that Mr Beatts is there, because with the poor weather, I spend my days rambling through their books. We have become quite good friends.'

Several things now made sense to Jane. 'Is that how you knew about Lord Eldon's bill?'

'Oh, no! That is from Mr O'Brien.' She cast a confiding glance at her sister. 'We talk politics. I am becoming quite bookish. I am even thinking of acquiring spectacles.'

Jane laughed aloud at the thought of her sister as pedantic

scholar. 'Forgive me. I do not doubt your intelligence, but it is hard to picture you as an old maid with your hair pulled back and spectacles settled upon your nose.'

Looking at the walk, Melody replied, 'I do not have such a difficult time imagining myself an old maid.'

'Stop. You could have attached any man at Mr Colgrove's if you chose.' Trying to influence her sister's thoughts, Jane said, 'Major Curry seemed quite taken with you.'

Sighing, Melody nodded. 'Is it awful that I know this? But knowing it makes it difficult to trust them. How much is about me, and how much is about who they perceive me to be?'

'Are they so very different?'

They walked past several shops, avoiding a grocer's stand and a Punch and Judy puppet show, before Melody answered. 'Sometimes. Sometimes they are very different. I—I am sorry that I snapped at you at Mr Colgrove's. I know you meant well.'

Jane squeezed her arm. 'Did you snap? I did not notice.'

Melody tilted her head back and laughed, one of the gay silver laughs that gentlemen found so charming. 'Oh, Jane. If you are going to have me believe that, you had best learn to control your complexion. You went quite red.'

'I suppose I did.' Joining in her sister's laughter, Jane walked happily beside her. She had learned to govern her features, but her tendency to flush red would prevent her from ever being truly in command of her countenance.

Melody nodded at a milliner's shop. 'Miss Godwin recommends them.'

'Shall we stop in, then?' Jane did not wait for an answer, but turned them into the shop. They spent a delightful half hour trying on bonnets of every shape and description. Pink satin, roses, pheasant feathers, lavender and ostrich feathers filled the shop with all things feminine.

One straw bonnet, with several ears of Indian corn on it, made Jane to break into peals of laughter when the thing slipped over her eyes. It was lovely but somewhat cumbersome. The milliner, a little woman with pinched features, eyed them with some suspicion and no small amount of disdain as Jane pulled it off her head, still giggling.

Melody governed her laughter long enough to say, 'Do not mind Lady Vincent. She is fond of experimenting with fashion.'

This nearly undid Jane again. She was saved only when the milliner sat up a little and said, 'Not *the* Lady Vincent, the Prince Regent's glamourist?'

'I—well, yes.' Jane supposed it was as accurate a representation as any other for what she did. 'Though we are not presently working on a commission for His Royal Highness.'

'That hardly matters, madam.' The milliner's features loosened some. 'I've had plenty of my customers describe your glamurals. Lady Hertford, one of my regulars, raved about you. Couldn't say enough nice things, could she?'

'How very gratifying.' Jane glanced at Melody to see if she had also taken note of the milliner's change in manner.

'Now . . . you ladies sit yourselves down. I think I have something that will suit you a little better than the Corn Maiden bonnet.' She bustled behind the curtain at the back of the shop.

Melody sat down on the low couch, which stood against one wall, and patted the seat. 'You heard her, Lady Vincent. We must sit.'

'Of course, Miss Ellsworth.' In great state, Jane sat next to

Melody, biting the inside of her cheek to keep from laughing again.

Her sister leaned close and murmured, 'You seem surprised, Jane.'

'I am.' Jane smoothed the folds of her pelisse. 'I am unused to being noticed.'

'Well, become used to it, Lady Vincent. I am quite certain more recognition is coming your way. Lord knows you deserve it.' Lifting her voice she expressed a cry of pleasure as the little milliner returned from the back room. 'Oh! My!'

Her sister's approbation was praise that Jane had not known that she needed. She waited a moment longer before she felt sufficient command of herself to lift her eyes. When she did, she took a breath in awe. The bonnets that the milliner had brought from the back might have been fashioned especially for her and Melody.

On the right, the one that drew Jane was a delicate straw with turned-back brim and a high crown that had been covered with pale pink silk and trimmed with fawn ribbons, completed by blond lace. Sprays of the palest roses seemed to blossom from the side of the bonnet, softening it still further.

Melody had already stood, reaching for the other bonnet. Made of a cream silk taffeta, it was trimmed round with the whitest Venetian lace and ornamented with celestial-blue ostrich feathers that were bent to wrap the crown. 'May I?'

'Of course!' The little milliner helped Melody settle it upon her head, fussing with getting the ribbon tied just so under her chin. The feathers brought out the colour of Melody's eyes and framed her golden curls to perfection.

Jane lifted the other hat and put it on, delaying the moment when she turned to the mirror to see how it fit. The bonnet was so lovely that she did not want to have that moment of disappointment, the moment when she was reminded of how plain she was.

'Oh, Lady Vincent, may I?' The milliner bustled over to her and pulled the hat off. She set it upon Jane's head again and retied the bow so that it was at the side opposite the roses rather than centred under Jane's chin. 'There. You are a vision, see?' She turned Jane towards the looking glass.

While she could do nothing for Jane's overlong nose, the way she had set the hat upon Jane's head had pushed her mouse-brown hair forward and made the hat appear to hide an abundance of curls. The ribbon, so gaily tied, framed her face and gave her some colour. 'It is a lovely hat.'

'You should get it, Jane! It is so becoming.' Melody bounded over to her with her own chapeau fetchingly perched upon her head.

Well. They were supposed to be having a shopping excursion. 'I think we should take both.'

In short order they arranged to have their old hats boxed up and sent back to Schomberg House, both agreeing that anything but these hats were inferior. Privately, Jane's sense of economy argued for keeping the old hats to remake them into a newer style, but for the moment she was more than happy to enjoy the simple pleasure of a new bonnet.

Stepping out into the street again, Jane and Melody continued on, pausing to look at gloves, ribbons and print shops. As they stood outside a stationer's shop, Jane noticed Mr O'Brien in the reflection. His red hair was indisputable, even warped in the glass. She turned to look across the street and stopped in surprise.

Mr O'Brien was speaking with the Earl of Verbury.

Jane turned back to the window hastily. 'Shall we go in, Melody?'

'What? Oh. I suppose. Though I have no scarcity of papers.'

'They might have something for Vincent's birthday.' Jane took her sister's arm and directed her into the shop with as little haste as she could manage. If she had been asked, she would have been unable to state whether she was running from Lord Verbury's notice, or keeping Melody from coming to the attention of Mr O'Brien.

The interior of the shop came as a relief. Tall cases lined the walls, filled with paper of every sort. Immense wooden tables ran down the centre of the shop, covered with thick portfolios. Several short glass vases were filled with pens of various sorts, some with the plumes still intact, others trimmed down to look like little more than white sticks. Melody picked up a sheet of marbled paper. 'What do you think he would like?'

'Some writing paper suitable for sending to Binche. Perhaps some drawing papers, if they have any.'

'I am certain if I tell them it is for the Prince Regent's glamourist they would,' Melody teased, and wandered further into the shop.

Jane stood by the window, looking across the street at Mr O'Brien and Lord Verbury. Why in heaven's name was he speaking with the Earl? Particularly in light of the conversation at Mr Colgrove's birthday party, she could make no sense of it. She was quite sure that Lord Verbury had said he did not know Lord Stratton. Why, then, would he be speaking to the son?

They stood under an awning. She could not see Mr O'Brien's face well enough to make out his expression, but the Earl was all smiles and charm. Jane was almost tempted to try to weave a *lointaine vision*, pass it across the street to where they stood, and eavesdrop upon their conversation. Even had it been morally acceptable, she could never have pushed a fold so far. Still, she was tempted. What business could they have together?

The Earl's disdain of the Irish had seemed clear enough. The Catholic problem would take care of itself, he said. Biting her lip, Jane turned from the window and tried to distract herself with items on the shelves. She ought not to care. Jane picked up and set down a handful of things, not truly noticing what she held, simply turning them over idly as she thought. She glanced outside to see if they were still talking and heaved a sigh. The gentlemen were gone.

A jangle from the bell hanging above the door checked her relief. Lord Verbury stepped into the shop, removing his top hat as he entered. Looking around, he spied Jane and approached her with remarkable nonchalance. At first he said nothing, merely looked down his nose at her. Jane lifted her chin to meet his gaze but did not grant him the recognition of speech.

At last, he smiled. 'What are you doing here?'

'Shopping for Vincent's birthday.' She held out the item in her hand, dimly surprised to find that it was a leather drawing book that would actually suit her husband. 'I might ask the same of you.'

'You might.' His smile stayed fixed upon his face. 'Would you ask Vincent to give my regards to Miss de Clare?' With no more ceremony than that, he lifted his hat, saluted her, and quit the shop.

Jane shivered in the chill he left in his passage. If Lord Verbury could not strike at Vincent directly, might he employ another to help? Vincent would tell her that she was seeing plots where there were none, and yet . . . she no longer had any doubt about why Lord Verbury had spoken to Mr O'Brien. Whatever plot he had wanted Vincent's aid in seemed to involve the young man. The question was: how?

Jane was not at all surprised that they got back to Schomberg House before Vincent. Though she was tempted to go to Lord Stratton's to fetch him, he had not yet stayed so late that she had cause to worry. Once home, she and Melody dropped their various parcels, then separated to pursue different activities. Melody settled into the drawing room with tea and Cook's excellent cakes, to occupy herself with a newspaper, of all things, while Jane went up to the studio to do some work.

She had a table under the skylights, which she found useful for working out design concepts, even at night. While their finished work would be rendered in glamour, she could not weave a glamour here and carry it with her to show their client, so she often drew or painted a design as a preliminary step. The general theme of birds and forests was agreed upon, but Jane preferred to settle what points she could on paper before committing to it in the glamural. In this instance, she had been having difficulty with the cardinal that their patron had requested. Something about the bird's top-knot did not suit her.

Vincent came upstairs well before the dinner hour and dropped heavily into a chair by her table. 'Well. I am sorry I told you that I did not need you today.'

'That does not sound good.' Jane dipped her brush into the pot of water she kept on hand.

'Mr O'Brien came in this afternoon and had a design change.'

'Oh?' She held the brush still in the water, watching her husband.

He rolled his eyes. 'Not properly a design change, I suppose. An addition. He wants us to add an area of silence to one end of the musicians' gallery so they might have a space for their breaks. I tried to point out that they could leave the gallery, but he was most insistent.'

Jane set her brush down. 'What time did he ask this?'

'Hm? I did not pay any attention. After I paused for a nuncheon – and note, Muse, that I did pause – so it must have been past two o'clock.'

'I also note that you paused to eat far later than when I am there.' Jane smoothed her mobcap with both hands, trying to order her thoughts. Two o'clock was after she had seen Mr O'Brien speak to Lord Verbury. Sighing, she let her hands drop to her lap and related what she had seen that afternoon.

Vincent wore a deep frown by the time she had finished. 'I hardly know where to start with this. He—you are certain that it was Mr O'Brien?'

Jane hesitated, thinking back. She had seen him first in the reflection, but then had turned. She nodded slowly. 'Yes . . . yes, I watched from inside the store later and saw his face.'

Vincent made a noise of astonishment and leaned against his chair back. 'That makes no sense.'

'I know.' Jane turned the conversation over in her head again. 'Afterwards, Lord Verbury came inside and spoke to me. I am to ask you to give his regards to Miss de Clare.'

Vincent stopped breathing. His face went pale. Clearing his throat, he asked, 'Did he say anything else?'

'No.' Jane waited, giving Vincent time to sort out his thoughts. She held back the question about who Miss de Clare was, knowing that he must be aware of her curiosity on the subject. Clearly, it was a topic that his father had introduced to cause him some pain.

Some minutes passed, in which Vincent stared at the ceiling, working his jaw in thought. At last, he rose and paced around the room with his fingers knit together behind his neck, pulling his head down. He stopped by one of the windows lining the top floor and stared out at the dark beyond. 'So. What do we know? Mr O'Brien appears to want to march on Parliament. He seems to know my father. They met, and then Mr O'Brien changed the design.'

'It could be used to . . . one could have meetings without fear of being overheard.'

Vincent sighed heavily and drew his finger across the condensation on the window. 'The difficulty I face is that it would not be unlike my father to use our own fears against us. In fact, nothing untoward may be happening. But he can twist innocence . . . oh, can he.'

'But why?'

'It could be related to the "commission" he wanted us for. Or it could be spite. It is impossible to guess without knowing who his object is. Us? Lord Stratton? Someone else entirely? Certainly, he has no scarcity of enemies.' Vincent scrubbed his face again with both hands and held his temples. 'Jane?'

'Yes, my love?'

He wheeled around to face her, dropping his hands to his side. 'Miss de Clare was—she was a prostitute. Is. She is a prostitute.'

'I—I . . . she was, I mean, you . . . you frequented her establishment?' If Jane's voice, after the initial struggle, was creditably steady, her nerves were anything but.

'Yes.'

'How long?'

'Four years.' He took a half step closer and checked himself. Standing by the window, Vincent clenched and unclenched his fists. 'May I explain?'

Jane lifted her paintbrush and dipped it into the water, stirring to clean it of paint. The water splashed up the sides of her cup, almost spilling out the top. She cleared her throat. Inside her head, the thoughts were so foreign that she could not find words even to express herself. She had no understanding of her own feelings. He wanted to explain. Good. Did she want to know? Hand shaking, she lifted the brush out of the water and laid it on the table. Starting and dismissing four or five sentences, Jane finally settled on, 'Do you think an explanation would be productive?'

'I was sixteen. My father took me to her for my birthday. Years later, I realised that he had thought I was effeminate. Because of the glamour. At the time . . . he was generous so rarely. I thought—I believed him when he said the trip was a gift.'

'And afterwards?'

'She was kind to me.' He looked at the floor, digging his thumbnail into the side of his finger. 'I know that she was paid to be, but . . . but because of that, I was sure of her. She was safe, at a time when I very much needed a place to feel safe.'

Jane caught the next words before she spoke them. She did not ask Vincent whether he would feel safer with *her* if he paid her. 'This is why he wanted me to ask.'

Vincent nodded. He held his lower lip between his teeth, still staring at the floor.

It was a mark of cruelty. Jane could look at the marks of manipulation that Lord Verbury had employed. She could recognise them for what they were. And yet that did little to ease her disquiet. She was not so naive as to be unaware of the tendencies of young noblemen. It should not shock her that Vincent had been with a woman before they wed. Nevertheless, it did. Regardless of how her mind might wish her to behave, the mores she had been raised with left her chilled. But she possessed, she hoped, more quickness than Lord Verbury gave her credit for. Marshalling her resources, Jane straightened her back and faced her husband directly. 'Thank you for telling me.'

He peeked at her, without lifting his head. 'It is in a part of my life I would rather were forgotten.'

'Undoubtedly.' Jane stood, smoothing out her gown. 'I am going down to dress for dinner.'

'Do you— do you need help?'

'Not tonight, thank you.' She bit her lip and looked towards the stairs.

'Jane, I—' He stopped and sighed. 'Of course. I will be down later.'

'Thank you.' Jane went downstairs alone.

# ELEVEN

# A Concurrence of Feeling

Though Jane had no wish to allow Lord Verbury to control her actions, she was all too conscious when alone with Vincent. A part of her wanted to ask him to tell her everything so that, knowing, she could stop imagining. Another part wished that she could undo the knowledge. She thought of this before dinner and during dinner. After dinner, she simply pretended the conversation had not happened. Remembering how she had behaved on days before she had known of Miss de Clare, Jane attempted to act the part. She told herself that it was for Melody's sake. Her sister should not be a party to this.

In truth, she was not so considerate. It was to maintain her own reason that she avoided the topic so scrupulously.

She could not continue to ignore it when it came time for bed.

Vincent stood by the door on the other side of their bedchamber as if set to quit the room. His coat, which he usually shed the moment he was through the door, remained on his shoulders. 'Do you want me to sleep elsewhere?'

'No.' Jane lifted her dressing gown, which had been laid out to warm by the fire. 'Mrs Brackett would ask questions.'

'Well, we would not want that, would we?' Vincent tugged his cravat free and tossed it on a chair.

'I am trying.' Jane stopped and wrapped her fingers in her dressing gown. 'I am trying to have a measured response, but you cannot expect me to have none.'

He rested his hands on the back of the chair and braced himself there. 'No.' Blowing out a breath that was not quite a laugh, he bent his head lower. 'I have figured out why he mentioned her. During dinner. I could think of nothing else.'

There was no doubt about which He or which Her Vincent meant. 'To drive me away. He thinks to punish you for refusing him.'

He lifted his head sharply and stared at her with earnest longing. 'If you understand—'

'Understanding his goal does not make the blow to my sensibilities any less. It only allows me to govern it until I master my emotions again.' She set down the dressing gown again, arranging the sleeves so that they hung straight. 'I also thought on it through dinner. I expect I will think on it through the night and tomorrow and . . . I am trying.'

Vincent wiped his mouth, nodding. He straightened, with a face that presented a controlled tranquillity. He shrugged his coat off and hung it over the back of the chair, avoiding her gaze.

Jane pulled at the ties on her gown. Lord Verbury had done this to his son with a coldness that repulsed her. Her every action to keep Vincent at a distance only assisted a man whom she abhorred. Vincent was her husband.

To be more specific, Sir David Vincent was her husband. Whatever had happened with Miss de Clare happened when he was the Honourable Mr Vincent Hamilton. She began to understand more fully why he kept the boundary between his two selves so inviolable. Wetting her lips, she lifted a hand to the tie at the back of her gown. 'Vincent? Can you help me with this knot?'

He met her gaze, all motion arrested. He nodded. The only sound in the room was the fire crackling and the rough edge of his breath.

She stood with her back to the fire and waited as he crossed the room. His fingers, usually so sure, fumbled with the sash at her waist. Jane trembled as his warm breath brushed her neck. An answer occurred to her then, to a question that it had never occurred to her to ask during the course of their marriage.

She now knew how Vincent had come to be so certain with undoing the ties and laces of feminine clothes. Jane wished she did not know, that she did not have the answers to a thousand other unasked questions pouring into her mind. But she held still and let him help her prepare for bed. He needed that regularity. No matter how Jane might beat against the walls of her mind in denial, she would not allow Lord Verbury to hurt her husband again, and certainly not through her offices.

Let us not pretend that the passage of a single night restored the Vincents to their prior state. Lord Verbury had laid a seed of doubt in both of their hearts, but neither had any intention of giving him the satisfaction of succeeding. What his actions accomplished, however, was that Jane became all the more determined to understand what Lord Verbury was about.

When she should have been attending to stitches of glamour that composed the texture of feathers, she was thinking of how to approach him. When she should have been thinking of the play of light across the limb of a tree, her thoughts turned instead to Mr O'Brien's character. If she only knew whether he were an ally of Lord Verbury or a dupe, she would rest easier.

Jane pulled too hard on the fold she was managing and stretched out the arrangement of threads on either side of it. The sunbeam she was rendering warped, snarled on the tree branch and drew it into a grotesque parody. If the tree were swollen and purple with infection, then it would look more natural than this error.

There was little to do but to tear the folds out. Jane fumed and chafed under her breath as she did so. Then another thread sprang loose of its binding. With a flash of colour like a prism dropping through sunlight, the glamour shivered into a rainbow. Jane tried to catch it before it vanished back into the ether, but succeeded only in knocking the thread away from her. The trailing end of it caught the folds of glamour that created one of the illusory trees adorning the ballroom, and caused the skein that made up the rough outer layer of the bark to fray and dissipate. Jane bit back a cry of dismay as the detail on the tree dissolved, leaving only a raw outline of the trunk.

'What is—? Oh.' Vincent saw the offending strands and scowled at the work to be repeated. A moment later, he conquered his expression and said only, 'That is unfortunate.'

'I should have been paying more attention.' Jane let the strands dissolve back into the ether.

'I must—I will own to being somewhat distracted today, as well.' Vincent tied off the fold he held. It circled into a coppice of maple trees he had been creating in the corner.

'Well, you have not spoiled your work.'

'This is the third time I have rendered that tree.'

Jane snorted and peered into the ether. She pulled apart the strands she had misplaced to see them better. 'I think I will have to pull these out as well.'

Vincent rolled his head, stretching his neck with an audible pop. 'Shall we end early, then?' At her look of surprise, he held out his hands in defence. 'If I am wrong, say so, but I thought that . . . a change might do us both some good?'

Undoubtedly, he was correct. She was accustomed to using glamour as an escape. Today, it was too closely tied to the business at hand to offer the relief that she sought. 'What did you have in mind?'

Vincent scrubbed his hair, thinking. 'Astley's Circus?'

Jane had absolutely no desire to see a circus. Watching riders do horse tricks had as much appeal as listening to a recital of Fordyce's *Sermons to Young Women*. However . . . however, Vincent had suggested it, and she was fighting with her own sensibility to keep him from feeling rejected by her distance. 'That sounds as though it might be interesting.'

'Good.' He took one last look at the tree he was working on and said again, 'Good.'

Jane wiped her hands off on her apron and joined him in preparing for departure. It took very little time to tidy their working place, blowing out candles and repacking her basket.

Vincent helped her don her pelisse and then they left the ballroom to head outside. As they stepped out the front door, a gust of wind caught them, pushing Jane against Vincent. He steadied her with a hand at her waist, then released her, as though she were a mere acquaintance that he might offend with familiarity. She claimed his arm and secured herself with a hand around his elbow.

As they descended the stairs, Jane caught sight of Mr O'Brien halfway down the street and walking rapidly away from them.

'Where do you think he is off to?'

'I cannot imagine.'

Jane chewed the inside of her cheek. 'I find that I should like to know.'

'You think he will meet with my father again? Jane, I must point out that there are many more reasons than that to step out. He might be going to his club, or just out for a stroll.'

'Then it will do no harm if I were to follow him.'

Vincent's mouth hung open for a moment. 'Oh, no. This is not a good plan.'

'It can do no harm simply to follow.' She turned their steps in the direction of Mr O'Brien. 'If you are not comfortable, I shall go on my own.'

'And if he were to see you?'

'In this crowd? Hardly likely.' She paused to look up at him. 'You, however . . . with your height, you are more conspicuous than I.'

He frowned at her, even as they walked together down the street. 'In spite of my previous statement, you cannot think that I would let you go alone.'

Jane patted his hand. 'No. But I think it might be best. You are right that we might be spotted.'

'To what end? What possible good can come of following him?' Vincent guided her around a carter delivering a grandfather clock. 'So you know where he is bound. Then what?' He did have a valid point, but she noticed that he did not slow his pace, nor lose sight of Mr O'Brien.

'Then I would at least have some peace of mind. And if his destination implicates him in any way, then I know to keep Melody from him.' Jane disengaged her hand from his arm, becoming more determined the longer they talked. What had been a whim became something that she felt she must do, though she knew it was not entirely rational. 'Please, love.'

'I like this not at all.' Vincent shoved his hands into his coat pockets. Even through the noise of the foot traffic and carriages, she could hear the small slow whine of his breath escaping. 'I will follow on the other side of the street, back some distance. No. No, do not ask me to go home. If you are correct and something criminal is afoot, then I can by no means simply . . . I will follow you, following him.'

'If I say no?'

He raised a brow and favoured her with a half smile. 'How will you stop me?'

'Fair point.'

When they next came to a crossing, Vincent let her go ahead. Jane glanced once over her shoulder and spied him a street behind, on the opposite side. He was not inconspicuous, but far enough behind Mr O'Brien that she thought it safe. As for that gentleman, he walked at a rapid clip through the streets of London. Jane followed him down a cobbled road, aware of the ceaseless tapping of her boots. She was tempted to walk on tiptoe, though she knew her footsteps were lost amidst the heavy rumble of carts and drays and the constant hawking of newsboys.

When he turned off Strand, Jane looked back to Vincent to make certain that he saw her stepping off the main thorough-fare and onto the less-reputable side street. The street narrowed and the houses crowded together as though for warmth. Jane kept her reticule close, regretting that she had not tucked it inside her coat before she started down this road.

Gin establishments packed the street, identifiable by the litter of blue bottles near them and the staggering inebriates.

Men, women and children alike showed the effects of the Blue Ruin in their slovenly and indolent nature. The streets here went unswept, and the rubbish piled the gutters. Jane had to hold her hem high and pick her way carefully at some points to avoid becoming mired in filth.

She took increasing comfort in the knowledge that Vincent was behind her. When they got home, she might even let him know that he had been correct; she did not feel safe following Mr O'Brien through streets such as these. But Vincent would also have to admit that something was not right. The further they went, the more she wondered what Mr O'Brien was about.

The street bent to the left and she lost sight of Mr O'Brien for a moment. Jane hurried ahead to catch him again, just spying him as he stepped through an iron gate set in a high stone wall. At intervals, the wall was broken with tall iron palisades allowing glimpses into the quadrangle beyond.

Jane stopped shy of the gate, waiting for Vincent to catch up with her. She looked up at the iron banner across the top. Why, she wondered, had Mr O'Brien gone into the Worshipful Company of Coldmongers?

Vincent drew Jane back from the gate and around the corner. 'We should go.'

'Are you not curious?' She looked back towards the gate.

'Yes, but I am known here.' He turned up the collar of his coat. 'Even if Mr O'Brien did not see me, the porter would surely recognise me from Chill Will's incident. We can return at another time, when Mr O'Brien is not here.'

'I am not known by the porter.'

'But you are a woman. The Worshipful Company only admits men.' Vincent tucked his chin into his coat and darted another look at the gate. 'Please, Jane, there is no reason to cause a confrontation.'

'But why would he be here?'

'Charitable work? Engaging a coldmonger? Perhaps he was following a spy.' Vincent threw out his hands in frustration. 'I do not know, but – but I think you might be – possibly you are being needlessly suspicious.'

Jane lifted her chin, nostrils flaring with anger. 'With Melody's history, I have a right to be cautious.'

'Yes. Of course.' Vincent wiped one hand down his face. 'But Jane, if she cannot marry him, why does it matter what he does? You are seeing plots where there probably are none. Yes. My father spoke to Mr O'Brien. Yes, my father harassed you. Yes, it is odd that Mr O'Brien is here. But these do not add up to a conspiracy.'

If Jane could articulate why she felt so sure that something larger was in the works, she would have argued for staying, but none of her arguments amounted to more than saying, 'But something is wrong.'

'I know. Or, rather, I understand. I am simply not convinced that I am seeing anything other than my own disquiet, and that disquiet may be explained by other events.'

He had hit upon some truth there. She sighed. 'Let me just inquire about William, and then we shall be off. That will provide all the excuse that we need if Mr O'Brien should see us.'

'If it will set your mind at ease . . .' Vincent relented, though his manner suggested that he was far from pleased by the prospect.

'Thank you. I know – I do know – that this is not an entirely rational urge.'

Vincent sighed heavily, his breath steaming white in the air. 'Permit me to remain a little back so that we do not attract too much attention. I can well imagine that word of my presence would reach Mr O'Brien.'

'Are you so certain of being recognised? You are usually more modest.'

Vincent gave a half-chuckle. 'Yes, well. You did not witness the . . . enthusiasm with which young William recounted the rescue. Half the yard made note of me.'

Jane squeezed his hand in thanks for indulging her. There was no other way she could describe acquiescing to an urge that even she must acknowledge was founded on irrational thought. But the idea would not leave her alone, so she strode up to the gate and inquired with the porter about William.

The porter knuckled his cap and sent a young messenger off to fetch the boy. 'Sorry I cannot let you in, m'lady. This here's an establishment for gentlemen only.'

'I quite understand.' She was grateful, in some ways, because it meant that she did not have to worry about encountering Mr O'Brien in the interior. Regardless of her desire to know his business, she did not wish him to discover their presence.

In a few minutes, William came out with a smile. The cut upon his temple had healed nicely, leaving only a thin red line that would fade with time. 'Lady Vincent! This is a surprise indeed. Let me call the lads out so they can meet you. I've told them all about you and Sir David.'

Jane stopped herself from wincing. She should have foreseen that as a possibility. 'I can only stay for a few moments. Are you well?'

'Getting by.' He shrugged deeper into his coat. 'There's no work, but that's true for all of us.'

'No work? But I saw a gentleman arrive ahead of me. Surely he was here on some commission.'

'Tall, red hair, with spectacles?' When Jane nodded, young William said, 'That's Mr O'Brien. He's a great friend to the Company, that's true. But it doesn't mean work for us.'

'I am sorry to hear that.' Jane kept watch out beyond him, upon the yard, in case that gentleman should reappear. She was astonished by the great number of children there. 'Does the Company run a school?'

'Eh?' He glanced over his shoulder. 'Oh, no. At least not for lads as old as this bunch. There's just a lot of us here now because there ain't no work. We got nowhere else to be.'

Jane had understood that coldmongers tended to be young, but she had not realised how young they started work. Appalled by the youth of boys involved in so treacherous a profession, Jane could barely master her expression. William would not, in the nature of boys, recognise that fourteen was very young indeed. To see boys even younger than he in the yard, waiting for work, sent a chill through her that had nothing to do with glamour.

'What do coldmongers do in winter?'

'We take time off and recover, most of us. The Company saves so we have funds to see us through.' He shrugged again, scowling. 'Don't look like there's going to be any work this year. It's not so cold as we can make ice, and not so warm that cooling would be needful. Looked for a while as though Lord Eldon would help but . . . he ain't.'

'The bill the Lord Chancellor was proposing, you mean?' She would have to ask Melody to tell her more about that. At the same time, Jane could not help but recollect that Vincent's father had been in an argument with Lord Eldon. 'He was a coldmonger's son, was he not?'

'Nah. Folks say he was, but his old man made his money in brokering coldmongers.' Seeing her look of incomprehension, William jerked a finger at the gates of the Company. 'This here takes care of us. We all pitch in, see? But to get work, you have to go through a broker. Someone who knows what your skills are and what the patron needs. Some of us is good at large rooms and breezes. Others at holding a weave of cold while walking. One feller is right quick in winter arts, and can make ice in any shape you imagine.'

Jane had not realised the full breadth of possibilities in cold-mongering. She knew that a coldmonger had more particular control over weaves of cold than a general glamourist, but had not understood how many different ways the skill could take shape. She wondered if Vincent were aware of this. It might present some interesting avenues for exploration.

Meanwhile, she had different avenues to explore. 'Well, I hope that something changes soon.' She hesitated. 'Perhaps we could hire you to work at our house?'

William scratched behind his ear and kicked at the street. 'That's right kind, Lady Vincent. You and I both know it'd be a charity, with the weather the way it is. You just remember me when it changes, all right?'

Jane promised to do so and took her leave of the young man. As she walked down the street, Vincent stepped out from the empty air. Jane jumped and shrieked with surprise.

'Sorry!' He held his hands up. 'I was just in a *Sphère Obscurcie*.'

Jane laid a hand upon her breast. 'And you think that *I* am being unreasonably cautious.'

Vincent blushed and ducked his head. 'I—um. Well. Did

you discover anything of moment?' She quickly related her conversation with young William, including her attempt to hire him.

'Perhaps we can have him in to instruct us in cold sometime. It might be useful if we attempt the glamour in glass again.' Vincent rubbed his chin in thought. 'Would you like to go dancing this evening?'

'Dancing? You are getting desperate to change the subject.' Jane turned their direction back towards their part of town. In the nearly two years of their marriage, they had never had occasion to dance – a fact that astonished her upon the face of it. 'But that will not keep me from taking merciless advantage of your offer.'

'I have no anxiety about that.' Vincent put his hand over hers, and the warmth encouraged her.

'Where did you think to go?'

'Well . . . I thought that Melody might enjoy Almack's Assembly.'

'She would, but one needs a voucher to attend.'

Vincent cleared his throat. 'I . . . ah . . . I have a pass for Almack's.'

Jane checked her pace. 'You do? You? The misanthrope who dislikes crowds above all else?'

A carriage rattled by, drowning his first response. Vincent waited until it was past and repeated himself. 'Before we met, Prinny and Lord Byron liked to attend, and made it clear that I needed to as well. So I did.'

The thought of her husband in the company of the Prince Regent and Lord Byron confounded her expectations. This must have been in his college days. The thought struck her before she could avoid it. 'Did you take—'

'No.' Vincent spoke quickly and with force, as though to stop someone from stepping into traffic. He looked down the street, showing her his fine, high profile. 'I am sorry, Jane. You know that, I hope?'

'I do.' She did not understand many of the events that surrounded them, but tonight she would let the past go and dance with her husband.

## TWELVE

# *Corinthians and Waltzes*

In spite of the patronesses who guarded the door to Almack's Assembly and denied entry to any they deemed unsuitable for society, the floor was thronged with couples. Decorated in blue and gold, designed to flatter, the ballroom did have a lustre of elegance, but the tall ceiling only served to allow the noise to echo around and become somehow louder.

Vincent's arm had tightened the moment they entered the room.

By contrast, Melody was in a state of rapture. She clung to Jane's arm and exclaimed as they crossed the threshold. 'Oh, Jane! Look at that ivory gown. The ruffle at the bottom is elegance embodied. And there! Oh, the gentleman with the blue jacket.'

'Everyone has blue jackets,' Vincent muttered. 'Including me.'

'And I must say, it suits you handsomely,' Jane said. Vincent's grumbles ought not amuse her, but they always did.

It was Vincent's habit to play the artist and pay indifferent attention to his dress, so it always took Jane by surprise when he turned himself out in fashionable attire. She had married a very handsome man.

She could admire his broad shoulders and fine profile, regardless of what he wore. However, there was something about a blue coat of superfine wool to make those shoulders seem broader and his waist narrower. Did she need to add to the catalogue of her husband's merits the manner in which his knee breeches fit?

Another might say that his brow was too brooding or that his manner was not calculated to please, but Jane felt no compunction in thinking that her husband was, while not the most elegant, still quite the handsomest man in the room.

But before she could dance with Vincent, she needed to find a partner for Melody. From the way the heads of young men turned as they walked through the press, it was clear that a number of them would gladly ask Melody to dance if they had an introduction.

Jane knew too few people in London. She and Vincent spent all their time at work, and only mingled at the rare event. If she had followed through on her intentions to host parties, then perhaps they would not be in this awkward social position.

Then, through the crowd, she caught a glimpse of a figure with a warm, dark complexion and heavy black hair. Miss Godwin. 'Thank heavens.' If Miss Godwin was there, then perhaps Mr Colgrove was as well. He would need little encouragement to dance with Melody, and if he were not there, Miss Godwin could introduce Melody to her set and at least get things started.

Jane guided them through the multitude to the group of young people. 'Miss Godwin?' The lady did not turn. With the noise of conversation and music, it was not improbable that she had failed to hear Jane. 'Miss Godwin?'

One of the lady's friends masked a smirk, poorly, and winked at the lady, who turned with a frown. 'You have mistaken me.'

'Oh. I—' With a certainty, Jane had. Where Miss Godwin was tall and slender with an admirable form, this lady tended towards plump. Indeed, once she turned, the only real thing the two women had in common was their complexion. 'Yes. I have. My apologies.'

The lady worked her fan, as though to dismiss Jane, before turning back to her set. Still blushing from her mistake, Jane retreated to Vincent. 'My love, do you see anyone you know?'

'A few, yes.'

She waited, then applied to him again. 'Do you think any of them might be willing to ask Melody to dance?'

'Hm?' He frowned first at her, then Melody in confusion before recalling himself. Wincing, he said, 'I am out of practice at this.'

'I will remind you that this was your idea.'

'And it should give you a fair idea as to the state of my mind that it was.' Vincent peered down at her. 'I jest, lest that is uncertain.'

'It is quite clear.' It was also not fully a jest, she was certain of that. 'May I impose, then?'

Vincent nodded with a tight jaw and offered Melody his arm. 'I have an acquaintance to whom I should like to make you acquainted.'

Jane stifled a laugh at the redundancy in his language. Her poor grumbling bear always retreated into taciturn silence or exaggerated formality when distressed. Tonight, he appeared to be doing both. There was little she could do for him now, but she hoped that once he had a task he would relax somewhat. Jane followed behind them as Vincent led Melody through the crowd, around a cluster of young gentlemen of the Corinthian model.

As they made their way, a man called, 'Lady Vincent!'

She stopped, turning in the throng to spy Major Curry. Of all things, this was the best of fortunes. She had been wishing to make Melody better acquainted with him, but had not yet had time to arrange the promised tea. 'What brings you here?'

'The Duke of Wellington.' He rolled his eyes, but only a little. 'His Grace says it is necessary to make social calls when in town, and this allows him to make them all at once. Everyone who is anyone, you know. However, he has left me at loose ends.'

'His loss, then, is our gain. Vincent and I were just searching for a dance partner for Melody. May I presume upon your kindness?'

'A privilege.' He bowed, and she thought he stood a little taller afterwards.

Together they caught up with Vincent and Melody, who had paused in their quest. Vincent was glaring over the heads of the crowd. 'The people I knew have moved.' His expression of displeasure brightened when he saw who was with Jane.

For a few moments they talked of the usual things: the press of the crowd, the lemonade and the quality of the cake. As soon as the pleasantries concluded, Major Curry turned to Melody and offered her a bow. 'May I have the honour of a dance?'

She accepted his offer with her hand. 'I should be delighted.'

Satisfied that her sister had been provided with the best part-ner Jane could wish for, she turned to Vincent. He glowered at the room, and she raised her eyebrows in expectation.

For a moment, he did not notice her questioning look, then he started. 'I told you we would dance.'

She nodded. Waiting.

With the noise surrounding them, she could not hear him hold his breath, but she could see his chest expand and his jaw set. Vincent rolled his shoulders as though he were preparing to work. He expelled the breath in a sigh.

As though a glamour had passed over him, Vincent's posture changed, becoming more erect, and Jane saw the man his father had wanted him to be. Extending his leg, Vincent offered her a full court bow with all the grace of a formal courtier. 'Lady Vincent. Would you do me the honour?'

'I—I would be delighted.' Astonished beyond measure, Jane placed her hand in his as he stood.

Keeping his eye on hers, he raised her hand to his lips and kissed it. 'Thank you, madam.'

All in wonder, Jane let him escort her to the floor. His carriage was smooth and elegant, but beneath her hand, his arm trembled with tension.

She pressed his arm. 'We do not have to dance.'

'I made a promise.' Vincent did not meet her gaze, but smiled – smiled! – and nodded at someone across the floor.

They reached the bottom of the set and took their places opposite each other. Beside all the fine ladies in their fashion, Jane felt all her old anxieties come back. Her carriage was poor. Her features too sharp. Her hair was all wrong. And across from her, Vincent played the part of the nobleman's son he had been born to. Had she met him then, would he have even noticed her?

He held out his hand and they progressed up the set, casting off in an arc around the next couple. The effort that had been put into his deportment showed in the way he glided over the floor, and the easy grace in his figures.

Jane was at once captivated by the sight of him dancing, and resolved never to ask him to dance again. When she thought about how each perfect movement had been purchased, of the privations and beatings that Vincent had endured for his failure, she could not rest easy with the result.

They danced through the set. Jane wanted to pull him off the floor, but she would not draw attention to either of them by creating a spectacle. Not with Melody and Major Curry four couples above them in the dance.

As they progressed, Melody and Major Curry reached the top of the set and began the turn back to the bottom. As a matter of course, they were soon in a group with Jane and Vincent.

Melody's eyes widened as she turned from their previous group to see Vincent offer his hand for the balance forward and back. 'Sir David! You astonish me. I did not know that you danced.'

'Only rarely, Miss Ellsworth.' He inclined his head to the perfect degree as they exchanged places, and offered a smile calculated to charm. 'It requires the greatest of temptations.'

Jane balanced forward and back with Major Curry. 'How are you enjoying the dance, Major?'

'Quite nicely.' He exchanged places with her smoothly. 'Your sister is an elegant dancer.'

He did not have time for more before Jane took hands and turned twice around with Melody. As the sisters swung each other in a tight circle, Melody said, 'What has come over Vincent? He is all elegance tonight.'

Jane shook her head. 'I hardly know him.'

Melody let go of Jane's hands and turned to change places again with Vincent. 'Indeed, I am not certain I would know him either.'

'I hardly know myself.' Vincent retreated to the corner of their set as Jane and Major Curry did a two-hand turn.

Passing her, the Major said, 'Have you enjoyed your stay in London?'

'It has been edifying, as always.' Jane dipped her head and retreated to her corner, turning to face Vincent again as he completed his two-hand turn with Melody.

He smiled at her with a degree of charm, but the wrinkles at the corners of his eyes seemed to her to be cracks of tension. He held his hand out, and the four of them joined hands to circle to the left.

Melody laughed as they spun. 'La! Vincent, I should think that it would be easier if you acted like this always.'

'But less true.' He gave her a short bow of his head as they all circled back to the right and turned to their new set.

Jane and Vincent's new partners were not known to them, and Jane was only too glad to allow anonymity to protect them from conversation. Without being forced to speak, Vincent glided through the steps with a grace that nearly stopped Jane's breath. She felt as though she danced with a stranger, which might almost be true. *Here* was Mr Vincent Hamilton, third son of the Earl of Verbury. She did not want him. She wanted her husband.

When that dance was finished, Jane put her hand to her chest and affected to be too winded to continue. Vincent guided her off the floor to a chair by the wall. 'Shall I get you some lemonade?'

'No.' Jane took his hand and ran her thumb over the back of it. 'I am sorry. I will not ask you to do that again.'

'It is not as bad as I make it out to be. It is only that I feel I am lying.' He looked across the floor with his head tilted to the side. 'Major Curry appears to be introducing Melody to some others.'

'I should not leave her alone.' Jane started to rise, but Vincent put his hand on her shoulder.

'Curry will not lead her astray. We can watch from here.' He raised a hand in a wave. 'There, she knows where we are now.'

'You are very good, you know.'

'That is because I have a lot of wickedness to atone for.'

'Vincent—'

'I shall get some lemonade for us.' He squeezed her shoulder and stepped away.

Jane caught his hand, and pulled him to a stop. 'Wait. Please. I am not thirsty, and you seem to be avoiding me too often.'

His brows rose in confusion. 'Avoiding? Oh, no, Muse . . .' He paused and studied the floor. 'No. I suppose that is fair. I will endeavour not to do so again.'

She tried to tease the disquiet out of him. 'Am I so alarming?'

'Losing you is.' Vincent's voice was so hushed that, had she been any further from him, she would not have heard it. He continued to stare at the floor as though counting the scratches there.

Engrossed as they were, the next voice caught both Vincents unaware. 'What a surprise!'

Vincent visibly started. A fine lady stood next to them dressed in a white crape frock over a satin slip; French Lama work in silver ornamented the hem, and delicate satin slippers peeked out from beneath the dress.

At her wrists and long, white throat, she wore a matched set of rubies, which brought out the warm tones in her cheeks.

The shape of her brow beneath her abundance of brunette curls was like Vincent's, refined into a feminine ideal.

'Are you not going to say good evening?' She patted him on the arm with her fan. 'I told Papa that he was approaching you all wrong.'

Clearing his throat, Vincent straightened and slipped that mask of civility over his features, but his eyes had no sparkle to them. 'This is Lady Penelope Essex. May I present my wife, Lady Vincent?'

'Oh, you are not still using that name, are you?' Lady Penelope wrinkled her nose at him. 'I suppose I cannot blame him, but I do wish that he would stop pretending that he is not my brother. I should wish you to be Lady Hamilton so that you and I might be properly sisters. Still, I do understand. Papa was always hardest on him.'

This charming lady was the one who had caused Vincent so much dread? Recalling Vincent pulling the mask over his features, Jane wondered if she could trust the lady's seemingly open manner. 'Vincent has spoken of you. I am delighted to make your acquaintance.'

'Spoken of me, only? Dear boy . . . not "with fondness"?' Leaning her head back, Lady Essex laughed as though it were a great joke. 'No. I suppose not. Though that is not my fault. You were always the wicked one. Oh, Lady Vincent, you would not believe the troubles he got my sister and myself into. Always undoing glamours, and making it appear as though it were our fault.'

'He has told me this story.'

'Has he! Oh, I am so glad. I was afraid that he would say nothing about us at all.'

During this conversation, Vincent had been staring fixedly

at Jane. Wetting his lips, he took a half-step forward. 'The music is about to recommence. Will you excuse us? I promised Lady Vincent that we would dance this evening.'

Jane kept her surprise hidden behind a mask of smooth pleasure. If he needed to beat a retreat, she would do all she could to help him. 'And a waltz! It is still something of a scandal in my parents' neighbourhood, so I have not had the opportunity.'

Lady Penelope flirted her fan open, not at all deceived, though she answered with graciousness. 'Of course. Only say that you will come to dinner on Monday and bring your sister. I do so want you to meet my husband and my little boy. A small family affair, I promise.' Leaning towards Jane, she said, 'Vincent does so despise crowds.'

'I have had ample opportunity to observe that myself.'

Again, Lady Penelope favoured her with a laugh. 'I am certain you have, my dear. To come here must be a sign that he loves you very much.'

Vincent took Jane's hand. 'I do. And so I would like to fulfil my promise to her.'

'Go. By all means, go.' She laid a hand on Vincent's arm, and for a moment dropped her air of playfulness. 'Only say you will come to dinner. Please?'

The simplicity of her request was deeply becoming. Vincent's chest set for a moment, then he exhaled. 'Yes. Thank you.'

With an exclamation of delight, Lady Penelope stood on her toes to kiss her brother on the cheek. 'I am so glad. Now, go and lead your good lady to dance.'

Taking their leave, Jane and Vincent walked to the floor. Jane waited until they were a good twenty paces from Lady Penelope. 'Are you all right?'

He chuckled. 'You were saying something about me avoiding people?'

'As long as you escape with me, I shall not object.'

Vincent raised her fingers to his lips and kissed them. 'As long as you will have me.'

Melody was still in the set preparing to dance, which pleased Jane, but she had exchanged partners for the new song. Standing at her side, ready to begin the shockingly wanton waltz, was Mr O'Brien. The couple chatted with great animation.

'Is his hand on her torso?' Beyond the intimacy of the dance, it was clear from the blush on his cheeks and the gentleness of his manner that Mr O'Brien had joined the ranks of young men smitten with her sister. More disturbingly, Melody appeared to be equally taken with the young Irishman.

'It appears so, yes.'

Since the waltz was not danced in a line, Jane led Vincent to where her sister stood. 'Are you going to waltz?'

'Oh!' Melody put her hand familiarly on her partner's arm. 'Yes. Mr O'Brien has offered to teach me how.'

'Has he, indeed?' Jane raised her eyebrows.

The young man flushed further and cleared his throat. 'I had occasion to learn while I was in Vienna. With my parents.'

Beside Jane, Vincent made a small humph of discovery. 'I have not, but I promised Ja—Lady Vincent a dance.'

'It is excessively simple. I can show you before we begin, if you like. There is a basic step, like so.' He sketched out a simple figure on the floor. 'Then one turns while dancing. Miss Ellsworth – would you assist?'

He held out his left hand and she placed her right in it. Melody's left went on his shoulder, but *his* left . . . Jane cleared her throat. 'It appears to involve being held rather close.'

142

If possible, Mr O'Brien became even redder. 'Ah—yes. I enjoy the dance because it allows one more opportunity for conversation, since one is not moving away from one's partner throughout the dance.'

'I see . . . for conversation.'

Melody laughed at her sister and patted Mr O'Brien's shoulder. 'Do not mind her. She is taking her part as my chaperon with over-seriousness.'

'Yes.' Vincent put his own hand on Jane's shoulder. 'And, for the moment, she has promised this dance to me. Now . . . this appears to be the dance position. Do I have this right?'

Mr O'Brien cleared his throat again and studied them. 'Yes. Only. Your hand should be . . . well. Here.'

'On her back?'

'Yes?' His voice cracked. 'At least, that is how they dance it in Vienna.'

'Ah.' Vincent slid his hand under Jane's arm to rest upon her upper back. She was aware of the warmth of his arm along her bosom, even through the layers of muslin.

The music began, then, and other couples moved into motion around them. Vincent stepped into the pattern of the dance, moving Jane away from her sister before she could object.

'What are you—'

'I am trying to enjoy dancing with my wife,' he murmured. 'I have just realised that this dance does not require me to talk to anyone besides you. I might find it tolerable.'

Tolerable was high praise indeed, for Vincent. If Jane were not so worried about her sister, she might look forward to the prospect of future waltzes.

# THIRTEEN

## A Congregation of Glamour

The faint silver light of dawn trickled through the curtains of the Vincents' bedchamber. Across the room, the shadowy shape of a maid knelt by the hearth to light the fire. Wood smoke teased Jane's nose, promising future warmth. She snuggled deeper under the counterpane, waiting for the fire to heat the room sufficiently to exit the bed. Quiet as a mouse, the housemaid crept out of the room with her basket of kindling and matches.

The door shut behind her with a click.

Vincent sat upright, throwing aside the counterpane and letting in a blast of cold air. Jane made a moue of protest and snatched the cover back over her as he sprang out of bed.

'Sorry, Muse.' He tucked the counterpane carefully around her shoulders. 'Idea.'

'About?'

'Glamural.' Dressed only in his nightshirt, he rooted around on the desk for a piece of paper and a quill.

Jane sat up, clutching the covers to her chest. 'My drawing book is in the top right drawer.'

He grunted his thanks and pulled the drawer open. Sitting at the desk, he started to write in the half light of the fire and the little bit of dawn visible through the curtains. Jane crept out of bed, wincing as her legs were exposed to the air, and pulled on her dressing gown. It should not be this cold in June, even in the morning.

She threw back the curtains, letting in the grey light from another day of rain. It was no wonder that illiterate members of the populace thought that the weather was so unnatural that some agent, such as coldmongers, must be to blame. She lit the candle on the desk and put it near Vincent's elbow to light his paper.

Standing at his back, she kneaded his shoulders absently. Not until he lifted his head and half-turned did she understand that their intimacy had become something to be noted and remarked on of late. Vincent wet his lips and returned to his work.

Jane did not allow her movements to falter, though she silently cursed Vincent's father. The whole of the fault lay in his quarter. To introduce so young a boy to a lady of easy virtue could only give the understanding that such things were acceptable. Small wonder that while he had remained in that house, Vincent had felt free to avail himself of her services. He had ceased going when he came of an age to understand – though another might suggest that Vincent had also left his father's house to go to university, and therefore it was not to be expected that he would continue to seek Miss de Clare out over so great a distance.

Jane could only reflect on what her husband had said about feeling safe. University had been a safe time for him in other ways, as was their life together now. His father sought to destroy that by saddling Vincent with old, painful recollections. Jane would have none of it.

She bent down to kiss Vincent's neck. 'I love you.'

His quill caught on the paper and ink spattered across his

words. Lifting the quill from the page, he laid it aside and turned in his seat. He took her hands, cradling them. His deep brown eyes were clear and expressive. 'If you do not know by now, you own me, heart, mind, body and soul.'

Jane felt a rush of heat from her toes to her middle. Words fled her capability. She bent to reassure him of the sincerity and conviction of her love.

Vincent wrapped his arms around her. 'Muse, you are trembling.'

'I am cold . . .' She found the tie at the neck of his nightshirt and pulled it open.

Without a word, Vincent stood and lifted her in his arms. He carried her to the fire, and together they lay before it.

After a period of delightful intimacy, made all the more precious because they had seen how easily it could be lost, the Vincents dozed by the fire with the counterpane pulled over them. The day had barely brightened as the sun fought through the clouds. Jane's head was cradled on Vincent's shoulder, and he smoothed her hair with his other hand as they watched the flames.

Jane ran her hand down his cheek. 'What was the idea you had?'

'The one you mercilessly distracted me from?'

'Yes, that one.'

'It occurred to me that it would be nice to give the glamural some birds' song.'

'But it would clash with the musicians when they play.'

'I thought to use the area of silence, which Mr O'Brien asked for, as a counter to that.' Vincent rolled onto his side, displacing her. Propping himself on his elbow, he sketched his idea in the air with quickly rendered glamour. 'I was trying to make notes so I would not forget, but . . . If I create another area here, which contains birds' song, and then create a sort of *bouclé torsadée* that can be changed from one to the other . . . you see?'

Jane narrowed her eyes and considered. Vincent had created a rough rendering of the ballroom, complete with musicians' gallery. Overlaid on that were glowing lines representing the glamour he was proposing. At one end of the musicians' gallery, a ball represented the birds' song. Next to the ball was the musicians' retreat that Mr O'Brien had requested. A twisted thread of glamour represented the *bouclé torsadée* and stretched from the ball to the closest bird cage. Rather than travelling in a tube through a house to carry orders, *this* would carry the sound across the ballroom, creating the illusion that the birds were singing.

If Jane understood what Vincent was proposing, all that would be required to silence the birds would be to move the *bouclé torsadée* from the area of birds' song to the area of silence. The chief advantage was that the two areas were close enough to each other that it would require only limited abilities with glamour to be able to move the thread between them. Many musicians had enough ability to manage that. Even if that were not the case, in all likelihood, the Strattons already employed someone conversant enough in folk glamour to manage it.

'You are surpassingly clever.' She traced a finger through the fine hair on his chest. 'What gave you the idea?'

'Last night's dancing, of all things.' He fell back on the carpet. 'As we were going up through the centre, I was thinking that it was much easier to bear than standing on the sides without you. It made me think of the speaking tube passing through the middle of the house. The jump from that to this . . . is more difficult to explain, I grant.'

'It is still ingenious, and I look forward to attempting it.'

Vincent stretched, pushing his arms over his head and arching his back with a moan of pleasure. He tilted his head to look at the window. 'Speaking of which, I suppose we had better go to work.'

Jane groaned. 'But it is so warm here.'

'You will be warm enough once you start managing glamour.' He sat up, again exposing her to the air, though this time she was wearing considerably less clothing.

With a small shriek, Jane snatched the counterpane back and huddled under it. 'This is most unfair.'

Vincent tugged the bottom of the blanket with a playful smile. 'I can make it more unfair.'

'Rogue.'

'Certainly.'

Rather than risk being exposed once again, Jane clambered to her feet. While one of the things she loved about Vincent was his devotion to his art, at times she wished that he would allow for distraction.

Still, she had to admit that she was excited about his idea. It was a variation on a few existing techniques, but the combination of them was particularly clever. Where Vincent's differed was . . .

Another thought struck Jane. 'If we do this, is there a reason not to offer multiple choices of sound?'

Vincent paused with his buckskin breeches in his hand. He stared at the fire, working his jaw in thought. 'Possibly . . .' He perched on the chair and pulled his breeches on. 'That might require devoting more area to the effect than is warranted. I thought of this because we already have the silenced area.'

'Hm . . .' Jane pulled her chemise on over her head.

They happily discussed the theory and practice of glamour as they dressed. By the time each was fully clothed, it was all Jane could do to convince Vincent to go down to breakfast rather than up to the studio to make a trial of the glamour. They could try it at the Strattons' house when they got there.

When they arrived in the breakfast room, Melody greeted them with such radiant spirits that Jane silently blessed her husband for thinking of dancing. Her sister had not wanted for partners the previous night, and though Jane might not approve of them all, there could be no denying that the attention had fully restored her bloom.

She had dressed carefully for breakfast, with her hair already in an artful arrangement. From the glow of her cheeks, no one would have guessed that she had spent half the night dancing. Rather than her usual linen morning dress, Melody wore one of her muslin frocks with a full ruche of lace around the hem. Around her neck, she had tucked the Brussels lace fichu that Jane had brought her from the Continent.

'You look lovely this morning.' Jane put some potatoes on her plate, glancing over at Melody. 'Are you going out?'

With a slight frown, Melody shook her head. 'No, today is an At Home day.'

The sausages looked nicely browned this morning. 'Ah. I had not realised that you had set up a routine. I am sorry that I have been out so much.'

'You cannot—' Melody set her fork down on her plate and bit her lower lip with distress. 'Jane, are you going to work today?'

'Yes, as soon as we finish breakfast.'

'Oh.' The note of disappointment in her voice was not successfully masked, but Melody did not say anything else.

149

Vincent reached past her for a slice of toast. 'Are you expecting anyone in particular?'

'I—well, yes.' Melody pushed her fork around with one finger. 'It is just . . . I mean . . . I do know that you have to work. Only. Only, after the dance last night . . . you see?'

Jane set her plate down on the table, trying to follow Melody's broken explanation. 'I am afraid I do not quite take your meaning.'

'It is just . . .' Melody looked miserable. 'I do understand that you have work to do.'

Vincent cleared his throat. 'It is often common for a young gentleman to call upon a lady with whom he danced on the morning following.'

'Ah.' Jane studied her sister, who in turn studied her plate. Growing up, Jane had rarely danced. There had been frequent dances in their neighbourhood, but once she had realised that no one would ask her to stand up except by necessity, she had offered to play the pianoforte instead. It had given her some relief to make it a decision to not dance, rather than a consequence of being plain and awkward. By the time Melody was Out, Jane had become so fixed in her place that she had not noticed this social nicety at play.

'I see.' Jane smoothed out her serviette and laid it in her lap. 'And you cannot receive these gentlemen without a chaperon.'

Melody nodded. 'But I do not want to be a bother. They may leave their cards. And perhaps Sir Prescott will call with Mr Colgrove. That would be all right, would it not? As they are cousins?'

Jane looked across the table at Vincent, who met her gaze with a disappointment as clear as Melody's. He bit his lower lip and idled with his knife. Inclining his head a little towards Melody, he nodded.

Jane sighed. She wanted to go with him. Oh, how she wanted to go and work. Her fingers fairly itched with the urge to pull glamour from the ether. And yet . . . and yet, she and Vincent had invited Melody to London with a purpose.

Though the matter was already decided between them, Jane asked aloud, for Melody's benefit. 'Do you need me today, Vincent?'

'I can get on quite well alone.' He compressed his lips in his private smile. 'And I promise to pause to eat.'

'Thank heavens for that.'

Vincent picked up his coffee cup and winked at her over the rim. 'Melody, that is the real reason that your sister insists that I not work alone.'

Melody raised her eyes from her plate, perceiving only the fact that Jane would stay. 'Are you certain?'

'Of course.' Jane was certain she would remain. She was less certain that she would enjoy it. Still, she had a fondness for her sister and enjoyed her company, so the day would have that, at the very least, to look forward to. If Mr O'Brien should call, then Jane had good reason to stay and keep an eye on the gentleman. She could not forget quickly the familiarity that he and Melody had shown each other the previous night. With luck, Major Curry would call as well, and she could have the pleasure of his company. Melody wanted only a little encouragement to look upon him favourably.

Nevertheless, when breakfast was over, Jane found that saying goodbye to Vincent at the front door was exceedingly difficult. This should be no different from any other time they had parted for an hour, two hours, or even a day, and yet, with their reconciliation so recent, Jane ached to go with him.

'Do you have your nuncheon?'

'I do.' He held up the basket.

'And you will not stay too late?'

'I will not.' Vincent kissed her cheek, then tilted his head to whisper in her ear. His breath was warm and it tickled. 'You provide remarkable encouragement to hurry home.'

'I can provide more encouragement, if you like.' Her hand found his waist and trailed down his thigh.

Vincent laughed and squirmed out of reach. 'I will see you this evening, Muse.'

After he went out, Jane stood for a few moments in the foyer, apparently regarding the wood grain on the door with great fondness. Heaving a sigh to collect her thoughts, she removed herself to the drawing room to attend to Melody.

Her sister had taken up a seat on the sofa facing the fire. She had added a blue shawl to accent her simple white muslin frock. 'This is quite the treat.'

'I should spend more time with you.' Jane sat on the sofa next to Melody.

Her sister laid a hand on her arm. 'No, Jane. You and Vincent are here for work, and I do understand that, truly. But it is still a pleasure to have you home.'

'I confess, I have forgotten how to have a day of leisure.' The parlour was in good order, though she could begin working on that glamural she had considered adding there . . . if not for the fact that she was supposed to be paying attention to Melody. 'What does one do when at home?'

'I read a little, although it tires me sometimes. I have been practising the pianoforte a good deal, but I sometimes feel that

I make no progress and the glamour line in the music remains beyond me.' Melody listed activities on her fingers. 'I am too dreadful at needlework to have any liking for it, but making a fringe can be diverting. Oh! And trimming bonnets.'

Jane well knew that she used to pass her days with such activities, and not so long ago. When she and Vincent had stayed with her parents during her recovery, she had spent entire days simply watching the light change on the lawn. To be so idle now made her very skin itch. 'I have lost much of the habit of this.'

'La! It fills the time, but does little for the mind, I will grant that.' Melody reached into her work-basket and pulled out a ball of string and a crochet hook. 'If you fetch your watercolours, we can converse as our hands work. You are not happy if you are not busy.'

Laughing, Jane rose to fetch her paints. 'You know me too well.'

With the aid of a footman, it did not take her long to move her watercolour supplies from the studio and set up a tolerable situation at a table by the drawing room window.

Setting her paints in order, Jane asked, 'Shall I paint you? It has been too long since I last took your portrait.'

Melody bent her head to her fringe. 'If you like, although I have not changed so much, I think.'

'No . . . but we do not have a painting of you here.' Pausing, Jane saw an opening for discussing the regard she had witnessed at Almack's. 'Or perhaps you have an admirer who would appreciate a mark of favour.'

As she expected, Melody flushed becomingly. 'No one to whom it would be appropriate to give such a gift.'

With relief, Jane picked up her pencil and opened to a fresh page in her drawing book. She had been afraid that Melody might have come to an understanding with Mr O'Brien during the hours that they had been together. That things had not progressed beyond that meant she still had some time to caution Melody before her preference was set. 'I confess that I was not certain after I saw you waltzing with Mr O'Brien last night.'

'Oh, do not tell Mama about that. She would die of mortification.' Melody wrinkled her nose in amusement. 'Can you imagine? La! Such a fuss over so simple a dance.'

'An intimate dance, you mean.'

'I suppose. Though, having tried it, I think there are few men with whom I would be willing to dance a waltz.'

'Oh?'

Melody adjusted the fringe on her lap and worked the crochet hook in and out of the thread for a few moments. The fire crackled in the hearth and the clock ticked upon the mantelpiece. Jane added the sound of her pencil sketching the line of Melody's cheek as she waited for her sister to answer.

Sighing, Melody shifted on the sofa to gaze into the fire. 'It is not the position of the dance that makes it intimate, though I own that it is shockingly close. It is that one does not trade partners. The opportunity for conversation. You see?'

'I do.' Jane saw all too well how much in danger her sister was of losing her heart. She was already repeating Mr O'Brien's conversation as if it were her own. 'What did you speak of?'

'He is excessively clever. We talk about music and what we are reading. Sometimes of politics. Alastar has the most astonishing ideas and, oh, Jane. He *listens* to me.' Melody seemed unaware that she had used Mr O'Brien's given name.

'He flatters you by requesting your input?'

'Very much so. Or, no—no, I do not think it is flattery, because that implies that it is insincere. He . . . I think, at least . . . he is genuinely interested in my thoughts.' She smiled in apparent remembrance. 'Sometimes we talk about you.'

All of Jane's senses now became alert, and any thought of drawing or painting vanished. 'How so?'

'Well . . . he wonders at your marriage. And to be frank, Jane, I cannot blame him. You are the oddest couple that ever walked the earth.' Melody shook her head, curls swaying against her cheek. 'Do not deny it. You know you are.'

'Not the oddest, I think.'

'No? Who else – name even one couple – who devotes their days to work as the two of you do? Most wives would be at home keeping house and tending to their childr—' Melody broke off, lowering her fringe with alarm. 'Oh, Jane. I did not mean . . .'

'I know you meant nothing by it. Fret not.' Jane had learned to keep a placid expression at references to her miscarriage. She thought that someday she and Vincent might have children, but it was difficult to imagine doing so now. It was hard enough to manage the needs of Melody against that of their work, and her sister was a grown woman. How much more difficult would an infant be? 'I am not certain that I am equal to hearing about Mr O'Brien's thoughts of us, but will trust that you do not drift towards any indiscretion.'

'Of course not. I am first and foremost your sister. I would never see any harm come to you, not even by chance.' Melody blushed again. 'I know that I have been sometimes thoughtless, but hope I have learned to value you since.'

Here, Jane saw the opening she needed to speak directly about the subject of Mr O'Brien. 'Then let me say that I also do not want to see any harm come to you. I am . . . I am too aware that past events were due at least in part to my unwillingness to speak frankly with you. May I address you now? Openly, about something that concerns me?'

Melody laid her fringe aside and turned to face Jane, with a stirring of alarm on her face. 'Please.'

'Mr O'Brien . . . I am nervous about his advances towards you.'

'Oh, but—'

'Hear me out, please.' Jane took a moment to smooth her dress and compose her thoughts. 'It is not that I think that any particular impropriety has yet been observed, but the whole of his manner promises something that he cannot provide. In short – though I am rambling a bit – you must see that his heritage makes him unable to address you.'

'I—Why?'

Jane paused with her mouth open. With a sinking heart, she realised that her sister, living in a country town as she did, would not have recognised his name as an indication of his ancestry. 'Ah . . . I made the same mistake when I met the family. They are Irish and Catholic.'

Melody looked down, her cheeks flaming. 'I know.'

'You know? And yet you continue to encourage his behaviour?'

'I do not understand why those two facts change the man. He is all that is courteous, and everything one could desire: easy manners, open and pleasing. A firm figure. Amiable character. If you could hear him talk about the plight of the coldmongers, you would not think so harshly. He is everything generous. Not at all the villain that the Irish are made out to be.'

Jane wet her lips, determined to try again, although she had some uneasiness about her own purpose. She must proceed, though, when she considered what her parents would say about Melody's preference. 'Even if I grant that, the greater trouble still remains. As a Catholic, he cannot marry you.'

'He . . . ? He cannot?'

'Depend upon it. Their Pope will not allow them to marry anyone but another Catholic. They think stooping to marry an Anglican would consign them to hell. Consider that even the Prince Regent could not marry the Catholic woman he was in love with.' Jane leaned forward to beseech her sister. 'I do not want to see your heart broken again. I fear the advantage Mr O'Brien takes with you by attempting to engage your affections when he cannot offer his own freely.'

'I—I had not thought of it in that light. Do you—do you really think he trifles with me?'

'If I did not, then I would keep silent. But he cannot marry you.' Jane bit her lip, sorry to see her sister look so downcast. It was good that she had not waited longer to speak – in fact, it would have been better if she had spoken sooner. 'When your callers come today, please, I beg of you, look at them not in light of who has the most pleasing manners, but who will give you a good life. Who can offer you a measure of happiness.'

Melody nodded, staring again into the fire. 'That is the other thing that Mr O'Brien and I discussed about you. It is so rare to find any marriage founded on love.'

'Vincent and I started with only mutual admiration.' Jane laughed, trying to lighten the mood. 'And, as you have noted, by disliking each other thoroughly.'

'Well then.' Melody wiped a hand under her eyes. 'I shall look for a man who is disagreeable and silent.'

The footman walked in bearing a card on a silver tray. Melody took it and gave a bitter laugh, leaving Jane no doubt as to whose card it was. 'Would you tell him that I am not at home?'

# FOURTEEN

# Family Matters

When Jane next accompanied Vincent to Stratton House, Mr O'Brien came out of the library to receive them, all smiles. He looked past them to the entry and his smile dimmed. 'Is Miss Ellsworth not with you today?'

'No, I am afraid that she decided to stay home.' Melody had shown admirable wisdom in removing herself from Mr O'Brien's influence.

'She has not suffered from one of her headaches, I hope?' He walked with them towards the ballroom. Vincent strode ahead, leaving Jane to manage the task of disappointing the young man.

'No, she was quite well when we left.' Jane kept her tone light. 'I think she only wanted a change.'

'Ah . . .' He studied the floor as they walked. 'Ah. Well. Thank you. I am glad that she is in good health.' After a few more pleasantries, Mr O'Brien excused himself and left her at the door to the ballroom.

Jane's conscience gave a pang then, because she thought that she had, perhaps, misjudged him. His disappointment seemed genuine, but there was nothing to be done for it. Separating the two now, before more damage was done to either heart, was necessary, though not without pain.

Melody had seemed cheerful enough at breakfast, talking about the variety of projects she would undertake that day, but in more than one quiet moment, Jane had found her staring into the middle distance with a melancholy look upon her face. Jane pushed the door to the ballroom open, thinking about her sister and the want of occupation she would face at home alone.

'Vincent, I hate to ask but . . . do you think I might leave off work from eleven to three today?'

He frowned as he removed his coat. 'You do not need to ask my permission, Muse.'

'No. I just wanted to be assured that you could do without me.' She glanced back at the door to make certain it was shut. 'I thought that if I could accompany Melody on her morning calls it might divert her tolerably.'

'I can hardly vouchsafe your time.' He rubbed the back of his neck. 'Do you think . . . we could have a dinner party?'

Jane stood on her toes to kiss Vincent on the cheek. 'I know how little you enjoy such things. Thank you. I will invite Major Curry so you may discuss glamour to your heart's content.' With the inclusion of Mr Colgrove and some of his set, Melody would have ample opportunity to see that she had other admirers. Jane had no doubt of her sister's ability to attach a gentleman. She only hoped that one of them could attract Melody's equal interest.

When Jane arrived at home early and suggested to Melody that they make morning calls together, her sister dropped her book so quickly that Jane might have thought she had not been reading at all. In very little time, Jane changed from her simple work dress to a sprigged muslin day dress with French knots in slate grey and coffee. Melody wore her celestial-blue pelisse, which did such lovely things for her eyes.

They set out, stopping first at Sir Prescott's to pay a call. Jane was embarrassed to recollect that the only time she had called on them was for Mr Colgrove's birthday party. She was a terrible relation, truly. Her mother would be appalled at her want of consideration, but the work had seemed so pressing.

She resolved to do better as she and Melody were shown into the front parlour.

Without the crush of people, the room's pleasant prospect was more apparent. It had a tall ceiling and ample modern furniture grouped around the room in picturesque arrangements.

In the chairs closest to the fire sat their cousins, facing Miss Godwin and an older woman, also from the East Indies. Seeing her deep brown complexion, Jane discovered that Miss Godwin was not so dark as she had first thought. Her complexion had been moderated by the English blood running through her veins.

Sir Prescott rose to receive them with delight, then drew up another set of chairs so they could join the group at the fire. 'You already know Miss Godwin, I believe. Allow me to introduce you to her mother, Mrs Godwin.'

'How do you do, madam.' Jane dropped a curtsy before taking her seat. While she had known that one of Miss Godwin's parents must be Indian, it still surprised her somehow and she endeavoured not to be so rude as to let that surprise show. Unbidden, Lord Verbury's words floated though Jane's head. *It is not as though she is Irish*. She felt abruptly ashamed.

'So charming. Mr Colgrove has spoken highly of your family. I am pleased to have the opportunity to meet you.' Mrs Godwin's voice danced, rising and falling with a modulation that flattered the ear.

Melody smiled at them both. 'Likewise. Your daughter has

been kindness itself to me. She knows ever so many more people than I do, and has been utter graciousness in making introductions.'

'You hardly need introductions.' Miss Godwin leaned over to her mother. 'Lady Vincent and her husband are the Prince Regent's glamourists.'

'Are you really?' Mrs Godwin clapped her hands and beamed at Jane. 'Oh! Well, this is not the time, but at some point I would very much like to talk to you about arranging the glamour for a wedding breakfast.'

Remembering Vincent's disdain for wedding glamours, Jane attempted to put Mrs Godwin off. 'I am flattered by your consideration, but I am afraid that we are not in the habit of performing at weddings.' A veil of reserve came over Mrs Godwin's features. Sudden fear washed through Jane, that Mrs Godwin thought that she was declining because of her heritage. 'Indeed, we declined the honour of Princess Charlotte's wedding.'

Sir Prescott cleared his throat and Jane's mortification deepened that even he seemed to notice her inadvertent gaffe. 'They—ah—they are often busy. We hired Mr Moyer for the glamural here, and he did a fine job.'

'Oh, but for family . . .' Mrs Godwin looked back to Jane. 'Surely you could fit in a family wedding.'

Her daughter blushed at her mother's presumption in discussing business at a social call. 'Mama . . . we have not properly announced it yet. It is too soon to make plans.'

Jane finally understood why Miss Godwin and her mother were calling upon Mr Colgrove. Her jaw did not drop, but it took her a moment to form the appropriate response. One only need meet Miss Godwin to realise the value of her company, but Jane could imagine her mother's astonishment at the connection. Jane herself was delighted with Miss Godwin, of course, but she had met her.

As she had met Mr O'Brien. As she had met his parents and knew them all to be of stout cloth and worthy acquaintances.

Melody clapped her hands, beaming at their cousin and his intended. 'Oh! Oh—am I to understand that we may wish you and Mr Colgrove joy? That is too, too wonderful.'

Wonderful, indeed. And yet, with Miss Godwin's thirty thousand pounds, society would find their engagement no wonder at all. If Mr O'Brien were merely Irish, then there would likely be no impediment to his advances to Melody. It was the fact that he was Catholic that was the true problem. She had done the correct thing to separate them, as he could not offer his hand.

They spent the rest of the call exclaiming over Miss Godwin and making all of the appropriate sounds of delight that one makes to the newly engaged. Freed from restraint by the acknowledgement, the two lovers were free with their affections.

Internally, Jane crossed Mr Colgrove off her list of suitors for Melody. The need to expand their circle of acquaintances was perhaps more pressing than she thought.

Before Jane could arrange a dinner at her own home, she first had to endure the promised dinner at Lady Penelope's home.

Though Lady Penelope had said that it would be a small family affair, Jane did not want to presume that they could attend in the half dress they favoured at home, but Vincent was no help at all in recommending the degree of formality to expect at dinner. Left to his own devices, he would have gone in his working clothes.

Consulting Melody proved far more efficacious. Together they decided that, since there had been the mention of meeting Lady Penelope's young son, a simple round gown was the safest course. Jane chose her pomona green one, and Melody settled on a figured white silk. Adorned with shawls, pearls and a minimum of feathers, they achieved elegance without dressing above their station. Jane had contrived to get Vincent to wear his blue superfine coat and breeches by mentioning how appealing she found the combination. He acquiesced with only a small amount of grumbling.

Even given the circumstances, Jane felt a degree of anxiety towards the event that surprised her. She half expected Lord Verbury to be in attendance, so by the time they called for the carriage and made their way to Essex House, she was in a state.

Vincent's sister lived in a grand town house stretching eleven windows across, facing Grosvenor Square on the fashionable end of the small park. The windows of the ground floor were bright with candles or the illusion of candles.

When they came into the entry hall, a flurry of footmen stepped forward to take their wraps. Jane nearly stumbled on the hem of her dress, staring. Each man wore the livery of Essex House: a deep green coat and knee breeches she had seen before. One of the men also looked familiar.

He was the servant who had been speaking to Mr O'Brien.

The footman saw her and paled to the shade of his wig, leaving no doubt as to his person. He averted his eyes and took Melody's wrap.

Vincent steadied Jane as she regained her balance. She opened her mouth to whisper to him, but at that moment, Lady Penelope came out of the drawing room to receive them. Jane bit the sentence off before she could utter it, determined to alert Vincent at the first opportunity. What in heaven's name had one of his sister's footmen been doing with Mr O'Brien?

Governing her expression, Jane greeted Lady Penelope with a smile.

Vincent's sister wore a full evening gown of amber crape over white satin, ornamented with rich silk trimming in Austrian blue. A profusion of ostrich feathers fluttered above her head. 'My dears! How lovely you look.'

'Thank you so much for inviting us.' Jane fought the urge to pat her own hair and surrender the single plume she had placed there.

'Come, I want you to meet my family.' She led them into the drawing room, all smiles.

Lord Verbury stood in the centre of the room in an attitude of relaxed enjoyment. On the couches and chairs in the elegant parlour were a profusion of lords and ladies. Although Jane had thought that the Earl might make an appearance, the reality still sent a jolt through her senses. She and Vincent had been promised a small family dinner, but it seemed Lady Penelope had included Vincent's parents and all his brothers and sisters.

Vincent stopped on the threshold, and Jane very nearly turned to go.

Lord Verbury smiled with cold civility. 'The fault for your surprise is mine. I told her that if you knew, you would not come.'

'Then perhaps that should have been reason to tell me.'

'Oh, Vincent . . . must you?' The oldest of the ladies present stood with admirable grace. 'Your father is apologising.'

Vincent swallowed and looked at the floor. Jane, in agony for him, felt that a retreat would only delay the reckoning. Melody shifted uncomfortably beside them. Jane tightened her pressure on Vincent's arm.

Gathering himself, he drew Jane further into the room. 'Mother, may I present my wife, Lady Vincent, and her sister, Miss Ellsworth. My mother, the Countess of Verbury.'

Vincent's mother was, as he had once reported to Jane, very beautiful. The Lady Verbury had a tall, upright figure, which had lost none of its vivacity with age. Though she had borne five children, she had the grace of a maid. The white column of her throat supported a face that would be well suited to a gallery, with a fine Grecian nose and full, soft lips. Where Jane could see her mark on Vincent most clearly was in her hands, which had an eloquence about them that seemed to draw pictures in the air, even without glamour.

As she took the part of hostess over from her daughter, Lady Verbury introduced them to each of her other children in turn. Jane felt confounded trying to remember them, though there were not so many names to recall.

Sir Waldo Essex, husband to Lady Penelope, was a stout figure of middle height and an unexceptionable manner. He was, fortunately for Jane, the only gentleman in the group who had lost his hair, and was therefore easy to remember. She was introduced in turn to Lady Merrick, Vincent's eldest sister, who he had called Caroline. She looked enough like Penelope to be a twin, save only that she had a few silver strands mixed among her brunette hair and faded blue eyes. Her husband, the Marquess of Merrick, was a small fox-faced man who watched the assembly with obvious forbearance.

Vincent's two brothers, of whom Jane had heard much, were cast from the same model as Vincent, though expressed in different ways. The eldest had followed the usual route of assuming one of his father's lesser titles and was styled the Viscount of Garland. Like Vincent, Lord Garland was tall, with a firm and upright figure. His face, though, had grown coarse and red from an excess of drink. His wife, Lady Garland, was a slender blonde whose colouring was so fair as to appear bleached, as if she were a glamour imperfectly rendered. The impression was strengthened by the want of regard that the rest of the family seemed to pay her.

Mr Richard Hamilton, the middle brother, had a delicacy to him that Jane found difficult to place – the movement of his hands, perhaps, or the softness of his features – which may have been some evidence of the 'propensities' that Lord Verbury feared use of glamour might produce in Vincent.

Once the introductions were finished, the assembled guests stood and looked at each other. Jane had the uneasy sense that they had placed a bet as to who would break the silence first.

The answer to that came from Melody. 'Are we too late to see your son, Lady Penelope? I had most particularly wanted to meet him.'

'How lovely of you.' Lady Penelope shook her head sadly. 'Alas, he has an ague, so Nurse is keeping him from us. He is such a delightful boy. So well grown and forward for his age.'

'Spoiled, you mean.' Lord Verbury looked down his nose at where his daughter sat on a divan.

'But of course, Papa.' She laughed, as though taking his remark as a joke. 'Who could mean anything else with boys?'

'I find it so myself,' Melody said. 'Our neighbours have the most charming little twin boys. They are forever getting into mischief, but one cannot mind them because their spirits are so irrepressible.'

A footman stepped into the room to announce that dinner was ready, saving them from further discussion of little boys. Lady Penelope stood and clapped her hands gaily. 'Now, the question is . . . since Vincent is now Sir David, does that mean he precedes you, Richard?'

Lady Penelope, for all her seeming good humour, was playing games with the order of precedence to deliver a sting to her family. By strictest rules, a knight did not rank above the son of an earl. If they were both Lord Verbury's sons, then Vincent's knighthood would push him above his brother in precedence in spite of the disparity in their ages. But if Vincent were to stand by his decision to cast off his family name, then he was not to be treated as Lord Verbury's son, and would rank below Mr Richard Hamilton.

Lady Penelope had, with a seemingly innocent question, laid open the entire trouble of this familial gathering.

Mr Richard Hamilton, who seemed to feel his sister's wit quite as much as anyone, said, 'Vincent should lead in, of course. As prodigal, his presence must be honoured. I shall take my usual place at the foot of the line.'

With a tilt of his head, which reminded Jane uncomfortably of Vincent, Lord Verbury gestured to Melody. 'Perhaps you might sit with Richard, then. After all, he is, strictly speaking, a commoner.'

His words might have been meant for his son, but Jane felt them for her sister. Melody's cheeks flushed. Wrinkling her nose and giving a little laugh, Melody snapped her fan open. 'La! Lord Verbury, you would have me think you are trying to make a match. How forward of you. But I will take the compliment as you meant it.'

Vincent, who, after the initial introductions had remained silent, coughed and covered his mouth. His face was quite red. For the first time that evening, Jane thought he was masking a smile. She wanted to commend her sister's ready wit, for even if Melody did not know the history of the family, she must be sensible of the tensions in the room.

Jane followed Lady Penelope into the dining room, taking precedence beyond her rank as the wife of the prodigal. The table was as elegant as she had come to expect from the establishment of a lady of fashion such as their hostess. Glamour had been used to dim the corners of the room so that the attention was on the candlelit tablecloth. A footman stood behind each chair, and the quantity of plate on the table was almost enough to blind.

As Lady Penelope took her place at the foot of the table, she caught Jane's arm. Lowering her voice, she gestured to the head of the table. 'Do sit by Sir Waldo. He understands what it is to be an outsider in this family. I am sorry that our teasing does not make it easy for you.'

She seemed so sincere that it was hard to credit her barbed wit but moments before. Still, Jane did not suspect she would find a safer place at the table than by their host's right hand. Melody sat across from her, seeming to have a similar thought as the other ladies took their places down the length of the table.

As the gentlemen processed in, Sir Waldo smiled upon seeing her. He pulled out his chair, saying, 'I had hoped we might have an opportunity to converse.'

'As did I.'

The chair to her left scraped as a footman pulled it out. Jane turned to her neighbour. Lord Verbury sat beside her. He inclined his head, and then turned his attention to Lady Garland, as was proper at a formal dinner. She would have to face him eventually, but for the first course, Jane was grateful that custom meant she had Sir Waldo as her dinner partner.

He was a tolerable conversationist, although staid in his choice of subject. They spoke at first of the weather, which both agreed was frightful. Finding common ground in that, they moved on to the more detailed question of the rain and whether it would cease, followed by astonishment that snow was still upon the hills, and finally winding up with the question of the harvest and if it would be late that year.

Jane was almost relieved when the table turned and she was faced with her new dinner partner, Lord Verbury. He gestured to the dishes close at hand. 'Would you care for ragout or the turbot?'

'The ragout, please.' Jane waited as he served her. She decided that since the weather had seen her safely through the first course, that she would employ it in the second. 'Have the rains given your estates much trouble?'

'Yes.' He poured a spoon of the vibrant red ragout on her plate.

'My father is struggling with the same issues. He had to replant after the late snow.'

'Indeed.' Lord Verbury set her plate down and helped himself to a slice of lamb.

'Did you have to replant as well?'

He reached for the peas and carrots. 'Yes.'

While Jane had been content to have a civil conversation, she was less willing to try when Lord Verbury made his contempt clear by uttering not a word beyond a monosyllable. Why had he taken a seat by her if he intended to slight her all evening?

Jane answered her own question. He took this seat precisely *because* of the opportunity to slight her all evening. Taking up her fork and knife, she cut a piece of beef in the ragout to size. Well then, she would present him with a question that could not be answered by a yes or a no. 'What sort of trouble have the coldmongers been giving? At your estate, I mean.'

169

He hesitated with his spoon suspended over the gravy. 'I have no coldmongers on staff.'

'Ah . . .' Jane took a bite of the beef, which was quite well prepared, and swallowed before continuing. 'It must confound you, then, as to why the cold weather continues on your estate if there are no coldmongers present. Or did I misunderstand your conversation with Lord Eldon?'

Across the table Lord Garland chuckled. 'Oh, Father has been trying to displace Lord Eldon these past two years.'

With a smile at his eldest son, Lord Verbury calmly pushed some peas onto the back of his fork. 'If he did his job as Lord Chancellor, I should not have any complaint with him.'

'No?' Jane sampled a slice of roast onion. 'I thought his parentage was an issue.'

'Father has yet to see anyone complete a job without wishing it done better,' Garland said. 'How is your meal, sir? Fancy a turn in the kitchen?'

'It is rare that anyone attains perfection. Few even see worth in the attempt.' Lord Verbury tucked his chin into his cravat in a movement so like Vincent – even to the desire to strive for perfection – that Jane had to suppress a shudder. 'It would be a great deal easier to replace Lord Eldon if I had the ear of the Prince Regent.' At that, he shot a look down to the end of the table, where Vincent sat by Lady Penelope.

His son met his gaze, then turned to his sister and resumed talking as if his father had not spoken.

'What is it about Lord Eldon's policies that you object to?' Jane lifted her glass and sipped some of the excellent claret.

Lord Verbury smiled at her, leniently, and returned his attention to his plate. 'How do you find the ragout?'

'Beautifully prepared. I must give my compliments to your daughter's cook.'

'It is over-spiced.' He lifted his glass and sniffed the wine. 'And pairs poorly with the claret.'

On Jane's other side, Sir Waldo paused in his speech to Melody, but did not turn to engage the Earl. Jane lifted a potato from the ragout. 'I suppose it depends on whether one enjoys spice. I do.'

They proceeded in silence for some minutes more before Jane attempted to engage him in conversation again. 'I would have thought that Lord Eldon's bill to help the working poor was a necessary thing given the climate and the shortness of food that follows.'

Melody turned briefly from Sir Waldo to join their conversation. 'I was just having the same conversation with our host. After reading the bill, it seems to me to provide temporary relief to the displaced workers, such as the coldmongers, without causing them to become burdens.'

Along with everyone else, Jane gaped at Melody, though on her side it was at least a little out of wonder that she had induced Sir Waldo to discuss anything but the weather.

Lord Verbury did not answer her, being concentrated on removing a trifle of fat from his lamb.

Sir Waldo nodded at Melody. 'I have not read it yet, but it does seem in line with all that the church teaches us about the worth of charity.' If he sympathised with the coldmongers, then that might account for his having sent a footman to Mr O'Brien. Could he, though, be said to sympathise if he were ignorant of the bill?

'I wish I had your confidence. I would never feel comfortable conversing about a bill I had not read.' Lord Verbury

171

# FIFTEEN

# A Studied Withdrawal

When the ladies removed to the drawing room, Jane was only too happy to escape the stifling atmosphere of the dinner table. Seated as she was at the opposite end of the table, Jane could do little to support Vincent. Had it been only his father present, she would have been willing to provoke more of a scene, but with the husbands of Vincent's sisters present, the wiser course was to let Lord Verbury's conduct speak for itself. She suspected that he was trying to spur her into exposing herself through irrational response, so she had endeavoured to meet his studied civility with her own.

The drawing room, on the other hand, offered a welcome opportunity to learn something of Vincent's mother, with whom she had thus far exchanged only a few words. As the ladies settled themselves around the room, Melody joined Lady Garland, the only other woman from outside the family. The pale woman seemed almost surprised to be addressed by anyone at all.

Jane sat on the sofa by Lady Verbury. She must have been a great beauty in her day, because her refined features still had more elegance than most younger women ever attained. She carried herself with an innate grace, turning to smile with welcome at Jane. 'Now, my dear, we shall be able to have a little tête-à-tête.'

'I am glad, as well, to have an opportunity to talk with you.' Jane glanced at the other ladies and used that subject for her opening. 'Your daughters are lovely.'

'Thank you. One might call them a blessing, as all daughters must be considered.'

'Are they very accomplished?'

'Their father felt it was important.' Which did not answer Jane's question about whether or not they had achieved any accomplishments. 'I understand you have some skill with glamour?'

Blushing, Jane smoothed her dress. 'I have been fortunate to have good teachers, such as your son.'

She sighed. 'His interest was such a disappointment to his father.'

'I—I have heard some stories . . . but do not wish to pry.'

'Hm . . .' Lady Verbury placed a confiding hand on Jane's arm. 'Then perhaps we should discuss the weather. I always find that a safe topic. Or Penelope's son. Such a charming boy, but then it is to be expected that I should dote on my grandson, and so I do.'

Jane tilted her head, frowning. 'Have you only the one grandson?'

'Oh, no. Caroline has three young sons and a daughter. Alas, neither Richard nor Philip have produced an heir. It frets the Earl dreadfully.' She glanced at the piano. 'Do you play, my dear? I believe I heard that you do.'

'Yes, it is a favourite diversion when we are not working.'

'Would you do me the favour, then, of playing?' Lady Verbury, too, eluded topics – not as though she were neglecting

Jane, but more as if she were unwilling to let any hint of her actual opinions pierce her beautiful countenance.

'But of course.' Jane had no interest in playing, but she did not wish to decline a request from Vincent's mother. She would like to be on good terms with at least one member of his family. After the trick that Lady Penelope had played on them, Jane had rather little trust for Vincent's sister.

Lady Verbury followed her to the pianoforte and leaned against the instrument with her back to the rest of the room. Jane turned through the music, settling on the Marche triomphale for piano in E Flat major, by Field, as having a pleasant air. It was a simple enough tune that it did not require her full attention, and the few strands of glamour that the score suggested to supplement the music allowed her to consider what an Essex footman might have been doing with Mr O'Brien. Her attention had been so absorbed since their arrival that she had thought of no way to ask about it.

If he had worn his wig – or if she had not overheard those pieces of conversations – then she might believe that he had been to Stratton House on a commonplace errand. It was puzzling in the extreme.

Lady Verbury leaned forward to look at the music, and turned the page for Jane. As she bent over Jane's shoulder, she whispered, 'My lord is very jealous. Vincent was right to get out. Tell him that I love him and miss him.'

Then the page was turned, and Lady Verbury was back in her place with the same placid smile as before. She stood so that if Jane had happened to look at her with astonishment – which she did not do – her expression would have been masked by the Countess's figure. It took all of Jane's will to continue to play without cessation.

The insipid chatter and smooth opinions that Lady Verbury expressed were a shield. If she felt the need to conceal, even from her daughters, this single expression of concern for Vincent, what must it say about how she lived her life? Vincent's stories of how his father treated him and his brothers came back to Jane. Lady Verbury must live her life in constant fear of saying the wrong thing or showing the wrong look.

The song, sadly, had only the one page turn. If Jane had realised the opportunity it offered, she might have chosen a piece that was rather longer. As it was, she was eager to select another and continue to play, but the gentlemen entered before she could move on. Lady Verbury turned from the piano with an expression of welcome on her face. Beckoning to Lady Penelope, she said, 'My dear, would you favour us with a tune so that Lady Vincent might have the opportunity to become better acquainted with our family?'

That lady was only too glad to oblige, standing with readiness to assume her place at the pianoforte. Jane relinquished her seat with some reluctance, but only because she had hoped to engage Lady Verbury in further conversation, so seeing Vincent's mother glide across the room to meet her husband made giving up the instrument that much easier. Jane moved to Vincent. Only by his compressed lips did he signal that he was at all uneasy.

She longed to have a private moment with him, but Mr Hamilton claimed her attention next. 'You have done wonders with him, you know.'

'Pardon?'

He walked her over to the fireplace and lowered his voice. 'No one else will admit it, but Vincent is much easier with you than he ever was at home.'

'I am not sure that I can take any credit for that, sir.' If Vincent's mood tonight counted as 'easy' among the family, she could only imagine how he had been before. She suspected his change in spirits had more to do with escaping his father than any influence of hers.

'No? I saw him smile at you twice tonight.' Mr Hamilton leaned against the fireplace and looked into it with as relaxed an attitude as any young dandy might affect.

Jane studied the flames with him. 'Had you seen him since he left?'

'No. God, no. His lordship made it clear that any of us who did would be cut off.' He glanced at her out of the corner of his eye. 'Now you are deciding if I am unfeeling, or a coward.'

This was too close to the truth for Jane's comfort, so she shifted the subject. 'Was he always brooding? As a child?'

'Hm? No . . . no, I do not think so. I recall him being a merry infant.' He shrugged easily. 'I think we all were.'

They were joined by Lord Garland, and any private conversation ceased. 'Vincent tells me you saved his life. Twice.'

'Oh . . .' Jane folded her hands together and examined the carpet. She had not actually thought of it as such.

'Look! She blushes. So charming . . . still, the war! I should like to have been there, but with Lady Garland increasing, it was not a choice I could make.'

'Have you children, then?' Jane frowned. She had been certain that Lady Verbury said they did not.

'Only a girl, so I could have gone after all with no fuss. More's the pity.' He clapped his brother on the back. 'But you never can tell, can you?'

'If you could, many things would be a good deal easier, eh?' Mr Hamilton laughed as though his brother had made a clever joke, but Jane failed to see the humour in it. She glanced over her shoulder at Vincent, who stood in conversation with Lord Merrick. Lady Verbury had taken a seat by Melody on the far side of the room, and the two seemed to be engaged in chatting placidly. Her sister had that tranquil expression she so often employed when listening. Occasionally she spoke earnestly, but the distance was too great to catch any hint of their conversation.

At the pianoforte, Lady Penelope brought her song to a close. 'Caroline, do come and take a turn. I want to hear that Italian aria you were working on.'

Lady Merrick waved a slender hand in denial. 'Oh, no, thank you. You have all tired of my playing, I am certain. I would rather hear Miss Ellsworth play.'

Melody jumped at her name and twitched her hands almost as though she were untying a glamour. 'Oh, no, thank you. I am wanting any real skill at any of the arts, I am afraid.'

'Oh, my dear. You must apply yourself.' Lady Merrick shook her head with an expression of genuine regret. 'A want of accomplishments will make it ever so much harder for a girl in your position to catch a husband.'

At so flagrant an attack on her sister, Jane decided she had had quite enough. She stepped away from the gentlemen. 'Sir David? I hate to call your attention to the hour, but we perhaps should take our leave. We do have to work tomorrow.'

'Ah yes . . . Vincent's hobby is now a profession,' Lord Verbury drawled. 'How amusing that a son of mine works for a living.'

'I think many people work, sir, but some do not know the wages they pay for their style of living. We, at least, know who our masters are.' Jane turned to Vincent and held out her hand. 'Sir David, shall we?'

'By all means, Lady Vincent.' He turned to his sister and offered her a full court bow. 'Lady Penelope. Sir Waldo. The pleasure has been indescribable.'

The carriage had barely left the drive of Essex House when Vincent sighed back against the cushions of the seat and pulled Jane's hand into his. 'That did not go nearly as badly as I thought it would.'

The sisters broke into a chorus of shocked outrage. 'How could you—' 'Not as badly?' 'That was nothing like good.' 'The worst possible—'

'No, truly.' He held up his hands as though to fend off their words. 'I knew that Penny might invite the rest of the family.'

'And you did not warn us?' Jane prodded him with her finger in outrage. 'You are as bad as they are.'

'I—no. I was not certain. I hoped not.' He fidgeted with one of the buttons at the knee of his breeches. 'Perhaps it is more accurate to say that I feared she would, but wanted to believe the fear irrational.'

'But why would she?' Melody frowned and pulled her shawl tighter.

Vincent shrugged. 'She was always my father's favourite. Whatever he asks, she delivers.'

Jane squeezed his hand. 'I do not see how you could survive such a parent. And your brothers and sisters are nearly as vicious.'

With a bitter chuckle low in his throat, Vincent looked out the window. 'Oh, my dear. They were all on good behaviour tonight.'

This brought stunned silence to the ladies in the carriage. Jane pulled away to peer at her husband's face, but as the carriage rolled through the streets, it was too dark to tell if he was jesting. 'I have a difficult time believing that.'

He shrugged. 'It does not matter. They are all creatures of my father. That Garland intervened for you is a sign that he liked you. No, truly. He was willing to needle my father on your behalf. He will pay for that infraction later, though he has more independence than the rest of them.'

Jane said, 'For my part, I cannot understand why you retained any tie to them, even the name Vincent.'

'I—I never told you? I named myself after my mother's father, who was always kind to me when he was alive.' He traced his finger around Jane's hand and stopped at the wedding band beneath her glove. 'My grandmother was an adept amateur glamourist who introduced me to the art. I am pleased to have another Lady Vincent in my life. Also, the name has always nettled my father.'

Melody cleared her throat. 'Which brings us to the most unusual conversation I had with Lady Verbury.'

Jane sat up. The brief sentence from Vincent's mother had been forgotten among the other events of the evening. 'I too—when I was at the pianoforte, she took the opportunity of turning the page to tell me that Vincent was "right to get out".' Vincent's breath caught at that and she laid her other hand on top of his, grateful that the dark interior of the carriage hid him from Melody. 'She said that she loved you and missed you.'

Jane could just catch the faint silhouette of his face staring at the ceiling. The carriage rocked over the cobbles to the clop-clopping of the horse, and the creak and groan of the springs. Outside, other carriages passed with a rush and rumble. Party-goers called boisterously to each other.

Vincent's exhalation almost blended with the night sounds of London. 'Well, Melody. What did she say to you?'

Melody's swallow was audible in the small confines of the carriage. 'She was afraid for you. She said . . . she said that Lord Verbury speaks in front of her because she "does not matter". She knows that you thwarted him, but not how.' Her voice got smaller. 'She wants you to be careful.'

Jane sat up, trying to see her sister through the gloom. 'When did she say all this to you?'

'On the couch. After the gentlemen came in. She said—she thought I had a similar want of consequence to the Earl, and so . . . so I was safer than Jane.' Melody's fan opened with a rattle and air finally stirred inside the carriage. 'La! I had so much difficulty keeping my composure.'

'I can imagine.' Vincent stirred on the seat, disengaging his hand from Jane's. 'She took quite a risk to speak to you.'

'There is more. She said that Jane had come too close to the point with her questions. Then we ran out of time.'

'I am sorry to have drawn you into my family's politics.'

Melody said, 'I do not mind. I am happy to help, if I can.' She hesitated and cleared her throat. 'You might ask Mr O'Brien about Lord Eldon. He is very well informed on the question of the coldmongers.'

Vincent humphed in surprise. 'Is that where you learned of the bill?'

'Yes.'

Jane winced, but there was nothing to be done. She longed to tell him of the footman and ask what he made of that, but she did not want to mention the existing connection to Mr O'Brien in Melody's hearing. Not when that subject was still so raw.

They rode in silence for some time. Jane could not stop turning the puzzle over in her head. So many pieces to consider, but the connections between them were perplexing. She leaned against Vincent and whispered, 'Do you think the message was genuine? Or—or was she acting on instruction from Lord Verbury?'

Vincent groaned and sat forward in the seat. His next words were subdued. 'I would wish that you had not learned to ask that question.'

Jane rubbed Vincent's back, wishing she could do more for him.

# SIXTEEN

## *Animated Spirits*

Vincent shut the door to their bedchamber and stood with his hand on the knob. 'Jane . . . I might go up to the studio for a while.'

'Shall I come?'

She could almost see the 'no' forming on his lips but he nodded instead. 'Please. My head is too full.'

'Oh, my dear . . . I wish—I so wish . . .'

The corner of his mouth bent, and he shrugged. 'I cannot help but wonder about my mother speaking to Melody like that. And to you. "Right to get out." Gah. Would that I could tell if she had been put up to it.' He scrubbed his face and stood with his hand wrapped in his hair. 'It is of no use thinking of it.'

'There is—there might be a reason to consider it.' Jane came to stand by him. 'Do you remember the servant that I told you I overheard at Mr O'Brien's? He is a footman at your sister's.'

'What—but . . . are you certain?'

She nodded. 'He started when he saw me, so I am quite certain.'

Vincent let go of the door and paced further into the room, lifting his other hand to wrap it in his hair as well. 'But . . . why? Muse, I will tell you that I was inclined to think that

184

you were seeing intrigue where there was none – out of concern for Melody, but still. Now, though . . . now . . . but why? What could the connection be?'

'Could . . . your brother said that Lord Verbury wants to take Eldon's seat as Lord Chancellor. We think that he wanted you to spy for him. Perhaps this is another avenue. Could he be using Mr O'Brien to get information from the coldmongers about Eldon?'

Vincent stopped in front of the window with his back to her. 'Surely simply engaging a coldmonger to spy would be easier.'

'Yes . . .' Jane chewed her lower lip, thinking. 'But recall how William would not accept charity? Perhaps the honour of the guild is too high.'

Vincent lowered his hands and wheeled to face her, with an expression that suggested that he had no such faith in the honesty of man. 'I could believe that of one man, but a group? Among them, there must be at least one, with a family in need, who would be willing to sell out his fellows for their sake.' He sighed and tucked his chin into his cravat. 'No . . . no . . . perhaps the answer is not in the coldmongers, but . . . consider that we have been back in the country for some time. Why should the Earl wait to approach us? Consider that he did not until we had been employed by Lord Stratton. Perhaps his interest lies there, and not with the coldmongers.'

'I almost wish that I had not suggested to Melody that she discourage Mr O'Brien. She might have been able to shed some light on his character.'

'Eh? Did you?' He lowered his head and scowled at the floor. 'I am sorry to hear that. He seemed sincerely attached to her.'

'But you know it is not possible. Why should Melody risk heartache?'

'I rather think—but she is your sister, of course.' He rolled his neck and straightened to face her again. 'The fact remains that your thought is correct. We need to know more about the gentleman than we do. I—I . . . Do I want to offer this? Yes. I have – had – some friends who would be likely to know all the gossip connected with the house.'

It was Jane's turn to hold her breath. He could not be suggesting . . . 'Miss de Clare?'

'What? Oh, Lord no. Jane, no.' He crossed the room in four great strides and gathered her hands. 'No. From that part of my life, yes, but never her.'

Jane found that she was crying.

Vincent pulled her close to his chest and wrapped his arms around her, soothing and murmuring to her. The sound of his voice rumbled in her ear, with no meaning, except that he loved her. She clung to him, utterly ashamed of weeping, of suspecting him, of giving in to his father's schemes. She held on to him and fought for control of her sensibilities once again.

She lifted a hand to brush the tears off her cheek. 'I am sorry.'

'No . . . no . . . hush.' He kissed the top of her head. 'I am sorry I suggested it.'

'It is reasonable.' She pushed back a little so she could see his face. His eyes were pink around the edges. 'I only regret that I let your father— No. I will not call him that, for he is no sort of father— that I let the Earl so infect my thinking.'

'It is what he does.'

Her heart broke all over again for him, to have grown up under that twisted grasp. 'Not to us.'

'Muse . . .'

'Rogue.'

Vincent bent to kiss her, and the room and the world beyond

was lost in the warmth of his lips. When they broke apart, Jane's heart beat against the confines of her stays.

Her husband traced the line of her jaw with his thumb and considered her. 'Now, Muse . . . now that we understand each other, let me explain what my offer meant. I can go to the club frequented by some of the gentlemen I knew at university. Skiffy will be there, likely, and some others. If there is gossip to be had, they will have it.'

Jane remembered Vincent at Almack's and hesitated to ask him to slip into that skin again. 'You do not mind it?'

'I have been thinking that I could let my father rot for his own sake, but if what he is doing chances to touch on you or Melody, I will not stand for it.' He bent closer. 'So, no. I do not mind it. Do you?'

She shook her head.

'Good.' He lifted her and spun her to the side. 'Then I shall be off. Do not wait up.'

She stared at him in surprise. 'But so late?'

'I am already dressed. I see no reason to wait.'

'I meant the hour. Will there be anyone to meet?'

'Muse . . .' Vincent paused by the door. 'They will only just be starting.'

In spite of Vincent's suggestion, Jane had no intention of falling asleep while he was out. She pulled the counterpane off the bed and settled herself on the bedroom's small sofa in front of the fire. She made some effort to read, but the late hour and her worry kept her from being able to engage in the book.

She closed her eyes, but only for a moment. When she opened them again, the candle had burned down, the fire was nearly cold, and she had a horrible cramp in her neck.

Vincent stood in the door with a candle in one hand and his shoes in the other.

Jane pushed herself into a sitting position, rubbing the back of her neck. 'I am awake. You do not need to be quiet.'

'I was hoping you would be asleep.' He shut the door carefully behind him. Vincent crossed the room and set the candle on the table a trifle too hard. He winced, then lowered himself into a chair facing her. He turned his head as though he were balancing a glass of water upon it. 'I am inebriated.'

'Are you?'

'Indeed.'

Jane had never seen him deep in his cups before, and found herself more amused than anything by the careful way in which he moved.

'Should you like to hear what I learned about Alastar O'Brien, or shall we wait until I am somewhat more respectable?' He spoke precisely, with an overemphasis on his consonants, as if to make up for his state.

'Will you remember in the morning?'

Vincent paused and tilted his head, considering the question with more seriousness than she had thought it had merited. 'I believe so, but I am also afraid that I mistook my capacity. It might be best to have my recital done with tonight.'

'Then please, continue.' Jane climbed off the sofa and went to the hearth to try to revive the fire. As she passed Vincent, she caught a waft of port wine.

'May I help?' He made as if to rise, but stopped when Jane shook her head.

'I am afraid you will combust should you come too near the flames.' She tucked her nightdress out of the way and pulled a log off the stack by the fireplace.

He chuckled. Rubbing his eyes, he yawned prodigiously. 'Ah, Muse . . . I am sorry you should see me in such a state.'

'So far, I have seen nothing to cause me any alarm, save for concern that you may have some discomfort tomorrow.' She tended the fire until the logs caught. 'Do you feel ill?'

'Thankfully, no.' He yawned again. 'I had that much judgement left. Skiffy and Poodle can be . . . insistent . . . and they would not share their information unless I indulged. They felt the need to "rechristen" me into the club.'

Jane settled herself at the end of the couch closest to him and pulled the counterpane over her again. 'So, what news did they have?'

'None. Or rather, they had much, but nothing that bears upon our questions.' He raised a hand and pulled at his cravat. 'As far as I can tell from their descriptions, apart from being an Irish Catholic, the young man has an irreproachable character. His father likewise. They have no debts and are widely considered to be good stewards of their property. They spent some time on the Continent giving Mr O'Brien a tour when he reached his majority and brought some nice marbles home. Lady Stratton is known for doing charitable works, and has visited the women's ward at the Marshalsea prison on more than one occasion. The only thing any of the men had to say about Mr O'Brien that was at all objectionable is that he had a red horse that Beau Brummell wanted and he would not sell it. Which turns out to be just as well since Beau has left town to escape his debts. I think they are irritated that O'Brien had the good sense not to be added to the list of people to whom Beau owes money.'

Jane frowned. 'Nothing about the coldmongers?'

Vincent shook his head. 'Nothing.'

'That seems to be an interesting omission, given how deeply

Melody implied that he was involved with them, and William's statement that he was a great friend of theirs.'

'This set is not likely to note charitable works as worthy of gossip. Lady Stratton's was so only because it involved a prison.' Vincent dropped his cravat on the floor. He bent his head to worry one of the buttons on his waistcoat free. 'I do not think there is anything more to it than that. His mentions of the coldmongers to your sister are likely nothing more than that she found the topic interesting, so he continued to speak on the subject. Speaking of your sister: according to Skiffy, she made quite the impression on the Prince Regent. Do tell her to watch out for him. He does not always act the gentleman.'

'I am well aware of that.' She could have used the reminder before the skating party. 'Was there any connection with your father?'

'That was harder to inquire about, but given that Skiffy knows my past, he would have found a way to bring it up if there had been anything relevant.' Vincent sat up further, still struggling with the same button.

'Do you need help, my love?'

He fidgeted with the button for a few more moments and then sighed heavily. 'Yes, please.'

Jane, resolutely, did not laugh at his impairment. She knelt in front of him and applied herself to undoing the various buttons on his clothing. As she did, she pondered what Vincent had learned, which was little enough. 'I must acknowledge that I have no real grounds for suspecting Mr O'Brien beyond seeing him speak to Lord Verbury.' She freed his waistcoat and turned her attention to the buttons on his trousers. 'No . . . that is not true. I heard him, most distinctly, say that they would march upon Parliament.'

'Likely a literary metaphor for a speech.' He grimaced and rubbed his head. 'I did inquire about Lord Verbury's plans as well. That he detests Lord Eldon for his common ancestry is generally known. He is also campaigning for the Lord Chancellor position, saying that Lord Eldon's policies will lead to a revolt among the working class, particularly the coldmongers. In specific, promoting the fear of coldmongers is gaining Verbury a substantial following. He insinuates that they are responsible for the weather, without going so far as to present unsound scientific theory. Still . . . it is having some effect, even among those who should know better. Do you know, I was pressed to admit that coldmongers could affect the weather, and when I would do no such thing, Poodle cursed me for making him lose a bet. No amount of detail would satisfy him about why it was not so. It was infamous conduct, really.'

'I am certain.' Jane finished with the last button on his breeches.

He yawned again, jaw cracking audibly. 'Ah, Muse . . . I am beyond tired.'

Jane glanced down. 'Not all of you appears to be weary.'

Her husband blushed and pulled his shirt lower. He stammered charmingly until Jane took pity on him and stood. 'Come, my love, let us get you to bed. I promise not to take advantage of your honour.'

He stood slowly, keeping one hand on the chair's arm for balance, and the other on the waistband of his breeches. 'You are very good to me.'

'I am no better to you than you deserve.' Jane walked him to bed and resolved to send a note to the Strattons in the morning to say that they would not be to work. She did not like to imagine Vincent's head when he awoke.

# SEVENTEEN

# Hidden in the Copse

Jane woke earlier than Vincent, who sprawled on the bed with his head half buried under a pillow. He snored. It was not unpleasant, his snore. Her husband had the slightest snore imaginable, rather like a small cat sleeping on its head than a broad-chested man. She sat in bed watching him sleep for some minutes, taking in the rise and fall of his chest and the shape of his shoulders under his nightshirt.

She had not heard the maid come in to light the fire, but it burned cheerfully in the grate, and the room had a tolerable warmth to it. She found it absurd that she should still require a fire in June, and began to wonder if the year would be entirely without a summer.

Sliding out from under the counterpane, Jane eased off the bed, trying not to disturb Vincent. His breathing did not change, and the slow wheeze of his snore continued. Jane dressed as silently as she could, wincing as she opened drawers and the quiet room exaggerated the sound of wood on wood.

On her toes, Jane crept out of their bedroom and shut the door behind her. It seemed unlikely that Vincent would be in any condition to work, so Jane made her first business of the day to send the note over to Stratton House to let them know not to look for the Vincents that day. Lord Stratton often sent a meal in for them, and Jane did not want the staff to go to the extra trouble if they were not there.

She went next to Mrs Brackett and asked her not to send anyone to tidy the room until Vincent arose on his own.

With those duties out of the way, Jane had time to seek her own breakfast and chat with Melody. Her sister was in the breakfast room with a newspaper open on the table before her.

'Good morning. Is there anything interesting today?' Jane put a slice of toast on her plate and considered the herring.

'It looks as though the price of grain will continue to go up. Crops are failing everywhere. The Luddites had another march in Bristol and destroyed three or four frames. Two of them were shot. The Luddites, I mean, not the frames. A volcano exploded on the isle of Tambora – that is in the Indies.' Melody tapped the paper and wrinkled her nose. 'Also, long sleeves are very much in vogue right now, which only makes sense with the weather. Oh! Do you think we might go to Fairfax's Symphonium sometime next week? They have a glamoured recording of the pianist John Field playing his newest composi-tion that I should like to hear.'

Jane raised her brow with some surprise at the range of items that Melody found interesting in the paper. 'Yes to Fairfax's – perhaps on Tuesday? Long sleeves make me glad. And more riots? That is a shocking thing.' It occurred to her that Melody might be better informed than she was about current events, a situation that she found uncommonly odd. 'Is there anything about the coldmongers?'

'Oh, the usual cries about their interference with the weather. La! You would think that people could understand

193

that it simply is not possible.' Melody rubbed her forehead. 'It makes me tired simply thinking of it.'

'You should see Vincent when he gets in form. Best keep the paper away from him.' Jane settled at the table next to Melody and applied herself to her breakfast.

'Where is Vincent this morning?'

'Still asleep. Last night took something of a toll on him, I am afraid.'

'I am hardly surprised. His family was horrid to him.'

'Mm . . . as a result, we are not going to the Strattons' today, so you and I do not need to rush our morning calls.'

'Oh . . .' Melody rubbed her head again and winced. 'I had actually thought to not make calls today.'

Jane looked at her sister with some concern. 'Do you feel unwell?'

'Only a headache.' Melody smiled, but it did not seem entirely sincere. 'I shall be quite comfortable later. You should go to the Strattons' without worry for me. I suppose last night took a toll on me as well.'

Jane frowned at her plate. In truth, she would very much like to get some work done. Vincent had done so much more on the glamural than she of late that the opportunity to even the balance intrigued her. The thought of working alone, in fact, had some appeal to it. She could set her own pace and not worry about him measuring her work. She resolved to leave a note for Vincent and then be on her way.

Jane found the empty ballroom to be a balm to her nerves. While the house was not quiet, with servants moving through the halls and the general bustle of a large establishment, none of it concerned her. She did not need to worry about Melody or Vincent or Lord Verbury. She could pay attention to her art.

She understood why Vincent had not objected to her spending time with Melody. Perhaps she should suggest that they stagger the hours they worked so that each of them might have some time alone on future projects.

Vincent had once explained to her that he thought art without passion was lifeless. He found it a way to channel strong emotions so that they might have an expression that was acceptable to modern society. Jane used that channel now, putting all the frenzy of the past weeks into the birds she sketched. She made a small flock of wrens that hopped from branch to branch, fluttering their wings. She stepped further into the illusory stand of trees, wanting to place some birds even deeper so that the motion came from back to front.

The sound of a door opening made her tie off the glamour and turn towards the ballroom doors to welcome Vincent, but the main doors were still shut. She realised that the sound had come from above.

A gentleman had entered the musicians' gallery. She caught the tail end of his speech. '. . . sees more clearly after our appointment.'

Another voice, with a pronounced Irish accent, spoke. 'Are you quite sure this is safe?'

'Yes. The Vincents are not here today, so the quiet area is disengaged.' The voice belonged to Mr O'Brien. 'You are certain that she marked you?'

'I turned that white when I saw her, and she almost fell on her—' The Irishman's voice cut off as he moved further into the gallery.

Jane could have no doubt as to who the gentleman with Mr O'Brien had been. The mysterious footman had come, undoubtedly to tell him that Jane had recognised him. It was as clear a mark of guilt as any she could think of. What she wanted to know now was what they were discussing that required that quiet zone in the musicians' gallery.

Jane bit the inside of her lip. She could not see them due to the glamural across the front of the gallery. If Vincent were here, he could weave a *lointaine vision* and record the conversation. The distance was greater than Jane thought she could manage, particularly since a *lointaine vision* had to be constantly spun by hand to work. Or . . . could she creep up the stairs and shorten the distance?

But then they might come down the stairs instead of going back the way they had come. Perhaps a *bouclé torsadée*? It was still a greater distance than she thought she could bridge, but at least she could tie off the glamour after it was spun. Grimacing, Jane sank to her haunches on the floor; she did not want to chance fainting and having her fall disclose her to the men upstairs. She took great breaths of air, trying to prepare herself for the weave she was about to attempt.

Jane grasped a fold of glamour and began pushing it out and up, towards the gallery. The weave itself demanded not only feeding glamour out in a long, slender ring but also winding it the entire time in even spirals. The glamour tried to sink to the floor, and Jane adjusted her grasp, aiming it more towards the ceiling. Her breath came quickly now. She had it almost to the gallery rail. Her pulse beat in her veins so loudly that she was surprised the sound did not carry through the *bouclé torsadée* to the men above. Sweat poured down the back of her neck and burned her eyes. Jane kept spinning the ring out.

Why had they put the quiet area on the far side of the

musicians' gallery? Only a few more feet remained until she reached where they sat.

'. . . the preparations for the march proceed,' Mr O'Brien said, and it was as if he were sitting next to her.

Jane held her mouth shut, trying to breathe quietly. She tied the glamour to itself and set it to spinning. Their conversation carried down to where she sat.

'What we need are some good banners to carry,' the Irish footman said. 'I can have the lads make some for us.'

'Good, good . . . what else do you think we ought to do?'

'Well . . . it seems to me that what the Luddites do to get attention is to burn the frames. Now, we don't have frames to burn, but some torches would not go amiss.'

A dark noise of pencil on paper. Mr O'Brien said, 'That might look fine. What else would you like me to take care of?'

She frowned. Did she have the voices backwards? It sounded as if Mr O'Brien were deferring to the footman. That made no sense, though. And yet, when the footman spoke again, the Irish brogue made it very clear who was who. 'I think you ought to be on your horse out front. It gives the lads heart to have someone like you leading them.'

'My friend, I wish you had more faith in your abilities. They would look up to you if you would let them.'

'Nay. Begging your lordship's pardon, but you don't sound Irish, and I do. You know how little trust I can get from them.'

'All too well.' Mr O'Brien's voice was dark. Another note marked on the paper. 'It shall be done, and we can discuss this afterwards. Now, I am afraid that I must be off, or I will be late for my appointment. I should not like to keep the lady waiting.'

The sound shifted as they stepped out of the zone and moved along the gallery to the servants' door. When she heard it close securely behind them, Jane stayed in the little woods, too stunned by what she had heard to think of what to do.

For some time, Jane sat among the illusory trees waiting for her heart to slow down. As her senses returned to her, she also felt it might be prudent to continue to hide for a time. Because Mr O'Brien appeared unaware that she was in the house, Jane wanted to be certain she gave him time to depart the property himself.

She waited a half hour, turning everything over again and fitting the pieces into what she already knew. Jane finally dragged herself to her feet and stepped out of the glamour she was hidden in. Her chemise clung to her back with sweat and left her chilled. Jane hurried to where she had set her pelisse, thankful that it had not been visible from the musicians' gallery.

The door to the ballroom opened. Jane jumped with a shriek.

Vincent scowled at her, with a hand to his head. 'Was that really necessary?'

'What are you doing here?'

He had dark circles under his reddened eyes and squinted as he looked at her. 'We have work to do. And yes, my head does ache abominably. Yes, I am irritable. And no. You may not talk me into going home.'

'My love, I assure you that is the furthest thing from my mind.'

'Good. I am in no condition for an argument.' He began to pull his greatcoat off.

'I am, in fact, very glad to see you.'

Vincent paused, one arm still in his coat sleeve. 'Why?'

'While I was working, Mr O'Brien came in.' She quickly explained what she had overheard, and her concerns.

Vincent stared at her, then his eyes went vague as he looked past the visible world at the glamour hanging in the room. He let out a low whistle. 'I did not know you could span such a distance.'

'Nor did I.' Jane paced in a small circle. 'What are we to do?'

He rubbed his head, frowning. 'I am thinking very slowly today. Bear with me.' Closing his eyes, he continued rubbing his temples. 'Where is Melody?'

'At home. She was not feeling well.'

'No . . .' He opened his eyes again. 'No, I am quite certain she is out, because Mrs Brackett asked after her as I was leaving. I thought she had gone with you.'

Jane covered her mouth. 'His appointment! He did not want to "keep the lady waiting". You do not think—?'

Vincent pulled his greatcoat back on. 'Get your pelisse. I shall call a carriage.'

Barely had the carriage come to a stop, when Jane was out of it. Vincent followed more slowly, stopping to pay the hack's driver. Running through the front passage, she lifted her petticoat and ran past the startled footman, up the stairs to Melody's bedroom.

Jane burst through the door of her sister's room, praying that she would find her at home. The room was at the front of the house, with a good prospect of the street below. The clear light through the windows left no doubt that the room was unoccupied. A maid had already been in to make up the bed and hang Melody's clothes. Jane snatched the wardrobe door open.

Melody's sky-blue pelisse was gone, along with the bonnet

that they had purchased together. Jane was not certain, but it seemed as if some of her other clothes were missing as well.

'Mrs Brackett says that no one saw her this morning after breakfast.' Vincent appeared in the door. A deep crease bent his brows together. 'Any sign?'

Jane shook her head and turned to her sister's dressing table. Her brush and comb were still there, as were her perfume bottle, the little china dog she was fond of and her work-basket. Jane crossed the room and snatched up the basket, digging through the half-finished crochet work until she found her sister's appointment book. Dropping the work-basket on the table, Jane turned through the pages to the current date. Her breath caught.

'Jane?' Vincent put a hand on her waist to steady her.

She showed him the entry and sank to the dressing table's low bench. 'This is my fault.'

*Alastar – No. 3 Bond Street – 2.00*

Around the words, Melody had drawn hearts with arrows through them. In the lowest corner of the page, Melody had erased two words, but they were still partially visible. *Mrs O'Brien.* Her sister was eloping.

# EIGHTEEN

# Vision Restored

Jane leaned forward again to look out of the carriage window. They were still on Piccadilly, and the traffic had slowed to a crawl. 'Perhaps we should get out and walk.'

Vincent took her by the shoulders and pulled her back. 'We will not get there any faster.'

She shrugged his hands away. How could she have been so foolish? Knowing Melody's history, she had no reason to think that her sister would listen to reason with regard to her heart. 'What am I going to tell my parents?'

'They cannot have gone far. It is only a quarter past two, and there is no business they could contract—'

'They could be married by now.'

'Not in London.' Vincent leaned forward with his elbows on his knees and knotted his hands together. 'Jane, if they were to elope, it would be more sensible for Mr O'Brien to collect her in his carriage.'

'Not if he thought we would see him. Recall that he thought we were at home.'

'Yes. But not until today.'

'Are you defending him?'

'No.' Vincent loosened his hands and put one on her

knee. 'I am trying to keep you from working yourself into a frenzy.'

'Much luck with that.' She would not be in a frenzy when she had Melody safely at home. The carriage turned onto Bond Street and Jane sat forward again, looking at the shop numbers. 'There!'

The driver pulled to a halt before Vincent could bang on the roof to stop him. Jane flung the door open and climbed out. Vincent followed, asking the driver to wait for them.

The address they had stopped in front of had large plate glass windows, through which optical instruments were visible. Above the shop's door was a large pair of spectacles with the note WILLIAM FRASER, OCULIST. Jane frowned, looking up and down the street. She had expected a church, or an inn, or a gambling den – but an oculist? 'We wrote the address down wrong.'

Vincent produced Melody's appointment diary from his coat pocket. 'No. This is correct.'

'You brought it with you?'

'It seemed prudent. Perhaps the establishment is a counterfeit and hides something else.' He went up the two short steps to the door, with Jane close behind him, and pushed it open. The doorbell rang merrily overhead.

Inside the shop, Melody sat in a chair with her back to the door facing a man in his middle years with ruffled black hair. Mr O'Brien stood at her side with his hand on the back of her chair. He glanced over his shoulder at the bell, then jerked around. 'Sir David! Lady—'

'Jane?' Melody spun in her chair. She wore a pair of spectacles.

For a moment, Jane could only gape at her sister. She had so expected them to be eloping that to find them in an oculist's trying on spectacles seemed beyond comprehension. 'What in heaven's name is happening here?'

'I am—Dr McCrimmon is just finishing fitting me.' Melody held her hand up in front of her and turned it over. 'It is . . . it is remarkable.'

'Mr O'Brien. It is most irregular to find you here, with my sister, unattended. I require an explanation.'

'They are not entirely unattended, Lady Vincent.' From a chair hidden by the door, Lady Stratton rose. 'My son asked me to accompany him to avoid any improprieties.'

Mr O'Brien cleared his throat. 'Miss Ellsworth—when we were looking at music, you see. She had so many headaches after, and then—well, her symptoms were so similar to mine that I was quite sure she had a vision impairment, so I made her an appointment with my oculist.'

The doctor took Melody's chin and turned her back to face him. 'The young lady is presbyopic.'

'Pardon?' Jane tilted her head, trying to understand.

'Far-sighted. It means that she can see things at a distance quite well, but has trouble with anything close to her.' Dr McCrimmon straightened the spectacles on Melody's face. 'The eye strain should not be a concern with these.'

'Far-sighted . . .' Jane looked to Vincent for support, but he looked as stunned as she was. 'Melody, why did you not simply ask me to take you to an oculist?' At times, Jane had wondered if Melody's trouble with detailed work was related to vision, but she had never pursued the idea, since her sister had never complained.

Melody bent her head and sighed. When she turned to face Jane, the light reflected off her new spectacles, hiding her eyes. 'Because I have said my whole life that I could not see music, or glamour, and that my eyes got tired when I read and . . . and you always told me to apply myself more.'

'I—I did not understand.'

'And when I asked for a lorgnette? To see better?'

Jane felt ill. 'You were ten. I thought . . . I thought you only wanted to be fashionable.'

'And last month, when I said I thought about getting spectacles? You laughed at me.'

Jane could find no response.

Melody looked down, cheeks quite red. 'When you said that you did not approve of Mr O'Brien, I felt that I could not tell you I was meeting with his oculist.'

Mr O'Brien stepped forward, his hands held a little out from his sides in supplication. 'Miss Ellsworth did not know I would be at this appointment. We had planned to go together, but then . . . I will grant that I should not have come after the situation was made clear.'

'Which is why he invited me.' Lady Stratton crossed the floor to stand in front of her son and glared at him. 'Though he did *not* tell me that you were unaware.'

'I only wanted to see how she got on.'

Melody spoke to the floor. 'I am glad you came, Mr O'Brien.'

'I am grateful for the service you have rendered my sister.' Jane kept her back straight and managed to look Mr O'Brien in the eye. 'However, you ought to have come to me, as her chaperon, to discuss this.'

'So you could send my card back out with the footman and say you were not at home?' He took a step closer to her.

Lady Stratton caught his arm. 'Alastar!'

He shrugged her off. 'You did not even know she had headaches, did you?'

'Of course I did.' Jane's voice faltered.

Melody said, 'But you thought I was feigning. Like Mama.'

She had, in fact, thought just that. Her mother had such a catalogue of injuries that Jane had become used to taking none of them seriously. Why should her sister, whose spirits were so like their mother's, be any different? 'Be that as it may, it was entirely improper for you to come here with this man.'

'I came by myself!' Melody stood, trembling visibly.

'Even worse, as you did not know Lady Stratton would be here.' Jane remembered herself, but only barely. 'For which I am grateful, madam.'

The doctor stood and cleared his throat. 'I have some things to attend to in the back, if you will pardon me.' No one paid him any mind as he slipped behind the curtain leading to the back of the shop, which appeared to be bigger on the inside than Jane would have suspected.

Mr O'Brien crossed his arms. 'Why do you disapprove of me? You are comfortable enough accepting my father's money.'

Jane pulled her head back, appalled. 'Your father is not trifling with my sister's affections.'

'Trifling? I assure you, madam, that I have never said anything to your sister with less than perfect sincerity.'

Vincent cleared his throat, but Jane continued. 'If that is true, then it is far worse. To engage her affections to no end but your own satisfaction is reprehensible. What would you have done with her? As a Catholic, you cannot offer marriage – so, yes, I call that trifling with her affections.'

Mr O'Brien lifted his chin, spectacles flashing. 'What can you mean by that?'

'It is a well-known fact that Catholics cannot marry outside their faith. Therefore—'

'Your *fact* is decidedly false.' Mr O'Brien's face had turned an alarming shade of red. He clenched his arms across his chest so hard that his knuckles had turned quite white. He spoke in a low, harsh voice. 'The report that we cannot marry outside our faith is spread by the Church of England, by *your* church, as part of a long effort against us. There is no truth in it. Does *that* change your feelings with regard to my eligibility as a suitor?'

Jane could only shake her head in denial. It was not possible that he was free to marry her sister. It was not possible that she could have been so in error. But had she ever studied the question? No. She had accepted the facts as she had been taught, without question.

Lady Stratton had lost any expression of sympathy. 'Pope Pius's Benedictine dispensation explicitly allows mixed marriages.'

The spectacles that Melody wore could not hide the fact that she was weeping.

'Jane, we should go.' Vincent went to Melody and offered her his handkerchief. 'Thank you, Lady Stratton, for your time and attention.'

Now Vincent was taking Mr O'Brien's part? Had he forgotten that this was not the only concern about Mr O'Brien, not when so much unaccountable conduct remained? 'I am sorry, I cannot allow him to stand before us with professions of openness while I know him to be in a secret league . . . when I have seen Mr O'Brien meeting with Lord Verbury.'

'What?' Mr O'Brien's mouth dropped. He appeared so openly confounded that Jane doubted her own recollection. 'I mean, yes. I have met the man, but can barely claim a speaking acquaintance.'

'I saw you on the street speaking with him.'

'So, you are accusing me of having a secret meeting on the street? The man stopped me and introduced himself as Sir David's father. I *thought* I was being polite.'

'What about the area of silence in the musicians' gallery?'

He looked even more confused. 'It is for them to take a break in.'

'You must do better than that. Why not have them simply leave the gallery?'

'Because, Lady Vincent,' Lady Stratton said, 'the string players need a place in which to tune their instruments. The temperature difference between the gallery and the hall would be too great in winter.'

Melody spoke up, then. 'Mr O'Brien is a cellist.'

He seemed to have a ready answer for everything.

'And yet, you have made use of it for private conversation. How do you account for the system of deceit – even espionage and treachery – which you have so recently undertaken? What of your meetings with the coldmongers? Do not deny your plans, sir. I was in the ballroom today and overheard your conversation.'

Mr O'Brien's expression soured. 'Aye. I see how it is. Being a Papist is not a black enough mark on my character for you. Now you would have me be a traitor to the Crown.' He looked as though he would spit upon the ground if they were outdoors. 'The work I do with the coldmongers is nothing that I am ashamed of, nor will I deny it.'

Lady Stratton said, 'I must ask why, if you thought my son was engaged in something so deplorable, you did not speak to Lord Stratton.'

'I— It was only supposition.' Jane could not put voice to her reason for not approaching the Baron.

'And it has nothing to do with the fact that we are Irish, I suppose?'

Jane flushed, feeling the warmth of mortification mount in her cheeks.

With her head high, Lady Stratton put her hand on her son's shoulder. 'I am proud of the good work that my son does.'

Vincent asked, 'May I ask what work that is?'

'We bear a responsibility to those who are less fortunate than us.' Mr O'Brien turned, seeming to speak to Melody more than anyone else in the room. 'The coldmonger in our house took ill and passed away last summer. I performed the office of returning his effects to the Coldmongers' Company before we left on our tour of the Continent. I learned that the illness which took him was common to coldmongers. Chilblains occur regularly among them, but in some, the ulceration of the skin becomes so severe that it sloughs off entirely. Infection sets in. They die. Did you know that the word is a corruption of "child bane"?'

'I did not.' Vincent still stood by Melody. He held his hands behind his back as though he were listening to any common lecture.

'Children have the constitution and strength to manage the skeins of cold. More importantly, they are too young to feel mortal. Until recently – and still in America – slaves served as coldmongers. *That* is how Lord Eldon's father first made his wealth.'

'I thought it was as a broker.'

'That is what he calls it now, to hide the fact that his wealth was made upon the backs of children. Is it any wonder that the coldmongers are outraged that they have been forgotten by him? He promised them that he would push a bill through to give them some relief, and has disregarded that.' Mr O'Brien beat his fist into his open palm. 'After our march to the Tower, I think that he will remember us.'

'My God.' As though someone had pulled a slipknot, the pieces of the glamour fell away and Jane could see the pattern at last. Lord Verbury had been playing upon the coldmongers' unhappiness to create a revolt. By suppressing them brutally, he would 'save' the city from the coldmongers and seem a hero. 'Vincent, is *this* the Earl's plan? Creating the march and then striking against it?'

He paled and cursed vehemently.

Melody lifted her head, eyes red from weeping. 'Oh, no. Please say that's not true . . . it is though, is it not?'

Mr O'Brien and Lady Stratton looked at each other. Confusion was writ large upon his face. 'Will someone explain?'

Vincent and Melody both looked to Jane. Swallowing the bile in her throat, she took a breath to try to steady her nerves. 'Lord Verbury wants to displace Lord Eldon as the Lord Chancellor. I believe that he plans to do so by creating a revolt. The footman who spoke with you this afternoon is in the employ of Verbury's daughter, and she is very much her father's creature. The march was the footman's idea, was it not?'

Mute, Mr O'Brien's face drained of colour.

Jane faltered. 'I am sorry – I thought you were knowingly entangled with Lord Verbury.'

He shook his head.

'When you gather, I think this same footman will tell Lord Verbury the time and place of the march. Verbury has said that the way to deal with such a revolt is by martial law. The cold-mongers will be fired upon by British soldiers to "restore order", and then all of Lord Verbury's predictions will come to pass.'

'And no one will complain about coldmongers being shot because too much of the populace faults them for the weather. It will be a massacre.' Lady Stratton pressed her hand to her mouth in horror.

'Pardon. I need to be away.' Mr O'Brien snatched up his hat. 'We are marching tonight.'

Vincent glanced at Jane, then tipped his head to Melody, suggesting that Jane take her home. She gave him a half-nod back. Pulling himself upright, Vincent turned to Mr O'Brien. 'I shall go with you. As I know Lord Verbury, my words may help you explain the situation.'

The offer stopped Mr O'Brien. 'I—thank you, sir. That is very generous of you.'

Melody picked up her pelisse and bonnet. 'I shall come as well.'

'No. We are going home,' said Jane.

When Melody opened her mouth to object, Lady Stratton shook her head. 'Go with your sister. The Coldmongers' Company does not admit women. We would only be in the way.'

'Sadly, correct.' Mr O'Brien crossed back to Melody and took her hand. 'I would rest easier knowing you were safe.' With an obstinate glance at Jane, he lifted Melody's hand and kissed it.

Once they were safely in the carriage, Jane strengthened her resolve to speak with her sister about her conduct. 'Melody, dear. I know that you are upset with me.'

'I am, and so I beg you not to speak.' Her eyes were still red from weeping, and strangely magnified by the spectacles she wore.

'I . . . all right.' It would be best for both of them if they waited until their heads were cooler.

For the rest of the carriage ride, Melody sat facing the window and staring out, at times lowering her spectacles and looking over their rims before restoring them to their place. Jane sat on the bench opposite, fidgeting with a tassel on her pelisse. She felt once again the mortification and shame of the moment when Mr O'Brien had said that there was no barrier to their marriage. Her conviction had been no better than those who thought that coldmongers controlled the weather: wild supposition instead of fact.

Jane rubbed her forehead as if she could massage her vexation away.

The distance between the oculist's and their home seemed to expand in the silence. She thought, more than once, that the driver had taken some longer route, but whenever she looked out the window, she saw Piccadilly passing by with its wealth of haberdashers, linen drapers and booksellers.

It was with greatest relief that they arrived at Schomberg House. Melody descended from the carriage in silence and went into the house without waiting for Jane. Jane settled with the driver and followed her sister inside.

Mrs Brackett met her in the foyer. 'You found her, I see.'

'Yes. The alarm was over nothing.' Jane could not allow gossip to spread through the servants' channels that Melody had run off. 'She had an appointment with an oculist and forgot to tell me it was today. Did you mark her new spectacles?'

'Yes, madam.' Mrs Brackett's mouth turned down as though they were distasteful. 'I confess that I was surprised. Most young ladies go to pains to avoid such things.'

'True.' Jane pulled off her coat and bonnet. 'But my sister

likes to read, and these are easier to manage. Did she go upstairs, or to the drawing room?'

'Upstairs to her room, madam.'

'Thank you.' Jane went up the stairs, not looking forward to the interview she was now to face. She knocked on Melody's door and waited, feeling older than her years.

'Come in.'

Jane let herself into the room. Melody sat at her dressing table holding a handkerchief close to her face. 'Did you know that cloth has individual fibres?'

Jane sighed. 'I am sorry that I did not believe you, but is it really necessary to rub my face in my error?'

Melody dropped the handkerchief and turned. 'Why must you always assume that I am trying some manoeuvre to play upon your sensibility? I am not a glamourist creating the world out of whole cloth. I am twenty years old and this is the first time—No. I reconsider. This is not an argument that is worth having.'

Pressing her hands to her temples, Jane tried again. 'I am sorry. That was unfair of me. I have been under considerable strain for the last week, and I thought you were in some danger.'

'I am sure you have been . . . but, Jane, you have not told me anything.' Melody picked up her hairbrush without seeming to recognise it and turned the thing over in her hands. 'You are my sister, and if you expect me to confide in you, then you must do the same. Why did you not simply tell me about Lord Verbury? Or your concerns about the coldmongers? I could have set your mind at ease on that, at least, or perhaps – imagine! – we might have worked together to stop events before they came to a head. La! But why ask your pretty little sister?'

212

'I did not approach you because it was all just suppositions. Until the footman spoke today, I was not certain of Mr O'Brien's guilt beyond his conduct towards you.'

'Which you must now confess has been irreproachable.'

Jane was not ready to admit that. 'He should not have invited you to the oculist's, and you should not have gone. I am certain you will see that when you have had time for rational reflection.' She turned and walked to the door before she could say anything more she would regret.

'For heaven's sake, Jane. His *mother* was there. What do you think—' Melody visibly gathered herself, tightening her grasp on the hairbrush as though bodily restraining her emotions. When she spoke, she was quite calm. 'I assure you that my anger is completely rational.'

Jane paused before leaving, her conscience stopping her. 'I know. I do know that.' She spoke to the door. 'My conduct has not been all that it might, either. Nevertheless—'

'Oh, stop! Stop. Can you not leave with an apology instead of an excuse?'

Jane swallowed and pulled the door open. Some small part of herself shouted that she was blaming Melody for things that were not her fault. 'I am sorry. That is as much as I can say at this time. Perhaps we may speak later, when we are both calmer.'

She slipped out and pulled the door shut behind her. Melody gave a garbled cry and something metal slammed against the closed door.

Jane squeezed her eyes shut. She wanted Vincent. Desperately, at this moment, she wanted to not be responsible for her sister's conduct or disappointment or anger. She was responsible for all of that and more. She bowed her head and pressed her hand against the wall, trying to anchor herself.

And now Vincent was trying to ease the predicament of the Coldmongers' Company. That trouble, at least, was simple to repair. Once Mr O'Brien explained what Lord Verbury planned, they could put off the march and make a new plan. Now that they knew about the footman, they could keep him from telling Lord Verbury about the change.

If he had only the one spy, that is. But a man such as that would have more than one way to accomplish his plans. Vincent would realise this the moment he had time to think, but in the meantime, chances were good that he was relating everything to someone who would betray them.

If they allowed women, Jane would go warn Vincent now. This was hardly the first time that wearing a gown was a barrier, but—

Jane lifted her head. She did not have to wear a gown.

Hurrying down the hall to her bedroom, Jane rang for Mrs Brackett. As she waited, she pulled off her dress and petticoat. She had worn men's clothing for two weeks in Binche, and she could do it again.

In a few moments the housekeeper entered, expression showing nothing at finding Jane in a state of dishabille. 'Lady Vincent?'

'As quickly as possible, I require a suit of gentlemen's clothing that will fit me, as well as a pair of boots.' Jane did not, at that moment, care to think about what sort of gossip would spread through London about her attire.

'But, madam—'

'If it makes it easier, I am going to a fancy dress party.' She and Vincent were artists. Surely she could be granted this oddity.

# NINETEEN

## Above the Clamour

The ride through London on horseback was much differ-ent than in a carriage. Jane had always been an indifferent horsewoman while riding side-saddle, but had come to under-stand that it was because the position itself was challenging. Though she felt exposed in her breeches, sitting above the foot traffic gave her a sense of being somehow more private. The hack that Mrs Brackett had sent the footman to hire for her was a calm mare, which Jane was grateful for, and she was able to guide it past the knots in carriage traffic with relative ease. The trip to the Coldmongers' Company took half the time that it had taken her formerly.

The porter knuckled his forehead when she presented her-self at the gate. 'What can I do for you, sir?'

Jane tried to keep her voice low enough that it would not arouse his suspicion. 'I am on an errand to find Sir David Vincent and Mr O'Brien.'

'I will send someone for them.' He turned from the gate.

'If you will not let me in, then Sir David is preferable.'

'Aye.' He whistled, and a boy of ten, with the warm gold skin of the West Indies, left his playfellows and scampered inside the main building.

Jane had expected to be allowed in. It made sense that they would be somewhat cautious about whom they admitted, particularly with the march in question. She swung her leg over the saddle and lowered herself to the ground. Though she landed heavily, it was still an improvement over a gown. With a riding habit, she always needed help to mount or even dismount a horse.

Waiting, she shifted her weight from one foot to the other. Wearing breeches in Binche did not seem as revealing as here on her native soil. If they would not allow her in, then there had been little point in changing clothes.

Vincent came out the door, frowning deeply. He looked past her for a moment, then his gaze snapped back. Even across the yard, she could see his nostrils flare with alarm. Vincent ran the last few yards to the gate. 'Let him in, please. I will vouch for him.'

'As you say, Sir David.' The porter touched his cap again, and pulled it open for Jane. 'What name do I put in the register?'

Vincent's mouth opened and hung that way. 'Um . . .'

'Henry Vincent. I am his cousin.'

'Why didn't you say so? I wouldn't have kept you waiting out here in the cold.' The porter turned to his register and paid them no more mind as Jane followed Vincent into the yard. She gave her horse to a lad with copper skin and shockingly blue eyes along with a shilling to watch the creature.

The moment they were out of hearing, Vincent lowered his head. 'What is the matter?'

'It occurred to me that the footman would not be Lord Verbury's only agent.'

Vincent cursed. 'I should have thought of that.'

'You were distracted.'

'Perhaps.' Vincent pulled the door open for her, then looked at her curiously. 'I suppose I should not do this while you are dressed so.'

'Men are not courteous to each other?' She went through the door into the small dark entry hall of the Company. A set of double doors stood open at the far end and let out on a larger sitting area, lined with benches. Beyond that she could hear shouting from a mass of people somewhere deeper in the building. 'Where is Mr O'Brien?'

'Speaking to the coldmongers. It is not going well, which makes me think your supposition is correct. They did not care about what I had to say at all.' Vincent scowled and hurried down a hall. 'And we *are* courteous. But the manner in which the door is held is different for a lady than a gentleman.'

'You will have to teach me someday.' Jane followed him, boots tapping against the bare wood floors.

'How is Melody?'

'She is unhappy, which is understandable.'

'Did you quarrel?'

'Why do you assume that it is my fault?'

'I do not.' Vincent stopped outside a set of massive double doors. The shouting came from behind those. 'I assume that a quarrel happened, but make no further conjecture. I merely wanted to know her state of mind.'

'We did.' Jane looked at the floor and was startled anew by the sight of her legs instead of a smooth sweep of fabric.

Vincent clapped her shoulder, as though she were a man. 'It will all work out.'

Nodding, Jane pulled the door open for Vincent. The wave of sound that rolled out was full of anger. With a wince, Vincent passed into the room. The assembly hall of the Worshipful Company of Coldmongers had a high ceiling, hung with banners showing the various guilds around the country. Tall, narrow windows set high in the walls let in thin beams of light, which were supplemented by heavy iron chandeliers. It seemed one part monastery and one part fortress. The room was filled with boys and men in every shade, from the dark Moor to the milk-white Scot. Many of them had abandoned the benches that faced the front of the room and stood, shouting at the three speakers on the dais.

Two of the speakers had the lean build of coldmongers and stood slightly to the side of the platform. The third was Mr O'Brien. His red hair was caught in one of the rare rays of sunlight, and it glowed in a fiery corona. He held up his hands, calling for silence. 'My friends, I beg you to reconsider. You have heard Sir David speak of the likelihood that the Crown will fire upon us.'

'And that's why we should march!' A young white man with yellow hair stood and raised his fist above his head. He had abandoned his coat in the absence of women, and his blue armband stood out sharply on his shirt sleeve. 'We've been cast aside, and must show that we will not be forgotten!'

'No, no, that is what they want. Please. Taking time to reconsider our plans will not harm the movement.'

'What about those of us who are being beaten any time we leave the gates?' A young man with light brown skin pushed himself up. 'Chill Will's been beaten twice, and Ice Mike almost lost an eye. Are we just going to let that keep happening? I say No. No! NO!'

The young men around him roared with approval. They were *all* young men, some no more than boys. No one here was over thirty. All were slender, some to the point of appearing emaciated. And she counted four men just among those near to her who were missing fingers. Their health was the price paid for cooling Jane in the summer or keeping produce fresh just that little bit longer. And yet, to say that she would not use coldmongers any more . . . what work would they have, then?

'If you march now, you will confirm every fear, every rumour that has been spread about you. For months it has been put about that coldmongers are a danger, and the march will be seen to confirm that.' Mr O'Brien stretched his hands towards them, pleading. 'Please, Mr Lucas. Please, consider the consequences. And let me plead that if you *are* set upon this, that the march give no cause for alarm. Let it be peaceful.'

'If they were afraid of us before, I say let's give them a reason.' Mr Lucas stood on a bench and addressed the group. 'Lord Eldon has turned his back on his heritage. This will get his attention. And if the people are more afraid of us? I say good. Perhaps they will leave us alone when we go out if we remind them how many coldmongers live in this city. Did we not assemble to march tonight? I say we march!'

The shout of approbation rattled though Jane's chest. Vincent pressed his hands to the side of his head and squeezed his eyes shut, though whether because his head still ached or from dismay, Jane could not be certain. She felt nothing but alarm and fear. If Mr Lucas was not the agent of Lord Verbury, then he was doing his work for him out of naïveté.

Mr Lucas faced Mr O'Brien and lowered his voice. 'My question to you, sir, is if you will also turn your back on us, or if you will march?'

The silence that followed that question rang almost as

violently as the shouts had. Mr O'Brien dropped his hands to his side, looking inexpressibly sad. 'Of course. I am with you.'

The anger carried the coldmongers outside. Mr O'Brien strode out after them, his face forbidding. In the yard they assembled, passing out signs and banners. Some of the coldmongers had horses and they swung up onto those. Two rode close to each other with a banner spread between them that read, REMEMBER THE COLDMONGERS – SUMMER IS COMING.

The wind had come up while they were indoors, making that slogan seem a lie. It swept through the quadrangle, stirring coat-tails and snatching hats. The horses' manes snapped in the cold breeze. Jane shivered and wished for a bonnet, which did more to keep out the cold than a top hat.

She looked at the barely contained chaos and turned to Vincent. He was staring at her with the strangest expression on his face. He blushed and looked away, wetting his lips. Still looking across the yard, he leaned down to whisper, 'I was thinking about what my father would say if he knew that I found you attractive in trousers.'

Her coat seemed too warm, suddenly. She whispered back, 'I do not care what he would say, if you like them.'

The corner of his eye wrinkled into his small private smile. A frown followed as the first torch was lit. 'Will you go home?'

'Will you?'

He hung his head, with a little laugh. 'There are times when I wish we were not so well matched in temperament.'

'Melody will never forgive me if something happens to him.' As she spoke, Mr O'Brien swung up onto his horse. Jane's heart sank as he did. 'Is that the horse that Beau Brummell wanted?'

Vincent turned and scowled. 'It is.'

The horse was tall, taller than even the Duke of Wellington's Copenhagen, and towered over the other horses like an equestrian statue cast in bronze. Its coat could be called bay, but that did no justice to the brilliance of its hide. It was a red horse, as red as Mr O'Brien's hair. There could be no other horse like it. 'And is it well known that he rides it?'

Vincent's face tightened as he made the same connection that Jane had. 'The Earl must be planning on making him a dupe. I will see if I can convince him to change horses.'

'I brought a horse. See if he will take it?'

As Vincent pressed through the crowd, Jane followed. She had little hope that he would succeed. When Mr O'Brien heard that Vincent thought the horse made him a mark, he would likely cling to it all the more. The effort must be made, however.

'Sir? A word, if you please.' Vincent looked up at Mr O'Brien.

'Of course.' Mr O'Brien glanced at Jane, but did not look beyond her clothing. His attention moved past them, taking in the coldmongers as they prepared to march.

'I think that the Earl of Verbury plans to mark you by—'

'Gods, no.' Mr O'Brien straightened in his saddle and looked past Vincent. Jane followed his gaze, wondering what had caught his attention. On the far side of the iron gate, she caught a shock of golden curls under a bonnet with blue ostrich feathers.

Jane grasped Vincent's coat sleeve. What in heaven's name was her sister thinking?

Mr O'Brien pushed his horse forward to the gate. Jane followed him through the press of people as he broke through some of the lines that formed as the coldmongers organised themselves.

Jane grasped the metal fence. 'Melody, what are you doing here?'

Melody looked at her, then looked again. Behind her spectacles, her eyes widened with alarm as she looked a third time. 'Jane?'

Now Mr O'Brien recognised her. 'Lady Vincent?'

'Yes and yes.' She frowned at Melody. 'You ought not be here. This is no place for a young lady to come alone.'

'It is no place for a woman at all.' Mr O'Brien swung down from his horse. 'Both of you should go back.'

'Melody, let me take you home.' Jane was aware of Vincent at her back, strong and alert for additional danger.

Melody shook her head. 'No. This is a just cause, and I want to add my voice to it.' She held up a placard, neatly written. ALL OUT OF WORK AND COLD FOR ACTION! – HENRY V. 'I made a sign.'

'But the Coldmongers' Company does not admit women.' Mr O'Brien twisted the reins of his horse. 'So, you see, there is nothing you can do here.'

The gates opened and the march tumbled onto the street. Melody lifted her chin and backed away from the fence. 'But when they are on the street, who will complain?' She turned and ran to join the ranks of young men, lifting her placard to join theirs.

Mr O'Brien cursed and swung up onto his saddle. He wheeled the horse and pressed forward into the marching ranks of coldmongers.

Jane started to run after Melody, then cursed, remembering the horse she had brought. She was not enough of a horsewoman to feel comfortable directing it in this crowd. She turned to Vincent. 'I hired a hack, the grey mare there.

Will you take her? I will have better luck catching Melody afoot.'

He hesitated, then nodded. 'Be careful.'

Jane ran after her sister. She had no idea what she would do to keep her safe, but she could not abandon her, either.

Melody seemed to have a sixth sense about where the rest of them were. She ducked through the lines of coldmongers and pulled away from Jane, Vincent or Mr O'Brien any time they neared. If they had not been marching, Jane might have tried to mask herself with glamour, but that was not an option while they were in motion.

As they went, they picked up followers. Neighbours and family came out in force, so that soon Melody was not the only woman marching. Fortified by this early support, the cold-mongers began to sing ' 'Twas in the Summer Warm'.

When they got to the third verse, Jane began to feel as though she had never heard the song before. Though not well trained, the profusion of young boys gave it an ethereal beauty, making the song a prayer for deliverance. Their voices drifted upward.

> *But I have, when the sun is high,*
> *put forth above the clamour*
> *'Tis winter deep in me, and I*
> *with heart and with my glamour*
> *O God, O brother let me give,*
> *the blessed cool to Thee*
> *that through your Grace I may yet live*
> *May pure and spotless be . . .*

In spite of the clouds overhead, which brought an early gloom to the evening, the torches made it seem all the brighter, but they added little to the warmth unless one stood close enough to be endangered by the flames when they gusted.

'Turn the collar of your coat up.' Vincent swung down from the horse to walk beside her. 'You are shivering.'

'I am nervous.' Jane glanced at the clouds. 'What if it snows? The people will think it due to the coldmongers.'

'It is not that cold.' Vincent turned and perused the marchers. 'William! A question.'

'Sir?' The young coldmonger drifted back two rows to join them, but showed no signs of recognising Jane.

'Is it cold enough to make it snow or do any ice work tonight?'

The boy held out his hand and rolled his fingers as though feeling the air. 'Naw. Not even close. I don't think even Ice Mike could.'

'There, you see?' The brisk air seemed to have refreshed Vincent. He walked with his head up, and much of the colour had returned to his cheeks. Jane could not feel so easy.

As they crossed over Quatre Bras Bridge, the tenor of the march changed. They continued down Quatre Bras Street and a flood of other marchers suddenly joined them, shouting and singing their own songs. More imposing than the coldmongers, these men carried sledgehammers and clubs in addition to their torches.

One of them ran past Jane, laughing boisterously. He slapped her on the back as he passed. 'Cheer up! Your Luddite brothers are here to support you!'

Hooting, another man thrust his torch to the sky. A third swept one of the smaller boys onto his shoulder and danced a jig as the little boy laughed and laughed. Thoroughly wild, they nevertheless fought back the gloomy night with much-needed cheer.

Jane, however, could think only of Major Curry and how he had been forced to fire upon the Luddites in the North. The danger of their situation seemed more apparent.

And the crowds they passed changed. The walkers crowded up against the walls of the shops by their passage scowled, or muttered imprecations, or even spat. The coldmongers gathered closer, but did not lose sight of their purpose. The Luddites shouted back, starting a chant of 'Shame! Shame!'

Behind them, a mob of people now followed, but not to support them. These were here to watch the chaos.

At the head of the group of coldmongers, Mr Lucas had pulled one of the younger boys up onto his saddle and rode with the lad kicking his heels in the air and singing lustily. By his side, impossible to miss, rode Mr O'Brien on his fire-red mount, carrying the banner of the coldmongers. He kept turning in his saddle to watch Melody.

Jane had yet to get close enough to her sister for speech.

William nodded at Mr O'Brien. 'He's something, ain't he, Sir David? Told you as he was a great friend to the coldmongers.'

'That he is.'

'Having you with us, too – the Prince Regent's glamourist – we got nothing to fear, now, do we?' The boy's hero worship was all too apparent.

Vincent blanched and turned to Jane, the expression upon his face clear to her. By coming with them, he had given the coldmongers unfounded courage. The Prince Regent did not know, nor likely care, that Vincent was here. Yet leaving them would do nothing to stop the march.

Vincent handed Jane the reins of the horse, without a word, and bent down to talk to a boy who could not have been older than six. The poor child was flagging from the walk. With a smile, Vincent picked him up and swung him onto the saddle of the mare. The boy seized the horse's mane with an infectious grin.

'Stop making it cold!' A gin bottle flew into the coldmongers' ranks and dashed against the pavement. Glass flew everywhere, but thankfully no one was hit. That bottle, though, gave the mob following them courage.

Another bottle flew into their midst and hit a little boy on the back of his head. He staggered forward and dropped to his knees, blood trickling down his scalp.

'Scottie!' One of the women marching with them hurried over and picked him up.

He clung to her, bawling, and she carried him to the side of the crowd, pressing her handkerchief to his head.

The coldmongers tightened their ranks and sped up to a trot, pressing the ones in front of them forward at an ever-quicker pace. They began to sing 'Joy to the World' with much spirit, making the song into an almost shouted chant.

> *No more let sins and sorrows grow,*
> *Nor thorns infest the ground;*
> *He comes to make His blessings flow*
> *Far as the curse is found,*
> *Far as the curse is found,*
> *Far as, far as, the curse is found.*

They turned onto Lower Thames Street and the Tower of London stood in front of them. The great causeway across the moat stood empty, with only the two ceremonial guards standing at the far end. Jane breathed a sigh of relief. She had never been so glad to be wrong.

All day – for weeks, it seemed – she had been drawing conclusions grounded in nothing but her own fears. It was a relief. A profound relief, to be wrong in this instance above all the others.

The marchers slowed as they entered the causeway. Broad though it was, it was narrower than the street they had been marching on. Jane took advantage of this crowding to finally reach Melody.

She grasped her sister's hand to keep her from getting away. 'I am sorry. I was wrong and wrong again.'

Melody pulled away. 'Let go.'

'I will.' She dropped her hand, knowing that this was no way to make her sister listen. 'Please. I was wrong about Mr O'Brien. I was wrong about how I treated you. I was wrong about—'

A cry went up from the front of the crowd, followed by shouts and a rush back. Mr O'Brien raised the banner higher and faced them. 'Be strong!'

She could not see over the heads of those in front of her to tell what had frightened them. The crowd in back of them heaved, also shouting with sudden fear.

From behind her, Vincent shouted, 'Jane!'

She turned to look at him and saw the thing that had so terrified the coldmongers. A great line of British militia was stepping onto the causeway, with rifles at ready. They appeared to pop out of the air. Her heart seized in her chest. They had been hidden by a *Sphère Obscurcie*.

She turned to the front again and now caught glimpses of red coats appearing in front of the Tower. The coldmongers were well and truly caught.

Jane pulled Melody by the hand, trying to work her way to

the side, where the space seemed somewhat clearer. Vincent was trying to reach them, but was caught in a pocket of coldmongers. Even if Jane could get to the side, she did not know what good that would do, since the only escape left was over the edge and into the putrid moat below.

A shout, almost lost in the crowd.

Then a shot.

Screaming began in earnest. The militia opened fire on them, driving the coldmongers into the middle of the bridge.

The little boy on her horse dropped, a single spot of red on his coat.

'Jane!' Vincent shouted. A mass of boys and red coats had him pinned, unable to reach her. Vincent twisted his hands, and an explosion seemed to rock the bridge.

She used the shock to push through the crowd and pull Melody to the edge. Jane threw her down by the stone wall, dropping beside her. If nothing else, they should stay low on the ground. Melody fought her, wildly. 'Let go!'

'We have to stay down.'

'Alastar!' Melody reached her hand towards Mr O'Brien.

He rode on his horse, turning it this way and that, trying to use its body to shield those that he could. The horse reared, whinnying, and the banner streamed against the sky. Red coats surrounded them and pulled Mr O'Brien down.

A moment later, someone in a red coat reached down for them. 'Miss Ellsworth! Come with me.' Major Curry, his rifle over his shoulder, pulled Melody to her feet. 'It is not safe here.'

Relieved beyond measure to see him, Jane scrambled up and helped him support her sister. Melody was in hysterics, fighting them to get to Mr O'Brien.

'Stop it. You can do nothing for him now.' Jane took Melody by the shoulders and held her until she stopped struggling. 'We need to go to a place where we can help.'

Major Curry did not waste time with words. Together they half carried, half dragged Melody back across the causeway. Curry's fellow soldiers strode among the coldmongers, beating them with their rifles. They were undiscerning as to the age of their victims, beating men and children alike, so long as they wore the blue armband of a coldmonger.

Vincent knelt on the ground supporting a limp body. Her husband held the boy's hand and whispered to him.

'Major Curry—my husband.'

The Major did not slow down, but turned their path towards Vincent. Making certain that the Major had Melody, Jane ran forward to Vincent. 'My love?'

'I think he is dead.' Vincent lifted his head, seeming to be unaware of the madness around them.

He held William.

The sign that the boy had been carrying lay next to them, the handle still in his grasp. Vincent held his other hand. 'He was not when I got here. But I think he is now.'

Blood stained the boy's shirt and coat and cooled between the cobbles on the bridge. His eyes had rolled back in his head so that the whites stared at the clouds. So much blood. Jane thought she had seen blood before, but it was as nothing to this.

Jane touched his throat, praying for a pulse, but found none.

TWENTY

# *By the Fire*

Somehow Major Curry managed to get them a carriage and send them home. Jane had few memories of the time in between. She went from the bridge, to a memory of Melody leaning against her in the carriage, to one of helping Vincent remove his bloodied clothing.

The sight of his breeches, drenched through with William's blood, reminded her too deeply of her miscarriage. She sent them out to be burned.

It did not seem possible, sitting in her bedroom beside Vincent, that they had been on a bridge being fired upon by British soldiers. It did not seem possible that William was dead.

William was dead. She tried the sound of that again in her mind. The young man who had been so excited to meet them, who had possessed too much pride to take a job when it was not needed, had been shot for carrying a sign to the Tower of London. It seemed too much to have saved him from the mob at the grocer's and have him meet this needlessly tragic end. They had taken his body to St. Margaret Pattens church and sent word to the Coldmongers' Company, hoping they would know his relations. Only a few coldmongers had returned from the march. More were detained. Many were dead.

As much as she tried to come to terms with what had happened, the enormity of it was too great, and Jane could only muster a stupefied ache. Vincent seemed more deeply affected. But then, he had held William as the life bled out of him.

Vincent stared into the fireplace with his arm around her. At times he would tremble, then it would pass, and he would go back to staring. Jane rubbed his chest and leaned her head upon his shoulder. Mrs Brackett had set out a cold supper for them, but neither Vincent nor she had the appetite for it. Melody had retreated to her room.

Vincent trembled and sighed. 'We have to tell Lord Stratton.'

Jane held still, remembering the confrontation in front of Lady Stratton. 'They will know, surely.'

'We were there. They deserve a first-hand account.' Vincent pulled his arm from around Jane and leaned forward to sit with his elbows on his knees. He supported his head on his hands. 'I feel particularly responsible, after today.'

'You tried everything in your power to stop the march.'

He made that small whine in the back of his throat. When he let his breath out fully, he said, 'I was thinking of the oculist's shop.'

Jane shifted on the sofa, pulling her shawl around her. 'That was unfortunate, but it has no bearing on his arrest.'

'No. Had we behaved differently, however, we could have prevented other events from coming to a head.'

'I do not know if I am equal to speaking to this.' Jane stood and walked around the room. 'I am ashamed.'

She paced from fireplace to bed and back again. What would she say to his parents? That she was sorry she had been wrong in her judgement of him? Something banal, such as: it was the worst of all possible outcomes?

'Are you suggesting that we should stay home tonight and then go to work tomorrow as if nothing had happened?'

'No . . . but I am ashamed,' Jane said again. 'Will they even condescend to see us?'

'If we can give them news of their son, I think, yes.' Vincent stood and shook himself like a bear throwing off water. 'Lady Stratton knew where he was going. She must suspect something, if they have not already heard.'

Jane chewed the inside of her lip. She did not want to go, because she felt more than ashamed; she felt guilty. She had done everything in her power to separate Melody from Mr O'Brien. Even after he was released, she doubted that her behaviour in this would allow his family to ever consider her sister as a suitable match. And yet . . . and yet, Lady Stratton had shown her sister a great kindness. How could Jane be so selfish as to stay home? How could she even consider not doing what she knew was right? 'You are correct. They should not hear this from a stranger.'

Vincent relaxed his shoulders and Jane realised that he had been holding his breath. If she had said no, he would have gone without her. This breach of hers would have been a far greater chasm between them than his indiscretion with Miss de Clare so many years ago. He had been a boy then, not knowing what was right. Jane had no such excuse.

'Thank you.'

He frowned. 'For what?'

'For being patient with me.'

'Muse . . .' He held out his hand and she went to him. Vincent kissed her on top of her head. 'You are far more patient with me.'

From the lights in Stratton House, it was evident that

232

the family was up. For a moment, Jane had hope that Mr O'Brien had returned home, but the anxious nature of the servants they passed made it clear that the master's son was still absent.

The butler showed the Vincents into a part of the house that they had not yet been in. It was a small chapel, done in the rococo style of the last century. The walls were ornamented heavily with china cupids and the stations of the cross. A font stood just inside the doors, carved out of marble. Five rows of pews faced the small altar at the front. Above it hung a crucifix, showing Christ as the carpenter's son he had been and not the starveling that Jane had sometimes seen.

At the front of the chapel, Lord and Lady Stratton knelt on the velvet kneeling rail. When the door opened, Lord Stratton raised his head. He glanced over his shoulder, showing alarm. Standing, he crossed himself, then came back to receive them.

His face was grave.

'You have heard, I see,' Vincent whispered. 'I apologise for troubling you so late. We were not certain.'

He nodded. 'You were there?'

'I am sorry.' Vincent glanced to where Lady Stratton still knelt. 'Should we step into the hall?'

'You may stop whispering.' Lady Stratton crossed herself and rose. 'I am too anxious to think of anything but what I am almost hearing.' She walked down the centre aisle with her back straight. The lines around her eyes seemed deeper than they had that afternoon.

'My apologies.' Vincent offered her a short bow.

'Accepted.' She raised her eyebrows and looked pointedly at Jane.

Blushing, Jane swallowed heavily. 'I owe you and Mr

O'Brien many apologies. For my doubts, for my conduct . . . for not coming to you sooner with my concern. This is, I think, my fault.' She took a breath, bracing herself. 'At the end of the march, the militia met us. Mr O'Brien was arrested. Had you known, you might have kept him away from the march.'

'Away?' Lady Stratton shook her head. 'As much as I might wish this undone, I would have encouraged him, had I thought that it was only the militia. No, your warning . . . I would have liked it as a sign of trust, but it would not have undone any of this. He still would have gone.'

Vincent cleared his throat. 'He was in good health when we saw him. They had taken him from his horse, but he had no injuries.'

'Thank God for that.' Lord Stratton placed his hand against his wife's back. 'You see?'

'For all the good that will do him.'

'Harriet . . .' Lord Stratton sighed and turned to Vincent. 'Forgive us. We are both discomposed.'

'May I set your mind somewhat at ease? I studied law at university. The charges for disorderly conduct are not so severe—'

'Sir David, forgive me.' Lord Stratton cut him off. 'But Alastar was not arrested for disorderly conduct. They are charging him with treason.'

Lady Stratton took her husband's hand. 'We are Irish, you see. What possible motive could any of us have for marching, except to overthrow the Crown?'

'Under the circumstances . . .' Lord Stratton cleared his throat and looked across the room to the first station of the cross. In the image, Christ stood with his arms bound behind him, a centurion guarding him with spear at ready. 'Under the circumstances, I hope you will understand that we no longer require your services.'

There had been little to say to the Strattons. Jane and Vincent took the time to collect their few effects from the ballroom and then were escorted to the door. Lord Stratton gave them the use of his carriage as a final courtesy, but the leather seats seemed to burn Jane all the way back to their house. Vincent held his silence for the entire ride.

Her thoughts rode ahead of her to Melody. Jane would have to tell Melody before she saw it in the paper. She walked into the house, dreading going upstairs to talk to her sister, but it needed to be done.

In the foyer, a bustle announced that someone had arrived. Trunks stood by the stairs, waiting to be carried to their proper place. Jane lifted her head, looking for Mrs Brackett to demand an explanation.

The door to the drawing room opened and her father walked out, beaming with delight. 'There you are!'

Mrs Ellsworth followed close on his heels, exclaiming, 'What a charming house! Such a desirable neighbourhood!'

Vincent inhaled sharply beside her. Jane's surprise was no less great. She crossed the floor, alarmed. 'Papa. What are you doing here?'

His face fell. 'Did you not get my letter?'

'No. I am so sorry.' Jane gathered herself and led them back into the drawing room. 'Let me welcome you properly.'

Vincent greeted her parents with solemn correctness. His usual taciturn nature was a benefit here, as it kept his lowered spirits from being so obvious. Jane had to exert herself to receive her parents with anything like animation. She would confide in her father at the first opportunity, but wanted to keep the events of the riot from her mother as much as possible. She would fall into hysterics at the mere thought of it.

Jane examined her hands to make certain, again, that she had really removed all the blood from them.

'Where is Melody?' Mr Ellsworth looked around, beaming. 'I most particularly want to talk to her.'

'She is upstairs resting.'

'She is not ill, is she? Oh, depend upon it, these mad London nights and the high society you keep will have quite ruined her health.' Mrs Ellsworth shook her head and settled into a chair by the fire. 'I should never have consented to her coming here without me.'

'Do not trouble her. I will see her soon enough.' Mr Ellsworth beamed and looked around with obvious satisfaction. 'The glamour here is very nicely done.'

'Oh. Thank you. The house came decorated in this manner. We have been quite fortunate.' Jane still had not had time to address it. 'As delighted as I am to have you here, since I did not receive your correspondence . . . what brings you to London?'

'Ah. I have had a most charming letter.' Mr Ellsworth patted his coat pocket. From the rustle that sounded, it was evident that the letter in question was there. 'A most charming letter.' More than that, he would not say.

'He will not even tell me, can you imagine that? You would not treat Jane so, would you, Sir David? No, of course not. Charles uses me abominably.'

Vincent stood by the fire with his hand on the mantelpiece. He did not need to be in here, plagued by her mother.

'Vincent, would you let Mrs Brackett know that she might prepare the south bedroom for my parents?'

'Of course.' The look he shot her was filled with relief and thanks.

Jane stayed in the room and chatted with her parents, trying to talk about innocuous things, but every topic she brought up seemed to bring them back around to some point of pain. At last, Mrs Brackett came in to let her know that the south bedroom was ready.

The housekeeper's mouth was turned down in another of her habitual frowns, as if to say that Jane and Vincent had deliberately withheld knowledge of the Ellsworths' arrival. Jane thanked her as if she had brought the news in with a smile. 'Would you show my mother up to her room so she might refresh herself?'

'Of course, Lady Vincent. Will madam follow me?'

'Oh! Quite.' Mrs Ellsworth stood. 'Are you coming, Charles?'

'In a moment. I just want to finish looking at this.' He held up a book and smiled at her.

'Oh, you and your books. I never saw such a man for reading.' She bustled off with Mrs Brackett, quite happy to have someone to whom she could freely express herself.

As soon as she was out of the room, Mr Ellsworth set the book down on the table. 'Now, Jane. Tell me what is the matter.'

Jane's relief at being able to disencumber herself to her father was extreme. In no order, she poured out the tale of the past month, holding back only some of Lord Verbury's cruelty. As much as she needed to relieve herself, she did not want her father to know about Miss de Clare. Nothing should damage her parents' good opinion of Vincent.

As she spoke, her father's face grew longer and he sat forward with his elbows on his knees, listening. He only paused her recital once or twice to ask for clarification. Otherwise, Jane spoke and Mr Ellsworth listened.

When she was finished, he sat back in his chair, astonished. 'This is very bad, Jane.'

'I know. Lord Stratton and his wife are beside themselves.'

'No—I mean . . .' He sighed heavily and pulled the letter from his pocket. 'You must not tell anyone about this. Not until we sort out what to do.'

Jane did not reach for the letter. 'I can keep no secrets from Vincent.'

He chewed on his lower lip for a moment and turned the letter over. 'That is not a concern. He understands discretion.'

'Papa, you are alarming me.'

'Oh. The letter is nothing bad. Or rather, it *was* not.' He sighed and opened it. 'Mr O'Brien had written to request permission to address Melody.'

Jane stared, stupefied. She had been so wrong, about every possible thing. 'Am I—am I to understand that he was planning to offer his hand?'

Her father nodded. 'In a most charming letter. Under the circumstances, I think it best if she not know right away. Not until his situation is certain. Your mother would . . . well. It is best to keep it quiet, I think.'

'Of course.'

Mr O'Brien had planned to marry her sister, and Jane had done everything in her power to separate them. Of all the evils surrounding Melody, Jane was persuaded that she must herself have been the worst.

# TWENTY-ONE

## *Apologies and Favours*

With the arrival of Mr and Mrs Ellsworth, it was important to Jane that Melody have a chance to prepare herself. No matter how much they esteemed their parents, the fact was that their mother was prone to effusions of emotion that might be difficult to bear under the current circumstances.

Jane slipped upstairs at the first opportunity to knock on Melody's door. 'Dear? May I come in?'

An audible sigh preceded the door opening. Melody stood by the door in her dressing gown and prevented Jane from coming in further. Her expression seemed almost blank, though her glasses still startled Jane.

Jane cleared her throat. 'Mother and Father have arrived.'

Melody's eyes widened at that, and she let Jane in. 'Here? Why?'

'Papa apparently wrote to say he was coming, but I did not get the letter.' Jane sat on one of the chairs by Melody's grate. The fire in the hearth did nothing to warm her. 'I told Papa about the march, but did not think it wise to tell Mama.'

Melody nodded. 'I could not bear it.'

Jane bit her lip and straightened the folds of her gown. 'I also wanted to apologise to you. I should have trusted you and did not. I am—I am not even certain where to begin with apologies. My offences seem endless.'

If Jane had hoped that Melody would stop her with a protest, that hope was sadly dashed. Her sister simply watched her, with more composure than Jane would have given her credit for in the past. Her eyes, behind the lenses, seemed curiously distant. The light refracted through her spectacles to make her eyes larger and bluer than Jane was used to. It was clear from their redness that Melody had been crying, but save for that, she appeared entirely calm. Jane did not trust this calmness.

No sooner had she the thought than she immediately rebuked herself. She had just apologised for not trusting Melody and was starting it all over again.

Jane tried again. 'I deeply regret that I did not take you to get glasses when you asked for them. I am sorry that I jumped to a conclusion regarding your purpose at the oculist. Although—' Jane stopped herself before she could point out the erased 'Mrs O'Brien' in the appointment diary. She was here to apologise, not to offer excuses for her conduct. 'Although I cannot be sorry that I followed you. I am glad, mortifying though the manner was, that I am no longer so mistaken about Mr O'Brien's character. He is an honourable man.'

'Yes. He is.' Melody bit her lower lip and sat across from Jane. 'Did you tell Papa that?'

'I did.' Jane winced, remembering why her father had come to London, and how Melody's prospects were seemingly at an end. 'And now . . . I have some news that I do not want you to come across by chance. Vincent and I went to see the Strattons this evening.'

Melody leaned forward, face brightening for the first time

that night. 'Is he there? Is he all—no. He is not, is he? Else you would not worry about me finding it out by chance.'

'No.' When had her sister become so adept at understanding Jane's moods? Perhaps she always had, and it was only Jane who misunderstood Melody's. 'He has been arrested and . . . and is to be tried for treason.'

Melody closed her eyes and clapped her hands to her mouth. A small sound of denial escaped, but she held still, displaying no sign of falling into hysterics as she had before. Lowering her hands, she let out a shaking breath. 'What must we do?'

'I do not know that we can do anything. We have no formal connection with the family, and—'

Without notice, the door to Melody's room opened. Mrs Ellsworth stood at the entry, looking all in a panic. 'Jane—Melody, my dear, you have glasses! Oh, but that is not why I am here. Jane, you must come downstairs at once! They have come for Sir David, and will not listen to reason. You must come.'

'What is the matter?' Jane stood, pressing her hand to her breast in alarm. Melody rose beside her, grasping Jane's free hand. 'Who has come for Vincent?'

'The Bow Street Runners. They are arresting him! For treason!' Mrs Ellsworth held out her hand to Jane. 'Come. You can always talk sense to people. Your father is trying to stop them but, oh me, he is having no success.'

The Bow Street Runners patrolled London and brought in criminals. If they were here for Vincent, then he must have been linked to Mr O'Brien's case. Jane rushed out of the room and down the stairs with Melody and her mother close behind her.

Mr Ellsworth stood in front of the door, red with fury. His

hands were on his hips and he blocked the door with his body. 'Sir David was knighted by the Prince Regent for his service in the war. You cannot suppose him to now be capable of committing treason. Leave him here, I tell you, until someone asks His Royal Highness if he really wants his friend arrested.'

Facing him, Vincent stood in shackles, guarded by two red coats. It was not merely the Bow Street Runners who had come for her husband, but His Majesty's Coldstream Regiment. Even with his back to her, Vincent's frustration was obvious in his posture. The last hope that Jane held fled at the sight of her husband bound. She had to struggle to hold on to her composure for his sake and for her father's.

With the guards were two gentlemen in the red waistcoats of the Bow Street Runners. One of them, an imposing giant, shook his head. 'That ain't our lookout. We been told to bring him in, and so we are.' He turned about at the sound of Jane's footsteps and jerked his head at her. 'Is that Lady Vincent?'

One of the redcoats turned around. Jane was shocked to see that it was Major Curry holding her husband. 'It is, Mr Miller.'

Mr Miller scratched under his arm, nodding. 'Heard she was wearing trousers earlier. Wish I'd seen that. A lady in trousers.'

The Major turned his head away. 'Lady Vincent, you must believe that this is my duty, and that I would have no part in it if I were given a choice.' He looked to Melody with inexpressible sadness. 'I do not expect you to forgive me.'

Pulling a set of shackles out of his pockets, the Bow Street Runner gestured to Jane to step closer. 'Lady Vincent, you are under arrest with a charge of treason against the Crown.'

Jane could not breathe. She shook her head in denial. Closing her eyes, she bit the inside of her lips until her breath was under her control. 'You have a job, and I understand that, but I believe you have been misled. We were there to try to stop the march.'

'Nice of you to say that, but we got evidence to the contrary.'

Melody said, 'Wait. What about me?'

Major Curry looked at her very carefully and said, 'No one has come forth as a witness to seeing you at the riot.'

Melody paled. Jane understood that expression all too well. The Major came very close to perjuring himself on her account by the spirit of what he said, if not the words themselves. Melody squeezed Jane's hand. 'We will get you out.'

Mr Miller stepped forward, shackles jangling. 'Will you come quietly, please? I don't want to hurt you getting these on.'

There seemed to be little other option. Jane held out her wrists and let him put the heavy metal bracelets around them. Seeing her submit, Mr Ellsworth's shoulders sank, and the Bow Street Runners pushed him aside with no gentleness, although the Major was kind enough to allow Melody to get Jane's pelisse for her. He promised to allow someone in her family bring a change of clothing to her later.

Jane followed the soldiers. Without ceremony, she and Vincent were placed in an enclosed wagon, which reeked of urine and sweat.

Major Curry swung up to sit inside with them. He said nothing until the door was shut, locked, and they were on their way. Then he removed his hat and held it in his hands, turning it over. 'I feel I should let you know that I think the charges against you are specious, but I have no proof of this. I will endeavour to get the Duke of Wellington involved on your behalf. We both remember your service to the Crown last summer too well to think that you would turn against it now.' He sighed and brushed a bit of powder off the brim of his hat.

'But . . . but one of the witnesses is an agent of the Crown. John Devenny swears that you were both involved.'

Jane shook her head in confusion 'Who? I do not know that name.'

'He was disguised as a footman at the house of Sir Waldo Essex, and had occasion to observe you there as well as at Stratton House.'

'Ah.' The pieces, which Jane had thought she had seen so clearly, rearranged themselves into another and deeper pattern.

It was clear to Jane that Major Curry had no idea that Lady Penelope Essex was Vincent's sister. 'He told us of a secret meeting area that you had created at Stratton House. If it was as he said . . . the case looks grave.'

'The musicians' gallery?' Vincent raised his eyebrows. 'It is hardly a secret area. We were following a commission so musicians could tune their instruments more easily.'

Jane had little faith that that explanation would hold water with anyone but a musician, since she had also believed the quiet area was evidence of criminal intentions.

'I am not the one you must convince,' Major Curry said. 'And the fact of the matter is that with such witnesses as Devenny and the Earl of Verbury, there is nothing I can do. The only latitude I am granted, I am exercising.' He continued to turn his hat over and over in his hands. 'No one, save me, recognised Miss Ellsworth, and I will do my utmost to make certain that she is not brought into this.'

'For that, I thank you.' Jane bowed her head and counted the few blessings that she had. 'What will happen to us?'

'We are on our way to Marshalsea. They will separate you and keep you there until your trial.'

'Is that where Mr O'Brien is as well?'

'Yes.'

Vincent cleared his throat. 'May I hold my wife's hand until we get there?'

Major Curry looked out the back of the wagon. 'I cannot stop something that I do not witness.'

Shackles clanking, Vincent reached for Jane. She put both of her hands into his. She studied the calluses on his palms and the fine hairs on the backs of his hands. The strong, broad tips of his fingers traced circles on her own hands. She held her husband's hands and tried to fix them in her memory.

They separated Jane from Vincent as soon as they walked through the door of the prison. She watched him as long as she could while they marched him down a hall to the men's side. His eyes were wild, looking back at her as the door shut between them.

Jane had thought she despaired before.

When the door closed, Jane nearly fell. Only the hands of her gaoler kept her upright. Mr Bradley had a paunch that strained his waistcoat and hung over his belt. He wore a clump of keys that clanked as he shuffled down the halls. The light from the lamp in his other hand glistened off his protruding lower lip.

He led Jane down halls and past rooms packed with women in the most distressing of conditions. As she walked, the faces of those women near their cell doors turned to follow her. A young woman, no older than Jane, watched them with a dull gaze, seeming to move her head more out of instinct than consciousness. In another cell, an old slattern sat with her arm around a girl of twelve, fondling the girl's hair. Her eyes gleamed as she watched Jane.

But the most dreadful thing about the place was the silence.

Only the small sounds of prisoners shifting position or a door shutting or Jane's own feet on the floor marred the quiet. It was as though the prison collectively held its breath.

Jane was led to a small room with one tiny window facing a stone wall. The cell itself was only five paces wide. As soon as she was inside, Mr Bradley began to speak. 'You're in luck that I've got such a nice place for you. Your family has seen you well taken care of. You may be certain that not everyone gets such nice accommodations.' Jane could not imagine how this had been arranged, since her family had been left behind at the house. The gaoler did not seem to notice her confusion, or perhaps was used to seeing people deranged, so paid it no mind. He tapped a card on the wall. 'There are rules here, even for folks with good connections. I won't do you the insult of thinking a fine lady like yourself can't read.'

Some response seemed called for, so Jane said, 'Thank you,' though gratitude was the furthest thing from her heart.

'Now, I won't scold you, since it's your first day and all, but you're not to speak. Not unless someone asks you a direct question. It's the first rule.' Her gaoler knelt and pulled a long clanking chain out from under the bed. A shackle was fixed to the end of it. 'Sit you down here, mind, so I can get this on.'

Jane sat on the very edge of the bed. The sheets were grey and had been repaired many times, but not well. A beetle of some sort crawled across the foot of the bed. Jane shuddered, imagining what else was inside the bed linens.

Producing a large key, Mr Bradley undid the shackle, then put the cold metal restraint around Jane's ankle. 'There now. If you ask your family when they come, I've got another chain that's a lighter weight. It don't cost much, but it'll make you ever so much more comfortable. You just ask them.'

Jane nodded. The weight was cold and awkward. The thin stockings she wore were unequal to the task of keeping the chill out, and the shackle bit into the skin at the top of her foot. She turned her head to the sign on the wall.

1. *No talking.*
2. *Baths every Monday.*
3. *No glamour.*

Pushing himself to his feet, the gaoler nodded. 'Did you bring anything with you? You may answer that one.'

'No. Just my pelisse. My father . . . later, I think.'

'I'll keep an eye out for him.' He sighed. 'Sorry that you didn't think to bring a candle with you.'

Jane opened her mouth to reply, but closed it at a look from him.

He smiled. 'You're a quick study. We'll get on fine. Not that I expect we'll have you long, not with the charges on your head. More's the pity.'

He walked to the door, shadow bounding from the single lamp. 'Try to get some rest, and I'll let you know when your family comes.'

When he pulled the door shut behind him, the room fell into darkness. Without the lamp light, the only glow came from the window, which, given the clouds overhead, was barely lighter than the walls.

Every sound was magnified in the dark. Wind hissed outside the glass. Somewhere in the abyss of Marshalsea, someone gave a single sob and was quickly silenced. The rustle of claws scuttled across the floor.

Jane stood, shackle clanking around her ankle, and walked

towards the window. She held her hands out in front of her, though she could not recall any furniture in the room aside from her bed. Her third step brought her to a halt as the chain attaching her to the wall tightened.

With her arm outstretched, leaning forward, she could just brush one finger against the cold glass. Not close enough to open it and let in a breeze. Not close enough to look out and see if there were some sign of Vincent.

Jane stood, almost at the window, and pulled her pelisse tighter, shivering.

Her father would come in the morning, and somehow he would make things better.

# TWENTY-TWO

# A Compact Visit

After a night which Jane spent huddled atop the bed linens wrapped in her pelisse and sleeping little, she was almost grateful when the early light from the small window woke her. She sat up and stared about the cell. If glamour had been allowed, she might have worked some to pass the time or to try to mask the bleak room. Jane had few illusions that she would be allowed such a luxury.

She scratched her head, grateful that she wore her hair short so she did not have to attempt to put it up without a mirror. She chewed the inside of her lip, trying to work out what to do. There must be *something*.

Without some activity, she would go mad.

Jane swung her feet over the side of the bed and stood, stretching to her full height. She let her arms drop back to her sides and looked about again. There was an abused tin chamber pot in one corner, none too clean. It was, however, the only thing in the room besides the bed and the sign upon the wall.

Jane tried again for the window, hoping that she might see out a little now that it was daylight. The chain rattled as she walked and rubbed against the large bone on the inside of her ankle.

By standing in a lunge with her shackled foot behind her,

Jane could tilt her head just enough to catch a corner of the sky. It was the same overcast grey that they had seen for weeks. She watched the slight changes of grey in the clouds and listened for sounds outside her cell.

What were they to do? She would talk about it with her father. He would find an attorney for them, of course. She scratched the back of her hand, idly, and her fingers stumbled over a series of bumps. Jane raised her hand to look at it. Three bug bites stood out in angry red sores.

Her other hand had one as well.

Pushing up her sleeves, Jane found more, and her whole body began to itch. She walked in a half circle as far as she could get from the bed. Pacing to put the itching out of her mind, she tried to work through what her options were. She could do little from inside the cell.

Jane had a moment of fancy in which she cast a *Sphère Obscurcie* and escaped when they left the door open, but the weight and rattle of the shackle quickly pulled her back to her senses. Even if she were to escape, what then? Vincent would still be chained, and there was a charge of treason against them. Perhaps one of Vincent's college chums could help. He had studied law at university, after all. Surely one of them must be adept. University – why was she so worried? Vincent had met the Prince Regent while at school. He would pardon them as soon as he heard that they had been arrested.

Footsteps sounded in the hall and Jane hurried towards the door, stopped short by her chain. Keys rattled outside the door. Please God, let that be the gaoler with her father, or the Prince Regent come to rescue them . . . not that the Prince would come himself. Jane wet her lips and tried to compose herself.

The lock scraped and then the door opened. The gaoler

was all smiles. 'There now, Lady Vincent. Here's the Solicitor General, come to see you.'

An older gentleman followed him into the cell, a withered man, no more than a rack of bones. He carried a leather satchel under one arm, which bulged with papers. 'Thank you, my good man.' He passed Mr Bradley a banknote. 'Could you see to it that Lady Vincent has a good breakfast?'

As the smiling gaoler pocketed the banknote, Jane found her voice. 'I am afraid you have the better of me, sir.'

'I am Sir Jeremiah Fisk.' The Solicitor General leafed through his papers. 'I apologise for leaving you here last night. We usually conduct our initial interviews at Bow Street, but due to the nature of the charges, you were all brought directly here.' He pulled out a paper. 'Ah. Here it is.'

Jane stood in front of him, waiting as he looked it over. Inhaling so that his nostrils widened, Sir Jeremiah pursed his lips. 'Now . . . given your husband's past service, I believe that we can come to an arrangement, if you will both cooperate fully with our investigation.'

'Of course. I am happy to cooperate.'

'Good. Good. I have some questions about Mr O'Brien that I want to ask. Before we begin, though, let us be clear: a man found guilty of treason will be drawn to the place of execution on a hurdle, hanged, cut down while still alive, and then disembowelled, castrated, beheaded and quartered. The state is lenient for women – they are only drawn and hanged till dead.' The solicitor looked down at the paper. 'In exchange for your assistance, I can arrange to have your sentence converted to transportation for life.'

What a question. Jane clasped her hands in front of her and raised her chin. 'You seem to be assuming our guilt.'

'The evidence against you is significant, I am afraid.' He frowned in consideration. 'You were, perhaps, misled by your husband? We might be able to pursue that angle, I suppose. If you are willing to testify against him. Given his history, I trust that will not be an issue.'

'His history? I do not take your meaning.'

'Ah . . . you did not know.' He looked back at his paper. 'I thought as much. It is often the case.'

'Know what?'

He hesitated. 'Your husband is not who he has presented himself to be. His true name is Vincent Hamilton—'

Jane laughed. She could not help herself, even knowing that the laughter made her sound as though her senses were quite deranged. 'Oh. That. Yes, I have known about that since he proposed. And no, I am afraid I cannot testify against him. Any other assistance you require, so long as I am not obliged to perjure myself, I am happy to provide.' Jane realised that perhaps the solicitor could help them. Knowing that the Prince Regent would vouch for them, it only required getting word to him of their difficulties. They were the Prince Regent's glamourists, after all – surely it could not be so difficult to ask the solicitor to carry a message? 'Sir Jeremiah, are you aware that my husband is a friend of the Prince Regent?'

The Solicitor General narrowed his gaze. 'I was aware that he had taken commissions from His Royal Highness. That is not quite the same thing.'

'But they met in their college days.' Jane kept her hands closed.

'As his Royal Highness is some twenty years older than your husband, I rather doubt that.'

Jane hesitated. It was true. They had not attended college

together. The Prince Regent had come down for a fête. Perhaps she was overstating their acquaintance. 'I am certain that, if it is possible to get a message to His Royal Highness, he can vouch for our innocence. Can you do that for me?'

'Yes . . . yes, I can. Though I make no promises, of course.' A complaisant smirk crossed the solicitor's lips. 'Many people claim a friendship with His Royal Highness when in a similar position.'

Jane dug her fingernails into the bug bites on the back of her hand. 'I see.' She looked to the wall where the list of rules was posted, concentrating on the tack in one of the corners so that the Solicitor General was only a shadow at the edge of her vision. Jane let her breath out slowly. The charges were specious. The Prince Regent held them in high regard. So long as she was honest, it was only a matter of time before they were free. 'Thank you, sir. Now, how may I help you?'

'First, I need to know exactly what your husband said about his part in the plot.'

'Once we realised that Lord Verbury had contrived the march to look like a revolt, Sir David and Mr O'Brien attempted to stop it—'

'Lady Vincent, please.' The solicitor's voice was entirely level. 'I am offering you a chance, which not many would. If you do not cooperate, then I will walk out of this room, and you will not get another.'

'But—but I am cooperating.'

'By inventing a conspiracy to cover up your own? I assure you, I am well aware of the differences between Lord Verbury and his son. Attacking him with your fancies will do you no good.'

'This is a dilemma. You ask me to be honest, then reprimand me for that honesty. What am I to do?' Jane's heart trembled. In the silence of the prison, she could hear only it and the solicitor's breathing. She stared at the tack, counting the holes in the paper where the notice had been pulled down and replaced. Seven times, it appeared.

'It seems we have nothing to discuss at this time, then. When you are on the witness stand, remember my offer to commute your sentence to transportation.' He shoved his papers back into his satchel.

'And your offer to contact the Prince Regent on our behalf?'

'Of course. I am a man of my word.' With a grunt of irritation, Sir Jeremiah swung around on his heel and strode out of the room. The door hung open behind him, showing Jane a view of the long hall and the cells bordering it.

She stared out the door, but it was beyond her reach.

The breakfast that Sir Jeremiah had so ostentatiously ordered for Jane never arrived. She suspected that he had cancelled the order on his way back out. Certainly, the gaoler was not in a good humour when he returned to lock her door.

Jane gathered her gown around her and sat down in the middle of the floor, not trusting the bed. She rested her head on her knees and tried to think. Thought came slowly. Her very mind seemed to fight her. Jane passed her time sitting on the floor, retracing her errors, pacing the room, or staring at the pocket of sky.

It had gotten significantly lighter, and Jane had time to regret the want of breakfast, before she heard footsteps again. The gaoler opened the door with fewer smiles, though still more cheerfully than when she had last seen him. 'Your father.'

Jane scrambled to her feet as Mr Ellsworth walked in. His face told her everything she needed to know about her state and their prospects in general. He carried a bandbox in one hand and a covered basket in the other. Tears dimming his eyes, he set both down and hurried across the room to wrap his arms around Jane. She clung to him and let herself fall apart, weeping as she had when she had been small. Her father murmured to her and patted her on the back, but Jane had no illusions that he could make anything all better.

'Oh, Papa. I am so glad to see you.'

He pulled back, beaming at her, but his face was wet and his chin trembled. 'I am sorry I could not be here earlier. I went round to our solicitor first.' He sighed and gestured to the covered basket. 'But we should eat something. That man said you had nothing to eat yet.'

Jane shook her head.

'Well.' He wiped his hands off and looked around at the bare cell. 'Hm. A moment.' Going to the door, he pulled it open. Briefly, Jane was afraid he would leave her. He called down the hall instead, voice shockingly loud in the hush. 'Sir!'

The gaoler was back in short order. From the sound of his footsteps, he had not gone far. Jane suspected he was used to this sort of thing. In fact, he brought a small folding table and two chairs with him. He did not, however, offer them to Mr Ellsworth until that latter worthy had presented him with a banknote.

'Thank you, sir.' The gaoler carried the table and chairs in and set them up. 'If I might suggest, sir, the young lady might be more comfortable with fresh linen and perhaps some candles.'

Mr Ellsworth's face turned red and a vein stood out on

his forehead. Jane realised that she had never seen her father truly angry before. He pulled his pocketbook back out of his coat and removed two fresh banknotes. 'I trust that I shall not hear of my daughter wanting for *anything* while she remains here.'

'Oh, no, sir.' The gaoler was unshaken. 'I think you and I understand each other well enough now. I can always just send a bill around if that would be easier.'

'Thank you.' Her father's teeth clacked against each other as he bit the words off. 'Now. If you will excuse us.'

'Of course, sir. Of course.' The gaoler bowed his way out, folding the money and putting it into his pocket.

Mr Ellsworth shuddered as the man left. 'Major Curry warned me that this would be the case. I was still not prepared.'

'He came to see you?'

'Yes. This morning.' Mr Ellsworth pulled out a chair for Jane and held it until she was seated. Even such a commonplace courtesy made her eyes water. 'He is why you have this cell instead of being in the general stews. He made arrangements for Vincent as well. I tried to restore his funds this morning, but he would not allow it.'

'He is a good man.'

Mr Ellsworth set the basket on the table and pulled out a meat pie and a small wheel of cheese. 'I recall you speaking fondly of him. Your mother is convinced he is the worst man in the world, in spite of my efforts to explain.'

Jane's mouth watered as her father set an orange on the table. 'I can well imagine.'

'She sends her love.' He put out a pair of tin plates. 'These were Melody's idea, by the way. I can leave them with you so you have something to eat on.'

Jane pulled the plate closer. 'By which I take it that the visit to the solicitor did not go well.'

Mr Ellsworth paused before setting a knife and fork on her plate. 'No. I am afraid it did not.'

'Ah. Well, the morning seems full of unhappy visits with solicitors. The Solicitor General came this morning to interview me.'

'Dare I ask how that went?'

'He wanted me to testify against Vincent. He offered to make my charges go away. I told him no.'

Her father spun, aghast. 'Call him back.'

'How could you?' It was not possible that her father could even contemplate such a thing. 'No.'

'Jane—' His voice shook and he clenched his hands into fists at his side. 'I do not think you understand. The punishment for treason is—'

'I know. But—during the war, when Vincent was a prisoner . . . no. I could not live if I were . . . No.' She turned in the chair to face him, her chain rattling against the chair leg. Her father looked down, wincing. 'Besides, the Prince Regent thinks highly of us. Once he hears that we are imprisoned, he will let us out.'

Her father looked at the floor and covered his face. He drew in a deep breath and then dropped his hands. Something like a smile was on his face. 'Well, then. Let us enjoy our meal, and we shall talk about this all later.'

He drew up a chair next to Jane's and cut a piece of pie for her. During the rest of his visit, he told her stories of Long Parkmead, and how their neighbours were, and other gossip from London. He would say nothing about the charges, or Mr O'Brien, or her situation at all.

When his visit came to an end, he reached into the basket and brought out a piece of paper and a pencil. 'I thought you might want to write a letter to Vincent. I shall see him next.'

Jane pulled the paper towards her, but could think of nothing to fill it with. Where could she even begin? There was so much to say that any words she imagined failed.

Her father stood at the window again, looking out.

'Can you see anything?'

'Hm? Yes, the river is just visible.'

She ran her finger over the page, imagining Vincent's face beneath her fingers. Taking up the pencil, she began to write.

*My dearest Vincent,*
*My room has a view of the river . . .*

# TWENTY-THREE

## *Volcanoes and Weather*

Every morning, Jane expected to hear that the Prince Regent had called for their release. Her father reported that Vincent had written to him, and yet they heard nothing. She tried very hard not to become vexed, but the continued silence – oh, the silence. It broke only when she had a visitor, and then Jane found herself inclined to chatter as if she could prevent the silence from returning.

Jane and her father fell into something of a routine over the next several days. True to his purchased word, the gaoler brought Jane clean sheets, a washbasin and even a rough chest to put her few possessions in. Her father brought Jane's work-basket from home, with letters from her mother and Melody. He refused, however to let either of them accompany him to see her.

By that, Jane guessed that they had a rosier picture of her environs than was the case, and that he did not want to undeceive them. Melody sent her several novels, including *St. Irvyne*, by A Gentleman of the University of Oxford; *The Sleeping Partner*, by Mrs Robins; and a translation of the German novel *Undine*, by Friedrich de la Motte Fouqué. She also sent along newspapers with interesting articles circled, though Jane noticed that others were cut out, and that the papers had no mention of the coldmongers. She asked them to stop cutting the articles out to no avail. Instead, Jane learned about the riot in Italy over Rossini's opera *The Barber of Seville*, that the latest colour for day dresses was mulberry, and more about the Tambora volcano explosion of the previous year in the East Indies. Next to that article, Melody had written, 'Mr Benjamin Franklin proposes in *Poor Richard's Almanack*, which I read at Beatts's, that volcanoes can cause unnaturally cool weather.'

Jane chuckled at that. Quietly.

The unnatural stillness of the prison weighed on her. It was broken only once, when a prisoner somewhere started screaming. The shrieks echoed off the walls and through the window. Jane pressed her hands to her ears, but nothing could keep out the raw terror.

She thought, *Thank God it was a woman*, and immediately hated herself for having so little compassion. But as long as it was not a man, it was not Vincent.

Footsteps ran through the halls, keys jangling, as the gaoler and guards attended to whatever had caused the screaming. Jane rocked back and forth in her chair, waiting for it to end. The sound was first muted, as if someone had pressed a hand against the woman's mouth, then slowly subsided into racking sobs. When the quiet returned, it was welcome.

Jane put her head on the small table, hiding her face with her arms. Why had the Prince Regent not answered? Had she mistaken his regard as well? He always seemed so amiable and approachable, so pleased with their work, and had showed them such attention that it was difficult to believe that he would let them languish like this. What had he been told about their involvement in the revolt? The keys rattled in the lock. Jane sat up, wiping her eyes and thinking, *Please, God, let it be someone from the Prince.* Her surprise could not be described when Lady Stratton entered her cell. She carried a work-basket and had a cape over one arm.

For a moment, Jane could only stare, before remembering herself, scrambling to her feet and dropping a curtsy.

When she straightened, Lady Stratton returned the courtesy, addressing her with calm civility. Looking about the room, she said, 'I am glad that your family is taking care of you. I only heard yesterday that you were here as well.' She stepped further into the room and set the basket on the table. 'I thought you might want for some necessaries.'

Jane's eyes burned at her unexpected generosity of spirit. 'Your ladyship is most kind.'

'I have volunteered in the school here and was familiar with the conditions.'

'There is a school?'

'Indeed. May I?' Jane nodded and Lady Stratton pulled out a chair and sat. She knit her hands together in front of her. 'I was able to get some of the coldmongers enrolled in it, so they have at least some relief while here.'

Jane sank back into the chair across from her. 'How is . . . how is Mr O'Brien?'

'He is more distressed for them than for himself.' Lady Stratton sighed and rubbed her temple with one finger. 'I—I must confess that I am here for not entirely disinterested reasons.'

Somehow, that confession relieved a measure of Jane's guilt at Lady Stratton's generous condescension in calling. It made the visit more understandable, and made Jane feel as though she might have some purpose. 'Will you tell me how I can help? I will do anything I can for Mr O'Brien.'

Lady Stratton's gaze lifted, eyes astonishingly blue. She relaxed and reached her hand for Jane. 'Thank you, my dear.' She took a shuddering breath, clearly more undone by recent events than she wished to admit. 'Our attorney would like to speak with you. He is hoping that you and Sir David can testify that Alastar did not have any intention of overthrowing the government. We are trying to convince his oculist to convey the conversation we had in his shop as a disinterested witness, but he is reluctant to be associated with my son at this point.'

'Of course.' This was testimony that Jane would provide willingly.

The rest of the call they talked over what Lady Stratton knew. She shared with Jane the details that her own family had kept from her. Mr O'Brien was being painted as the leader of a plot to overthrow the Crown in cooperation with the cold-mongers. The newspapers had named it 'The Coldmongers' Revolt' and sketched all those involved in the darkest possible light.

Though Jane was dismayed at what she heard, simply knowing gave her a purpose. Lady Stratton ended her call with a promise to send Mr Leighton, their attorney, to discuss the options for the defence. Talking to him was the least that Jane could do.

The sixth day she was imprisoned, Jane turned the pages of one of Melody's novels in a pretence of reading as she awaited her gaoler. Today was Mr O'Brien's trial, and his attorney had requested Jane's presence as a witness. She would not go on trial yet – each of the accused were to be tried separately – but she still looked forward to it as an opportunity to leave the prison, even for a short time. She had awakened early and dressed with care, but did not know how much time she would have until they came to take her to the Old Bailey for the trial. So she sat with her book, trying to lose herself in Mrs Robins's adventures of an agent of inquiry. Jane idly wondered if her sister had chosen *The Sleeping Partner* in order to give her hope that someone would prove her innocent.

Then she heard the gaoler's footsteps proceeding steadily towards her cell. She lifted her head from the page, counting the number of people with him. Four, she thought, just before they arrived at her door.

With a rattle, the gaoler unlocked the door and opened it. He was scowling. 'Pack your things.'

'What?'

'Did I give you leave to speak?'

Jane shook her head and stood. She had thought they were taking her to the trial, but they must be moving her to another cell. But why? Did someone pay more for this one? Jane had few possessions. Her second dress was already in the bandbox. She shoved the books on top of it and the plates atop that. She hesitated at the bed linens. Her first inclination was to leave them to be burned or given to someone else, but not knowing what her new environs would be, Jane removed the bedclothes and folded everything into a neat parcel.

The soldiers stood and watched as she did so. No one offered her any help.

Jane swallowed, wanting to ask if she should wear her pelisse or if she were just being moved within the building. Finally deciding that it would be harder to carry, she put it on along with her bonnet, then picked up the bandbox and the parcel of sheets to indicate her readiness to go.

'All right, then.' The gaoler stepped back and bowed her out the door. 'Off you go, your ladyship. I've washed my hands of you.'

Barely able to support herself, Jane walked back through the silent halls, accompanied by four soldiers in red and the quiet stares of the women in other cells. She was led all the way to the front, then through the gate into the yard.

A dark carriage sat in the yard with the livery covered.

Jane halted, struck by fear. She was outside – surely she was allowed to speak? 'Is that Lord Verbury's carriage?'

The soldier closest to her frowned. 'I am not at liberty to say, madam.'

'I cannot go. No.' Jane shook her head. She would have gone back into the prison to avoid that fate, had not a soldier at the rear stopped her.

'You will not be harmed.'

'Then you do not know him.' Short of throwing herself on the ground and screaming, there was nothing she could do, and even that would not keep her from ultimately being put into the carriage. Clutching the bandbox and the sheets, Jane let the soldiers lead her.

One of them opened the door. Another took the bandbox and sheets from her. A third helped her in.

'I thought you would not join us,' a masculine voice purred with self-satisfaction.

It took a moment before Jane's eyes fully adjusted to the darkness. Even then, she did not fully comprehend what she saw. Across from her sat Melody and the Prince Regent.

'Your Royal Highness,' she managed to gasp. 'Melody?' Then she sat forward, apprehending who was missing from the carriage. 'Vincent. Is he—'

'On his way. I could only have you fetched one at a time.'

His Royal Highness leaned against his seat, a picture of regal elegance. 'Are you well?'

Jane could not constrain a laugh. 'All things considered? I suppose that my state is now improved.' As much as she wanted to demand to know why he had left them to languish in the prison, it would not be advisable. Not now. Not when she still did not understand her fate. But the question would not be put off long – only altered into something less demanding. 'How are you come to be here?'

He shook his finger at her. 'Not until Sir David arrives.' He smiled, not without kindness. 'I only want to explain once.'

Jane looked to Melody for some explanation, but her sister would not meet her gaze, instead occupying herself with neatening the ribbon hanging from her gown. Jane could get nothing from either of them, and finally stopped trying. She had become used to silence these past few days.

It took only a little longer before the door opened. The carriage rocked as Vincent got in, and Jane's breath caught in her throat. Like her, he was blind for a moment as he stepped into the dim interior, so she put her hand out to guide him. 'Vincent?'

His movement checked, except for his head, which turned sharply towards her. 'Jane!' He sat next to her, insensible of the other two in the carriage. His cheeks were grizzled with the beginning of a beard and his hair was madly dishevelled.

Jane took his hands and pressed them between hers. 'Are you well?'

'Now? Yes.' Vincent leaned towards her, lips parting, and his eyes suspiciously bright.

The Prince Regent cleared his throat. 'I hesitate to interrupt – I understand that you have been under some strain – but we only have the length of this carriage ride to converse. And then there is the bother of a trial.'

The astonishment on Vincent's face was as great as Jane's had been.

'First of all, my apologies. I had not known you were involved in this situation or I would have given instructions for you to be let alone.'

Vincent frowned. 'I wrote to you. Twice.'

'And the Solicitor General said he would send a note as well,' Jane added.

'That is troubling. I was at Brighton, and knew nothing of it.' He rubbed his chin, looking thoughtful. 'Fortunately, your sister, Miss Ellsworth, came to plead your case most passionately.' The Prince put his hand on Melody's knee and patted it. Her sister looked downwards, but it did nothing to hide the deep blush on her cheeks. For the first time, Jane realised that Melody was not wearing her new spectacles. The implication stunned her. Melody had . . . had—

She was unequal to forming a response. Vincent made a low noise in his throat. 'Prinny—'

'Now, now, Sir David. You are well familiar with my habits, so I will reassure you that, though Miss Ellsworth was very kind in her offers, they were not necessary nor accepted.'

Jane's immediate relief that Melody's virtue was unblemished gave way to astonishment that her sister would even *contemplate* making such an impudent offer, let alone actually make it. And for her sake. Jane pressed her hand to her mouth, too stunned to think.

Vincent sought Jane's free hand and held it, running his thumb over the side of her palm. 'I am relieved to hear that.'

The Prince paused and leaned forward, suddenly casting

266

aside his appearance of polish. 'Even if your service to the Crown were not reason enough, I am familiar with your history with Lord Verbury. I acted as soon as someone let me know that you were imprisoned. That you both wrote to me is very troubling. I thought it a simple error that someone did not understand you were known to me. This hints at something more.'

'The whole of this business does more than hint.' Vincent ran his free hand through his hair, making it stand out even more. Quickly, and with more presence than Jane could summon, Vincent laid out their understanding of the events that had led to their imprisonment. The Prince Regent rubbed his chin as Vincent spoke, mouth turned down in thought.

'This is worse even than Miss Ellsworth portrayed it.'

'May I hope that the charges against us are dropped?'

'Entirely. Even without your recital. I have a letter stating that you are my agents and are cleared of all charges.' The Prince produced a paper with his seal and passed it to Vincent. Then he cleared his throat. 'But I can do nothing for O'Brien. In spite of Miss Ellsworth's plea.'

Jane straightened with surprise. The Prince Regent must not have understood Vincent's testimony. 'I can assure you that he is completely innocent.'

'Completely? He did march on the Tower, did he not?' The Prince Regent sighed, rubbing his brow. 'The trouble I face is that there must be a villain. The populace is too angry at the coldmongers. If Mr O'Brien was not responsible for the revolt, then they will look to Lord Eldon, and I will have my hands full keeping him from losing his seat.'

'The anger at the coldmongers is unjustifiable.' Vincent's hand tightened on Jane's. 'It is founded on absolute superstition. There is no possible way that they could affect the weather.'

'And you think that you can explain that?'

'Certainly. The principles of thermal transference are well understood.'

'To a layman?' In the silence that followed the Prince sighed again. 'It pains me. Our soldiers fired on children. If there was no revolt, then they acted without cause, so there must be a villain, someone for the populace to blame. Without substantial proof of his innocence, that person will be Mr O'Brien.'

Jane could scarcely believe what she had heard. The Prince Regent was willing to let an innocent man die – several innocents die – rather than let it be seen that his government had made a mistake. 'How are additional deaths going to make this right? You play into their hands by letting this go forward.'

'Do I?'

'Of course. They are already interfering with the information you are being given. What else will they do if they believe that they can so easily shape your decisions?'

'Who are *they*? If there is proof that there is someone to blame for this, then by all means tell me so that we can pursue them, but it cannot be a nameless *they*. There must be a villain for the populace to look to. The best I can do – which I will – is to change his sentence to transportation for life.'

Vincent whined at the back of his throat. A thin film of sweat was forming on his palm. He lowered his head and spoke to the floor. 'And if I can give you a villain?'

The carriage rocked back and forth over the cobbles. Jane could swear that she could hear the beating of all of their hearts in the silence. She had never before wished someone dead, and even now, with everything that Lord Verbury had done to them, some part of her drew back from the idea of a son giving up his father in such a way. But Lord Verbury had given his son up twice over, and had wished him dead in the bargain.

'It is a charge of treason.' The tone of the Prince Regent's voice made it clear that he, too, understood what Vincent was offering. 'I cannot change that. Not even for a peer. Especially if that peer is proved to have interfered with my business.'

'I understand that.'

'If you fail to convince the jury, though . . . Vincent, think what he will do to you. There is only so much protection I can offer.' The Prince Regent brushed a piece of lint off his knee. 'For all that I ostensibly rule England, I am good for very little besides throwing elaborate parties. It is why I put so much effort into them.'

'I understand.' Vincent's head stayed bowed. 'Can you send a messenger for me? I want to alert the Strattons' attorney of our change in situation.'

'Yes. I can do that, at least.'

Melody said, 'Is there anything I can do?'

The corner of Vincent's jaw worked as he considered. 'Yes, actually, there is one thing. Will you pay a call to my sister?'

# TWENTY-FOUR

# *At the Old Bailey*

The yard outside the Old Bailey was crowded with spectators when the Prince Regent's carriage arrived, though the doors were well guarded to prevent those who had not paid to see the spectacle from entering. The Prince Regent stayed in the carriage as they were let out, but he sent a paper in to the defence attorney. Melody remained behind as well, with a promise to run Vincent's errand with all possible speed.

Jane and Vincent were escorted through the throng and into the Old Bailey. The stench of the building made Jane's stomach turn. A miasma of the unwashed rolled out of the tunnel connecting the Old Bailey to the prison next door. Jane could only be grateful that they had not been held there. She pressed her hand over her nose as they entered the courtroom itself. The heads of the assembled turned as they entered, some standing for a better look at them. Jane shrank from the attention, pressing as close to Vincent as allowed.

At the front of the court, she had her first glimpse of Mr O'Brien since the troubles began. He stood at the bar with his hands resting on the smooth wooden plank. A mirror stood over him to focus the light from the windows on his face so that the jury could see it better. He had been given a clean suit of clothing, but, like Vincent, had not been allowed to shave for fear of what he might do with the razor. His stubble was so fair that it might have disappeared against his skin if the mirrored sun had not lit his face, making it look as though his cheeks had been brushed with sand. He had deep shadows under his eyes, but kept his chin up and stood in the box with a firm, erect posture.

Lord and Lady Stratton sat in attendance at the front of the spectators' gallery. Lady Stratton clenched a handkerchief in one hand and held it beneath her nose against the reek of bodies. As Jane and Vincent walked down the stairs to the floor of the court, Lord Stratton looked as though he wished to address them, but checked himself. Lady Stratton had eyes only for her son. A woman across the aisle let out a lament, drawing Jane's attention to where her mother was swooning against her father. As gratifying as her mother's concern was, Jane wished she could show a trifle more restraint. By the strength of the reaction, Jane could assume that her parents had not been told of Melody's visit to the Prince Regent. Jane tried to smile some encouragement to her father, but doubted that it helped, as his attention was occupied with her mother. The look he spared for Jane was grave and tormented.

To Jane's surprise, their cousin Sir Prescott had come and was sitting in the row behind her parents. The kindness he showed in supporting her mother was quite unexpected. Jane would have guessed him the type to distance himself from a relative in disgrace.

The court's usher led Jane and Vincent down the steps to the witness box in front of the gallery in the centre of the room. It seemed almost like a paddock with benches. He seated them facing the jury box and the gallery, which contained several young men who Jane recognised from the march. Mr Lucas had a contusion over one eye, and sat with his head bowed, as though the weight of the whole affair rested on his shoulders. His gaze shifted to them and away. The row of witnesses included Major Curry, splendid in his regimentals. He had deep lines around his mouth, and, while he presented a smart appearance, looked as though he had barely slept. If she could, Jane would tell each man that he was not the agent of their present misfortune. That honour was reserved for Lord Verbury.

The jury seemed composed of a jumble of gentlemen and merchants with one navy captain thrown in for good measure. They did not look like an ignoble lot, which gave Jane some hope. Surely once they heard that Mr O'Brien had tried to stop the march, they would not be able to continue to think him guilty. That they thought so currently, without hearing evidence, was obvious in the way they sneered at him.

'All rise.' The court clerk took his place in front of the judge's bench to their left. The judge arrived then, looking very severe in his red robe and white wig and was introduced by the clerk as the Lord Chief Justice Abbot. Even when imagining this moment, Jane had not thought of all the murmurings that took place in the courtroom. She had thought it would become silent once they started, that a hush would fall over the courtroom as a sign of respect and acknowledgement of the gravity of the proceedings.

She was far wrong. People who had seemed to be dozing now awoke and turned to their neighbours, asking, 'Didn't he look guilty?' or 'This is a hanging judge, ain't he?' or 'Did you ever see the like?' And one man said, 'Easy to spot the Irishman, at any rate.' The judge nodded to the clerk that he was ready for the charges to be read.

The clerk read from a sheet of vellum. 'Alastar O'Brien was

indicted, for that he—being a subject of our Lord the King, not having the fear of God in his heart, nor weighing the duty of his allegiance, but being moved and seduced by the instigation of the Devil as a false traitor against our said Lord the King; on the eleventh day of June, in the fifty-sixth year of the reign of our said present Sovereign, Lord George the Third, by the Grace of God of the United Kingdom of Great Britain, Faerie and Ireland, King, Defender of the Faith, with force and arms, maliciously and traitorously did compass, imagine, invent, devise, and intend to depose our said Lord the King. That is to say:

'Conspiring to levy war, and subvert the Constitution;

'Preparing an address to the King's subjects, containing therein that their tyrants were destroyed;

'Assembling with arms, with intent to murder the Prince Regent and divers of the Privy Council;

'To which indictment the prisoner pleaded Not Guilty.'

The severity of the charges which had been assembled whole cloth from innocuous events shocked Jane. She glanced to her right, where Mr O'Brien stood facing the judge with admirable calm. She, too, had thought the man capable of a conspiracy to overthrow the Crown, and she had the benefit of having met him. In the remembrance of his conduct, she could now see how his gentleness of manner and concern with being correct would have caused him to leave them on that first day – not because he disdained an artisan's sister as a connection, but because he did not want to be seen to press his attentions on one who might not be able to resist his advances due to her position in the household. Everything he had done, she had cast in the worst possible light. What could she expect from the jury already disposed to distrust him?

The Attorney General rose from his place at the great mahogany table at the front of the judges' bench. 'My Lords, with permission of your lordships, we will proceed to the trial of Alastar O'Brien.'

The judge responded in a musical voice, which would not have been out of place on the stage. 'Be it so.'

The first witness took his place. Until he climbed the stairs to the stand, Jane did not recognise him as the footman she had seen previously. He was now in the clothing of a gentleman, with knee breeches and a dark blue jacket over a buff silk waistcoat. The spots were gone from his cheeks and his hair was fashionably tousled.

The Solicitor General, Sir Jeremiah, took over for the Attorney General, rising to question the witness. In his thin figure, Jane could imagine that a skeletal death had come to try the case.

Sir Jeremiah cleared his throat. 'State your name, for the record, your residence and your occupation.'

With a nod, the footman spoke. 'My name is John Devenny.' Jane gaped. All trace of an Irish accent had gone from his voice, though the timbre was the same. A fold of glamour surrounded the witness box, attended by a glamourist at its side, which lifted his voice to the corners of the room. 'Until recently, I was in the employ of Sir Waldo Essex as a footman. This was in my situation as agent to the Crown.'

The court gasped at that. The young men on Jane and Vincent's bench displayed varying emotions, from obvious disbelief to a droop of hopelessness. Mr O'Brien went white, but continued to stare straight ahead with his chin up.

'And what was your role for the Crown?'

'We had heard rumours of a revolt among the coldmongers. I was sent to discover and penetrate any conspiracy.'

'What did you discover?'

'That it was worse than initial reports had given us cause to believe. It had been thought that it was labour unrest, like the Luddites, but the reality was that the Irishman, Mr Alastar O'Brien, was using the coldmongers as the first wave of a plot by a group of Irish to overthrow the government. Mr O'Brien was dissatisfied due to the circumstances regarding his father's seat in Parliament, and felt it unjust that he was prevented from taking the seat on account of being a Catholic. Rather than converting, he planned to use the coldmongers, and was successful in the first phase of his plan.'

His words caused the tension in the bench of the accused to shift. One boy shot a look of pure hate at Mr O'Brien. The one nearest him shifted away, as if to distance himself. Mr Lucas turned to regard him. Jane could not see his face, but when he turned back, he wore a deep frown.

Beside Jane, Vincent shifted anxiously. He bent his head as though to address her, then checked that motion, remembering where they were. She bit her lip, wondering what he had been about to say.

Vincent's hands moved in his lap, fingers pinching the air and rolling nothing. His breath sped a little.

Jane shifted her vision to the ether.

On the stand, Devenny continued to speak of the deplorable plans of Mr O'Brien, including a plot to kill certain members of Parliament as well as assassinate the Prince Regent. Even with her vision adjusted, Jane did not at first see what Vincent was doing. For a moment, she thought he might be fidgeting out of nervousness. Only when she looked very deep indeed, blotting all trace of the corporal world from her primary sight and using her second sight exclusively, could she see the gossamer weight of the glamour he wove. It had something to do with sound, but the fold was so thin she had trouble even seeing it, much less tracing the pattern.

Then she caught sight of the twist. It was a silence sphere, like the one that they had made for the gallery.

Vincent expanded it to surround them and the two men to either side of them. Understanding his purpose, Jane let her vision return to the corporal world.

After a moment, Vincent murmured, 'They should not be able to hear us so long as we speak softly and do not allow our lips much movement. A loud tone will likely be audible, though muted.'

The young man to Jane's left started visibly, but it appeared to look like a response to Devenny's assertion that Mr O'Brien planned to arm the coldmongers with explosives.

'My belief,' Vincent continued, 'is that they plan to divide us. We know that this man is, in fact, a spy, and works for the Earl of Verbury. He is lying.'

Keeping her lips as still as possible, Jane asked, 'How are we to prove that?'

'With honesty. We will be called to testify and it is important to stress that Mr O'Brien said none of the things we are hearing attributed to him.'

'That's because he was using us, wasn't he?' the boy to Vincent's right said.

'No.' Jane watched Devenny continue to answer questions. 'They want you to think he betrayed you, so that we turn on each other. Recall that he warned you of this plot, though we did not yet know the details. Why else would he ask you not to march?'

'The lady has the right of it,' her neighbour said.

'Good. Now that you understand what they are trying, we need to let the others know.' Vincent slid his hand towards Jane. 'I am going to pass Lady Vincent the weave. It is not the usual threads you handle, but I believe you should have no difficulty in passing it down the line. Alert the others.'

Jane took care to move slowly and wrapped her fingers around the gossamer threads. In her grasp they were as slight as a dream. She passed it to the coldmonger beside her, while Vincent spun a new one to send the opposite direction. With some satisfaction, she listened to her neighbour explain to his.

She spoke only once to draw their attention to the stand. 'Listen. He wants to break the Company.'

On the stand, Devenny was nodding. 'That is how it was explained to me. By adjusting the weather, the coldmongers would interrupt trade – as has already happened – and give them greater freedom within the unrest. From that first step, they could then put their own representative in power. It was something they already had some practice at. Lord Eldon is but one example.'

Again, a shock rolled through the courtroom.

'And can the coldmongers really affect the weather so severely?'

'They deny it to anyone not in their Company, of course, but working as a group—absolutely.' Devenny turned to address the jury directly. 'In a group, they can manage a more involved glamour than alone. If you have seen a coldmonger make an ice at the grocer's, it is much the same thing, but on a larger scale.'

'Thank you. No further questions.' The prosecution returned to his seat, swinging his coat-tails out behind him.

Next arose the defence for Mr O'Brien, a dignified older

man who might have worn the powdered wig of a solicitor when they were first in fashion. Mr Leighton carried a page of notes with him to the stand and peered at them through his spectacles.

The gesture reminded Jane of Melody. When would they have a chance to converse, so she could find out the details of her discussion with the Prince Regent? If Melody was willing to tell her.

Mr Leighton tapped his notes. 'My understanding is that you suggested the march to Mr O'Brien as well as recommended that the coldmongers follow the lead of the Luddites.'

Devenny looked confused for a moment. 'We had discussions about how to best effect an uprising, yes. I am certain that he would present it as stemming from me in an effort to clear himself of misconduct.'

'Oh, no. This is not from Mr O'Brien. We have another witness . . .' He let the question of who that witness was hang in the air. 'And you encouraged him to start a riot.'

'This is a common tactic to determine how serious dissidents are. An honest man will refuse to act against the Crown when offered an opportunity to do so.'

'So you first recommended the plan, not him. Thank you. I have no further questions.'

Frowning, Devenny left the stand. The prosecution resumed his questioning by calling a shop boy who testified that Mr O'Brien frequently came in on his way to the Coldmongers' Company.

Next was an arms dealer who had sold him several rifles, though the dealer hastened to add that he had thought they were for hunting. Had he known about the conspiracy, *of course* he would never have sold them.

Clearly, the dealer had bought the prosecution's line completely. The defence, who Jane was beginning to quite adore, asked if he sold rifles to other gentlemen as well. Yes, he did. Did he sell them in multiple sets? Yes, he did. So were all of these gentlemen plotting against the Crown? No, but they were *English*. Jane did not have to turn to see Lady Stratton bridle at the insinuation.

Next they called Mr Lucas, who stoutly refused to allow the prosecution to lead him into statements that might be interpreted as being against the Crown. In spite of Jane's earlier distrust of his role in the march, he steadfastly turned every answer into a discussion on the hardships endured by coldmongers and how the poor weather was affecting their guild. The defence also gave him the opportunity to speak about the general youth of the guild's members.

Jane glanced at the jury and was dismayed to see that they were inattentive. One man was actually dozing. Clearly, if there was not scandal or dreadful injury involved, they had little interest.

Then the prosecution consulted his notes and said, 'The Crown next calls Miss Rosalind de Clare.'

Why were they calling a prostitute as a witness?

# TWENTY-FIVE

# Duelling Sensibilities

At the sound of Miss de Clare's name, Vincent's face lost all colour. He covered his mouth and bent forward as if he were about to be ill.

There was a rustle of silk as someone rose behind them. Jane put her hand on Vincent's back, smoothing the fabric between his shoulders. He had stopped breathing. So had she, waiting to see who passed her on the way to the stand.

The woman was small and well proportioned, with an abundance of golden curls pinned up under a delicate lace cap. Her dress was a simple muslin round gown, embroidered with whitework around the hem.

When she turned on the stand, the last of Jane's breath left her body. Miss de Clare looked like Melody.

She did not have Melody's exquisite complexion, but her eyes were blue and her face heart-shaped. It was a passing resemblance only, but enough to shock Jane to stillness. Was this what first made Vincent pay attention to her family? That her younger sister looked like the whore he used to frequent? Vincent turned to face Jane with nothing but despair writ on his features. Jane drew a breath and had to use every conscious thought to remember how a good wife would behave when her husband was distressed. She lowered her hand to reach for his and smiled to comfort him.

This would pass. Then she would find Lord Verbury.

The prosecution, solemn now, approached Miss de Clare. 'You made the Home Office aware of the possible uprising. Would you tell the jury how you came to be aware of it?'

'Of course.' She looked very grave and tugged at her cuffs. 'I am employed at Madame Lydia's house—'

'As a prostitute, correct?'

She coloured very prettily, though this must be something she had been called before. 'Yes. Sir David Vincent has been a client of mine since he was sixteen and, in the manner of such things, has confided in me over the years. Several months ago, he began telling me about joining a movement to overthrow the Crown. Naturally, this alarmed me. In spite of my profession, I am a loyal British citizen, so I related this to another of my clients, who was then able to take action.'

'She is lying.' Vincent did not bother with the weave to mask his voice.

The judge scowled. 'No comments from the gallery, please.'

Vincent bowed his head and clung to Jane's hand. She leaned forward and whispered in his ear, 'I know.' Whatever other fears and doubts she may have, she did not doubt that Vincent loved her and was faithful to her now.

'To assure the jury . . . are there any distinguishing features that only one who had been familiar with Sir David would be aware of?'

'He has a mole behind his right shoulder, just above the shoulder blade.' She touched the spot on her own shoulder, shifting her lace fichu out of the way to display delicate skin.

Jane bit the inside of her cheek. He did have a mole there, though it had been largely obliterated by . . .

Jane's eyes widened and she dropped Vincent's hand, hunting in her reticule for a piece of paper and a bit of pencil. As the prosecution continued to question Miss de Clare, Jane wrote a hurried note to Mr Leighton. She waved an usher over and had it delivered to him, barely paying attention to the rest of the proceedings. Mr Leighton received the note and looked round to her, with his eyebrows raised in question. Jane nodded, putting her hand on Vincent's back again. Her husband leaned into her hand, exhaling slowly with his eyes closed.

The prosecution cleared his throat. 'Thank you. As to the conspiracy, did Sir David give you any particulars?'

'His work was first to create a secret area in the musicians' gallery at Mr O'Brien's home, which they planned to use to assassinate the Prince Regent—'

She had to stop here as the courtroom sprang into a dozen different conversations, all about the same topic.

After the judge had restored order, she continued, 'Once the uprising began, he was to use military glamours to confuse the opposition.' She wet her lips and glanced towards the spectators' gallery, then nodded and continued. 'He also had come up with additional techniques to allow the coldmongers to increase their ability with cold.'

Jane glanced behind her at the gallery. Lord Verbury leaned back on his bench, managing to appear to be lounging, in spite of his starched collar and white cravat. As Miss de Clare continued her recital, he would give a little nod any time she faltered.

How dare he? How dare he do this to her husband?

Mr Leighton rose when the prosecution had finished and approached Miss de Clare slowly. 'You say Sir David has a mole on his back?'

She glanced to the gallery.

'My dear, you must answer this yourself, without being prompted.' Mr Leighton lost some of his genial manner. 'Now, answer the question for me.'

'Yes. He does.'

'I see.' The defence nodded as if he saw something larger than that. He, too, glanced at Lord Verbury. 'Are there any other features you wish to mention?'

She blushed as though a woman with a character such as hers could be embarrassed. 'Well. He has a mole somewhere else, but I do not think I ought to say where.'

The courtroom laughed and Jane clenched her jaw with barely contained fury. The urge men had to fight duels became surpassingly clear to Jane. She had never so wished to rend or tear at someone as she did now.

Frowning, Mr Leighton shook his head. 'No further questions.'

The last witness called by the prosecution was Major Curry, who gave his testimony with dead solemnity. He stared straight ahead and recited the times and positions of the guard as well as confirming that he had seen Mr O'Brien there. 'He was particularly discernible because of his red horse and hair.'

When the defence got up, Mr Leighton asked only a single question. 'The average age of the marchers was only sixteen, and some were no more than ten years old. Do you think they were a clear danger to the Crown?'

Major Curry's composure broke, then, and he had to stare at the floor for some moments. 'No, sir, I do not.'

'That will be all.' He stood back to let Major Curry return to his seat and then yielded the floor to the prosecution.

The Attorney General rose to deliver his closing argument, after which Mr Leighton would have his turn to call witnesses to the stand for the defence. Jane braced herself for a harsh description of the events as he smoothed the stiff white cloth of his winged collar.

'Your honour, members of the jury, gentlemen. It is, thankfully, a rare occurrence to be called upon to try a case of treason that came so close to succeeding. We have heard from Mr Devenny, the Crown's agent, about the plan that these cold-mongers had embarked upon at the instigation of the Irishman, Alastar O'Brien. That they have already succeeded in disrupting our weather and causing an upset in trade is bad enough, but it is even worse to learn that if this conspiracy had continued, they would have made an attempt upon the Prince Regent and members of Parliament, with the ultimate goal of overthrowing the government entirely.'

A murmur of consternation went through the court at this, with more than one insult hurled at Mr O'Brien. The Attorney General paused, as though to let the jury hear the outrage the crowd felt. He tucked his hands into his waistcoat and continued his oration. He repeated key points made by the witnesses and assembled a damning wall of evidence. Even Jane, who knew better, found herself wondering if the coldmongers had a larger scheme in mind when they marched. She knew that they did not, but his argument still raised the thought that perhaps she *ought* to question the events.

Lowering the pitch of his voice to a dangerous rumble, the Attorney General concluded his oration. 'Can there be any doubt based on the testimonies that you have heard today that guilt most foul stains the hands of the men brought before you? And I do say "men". The defence will try to have you believe that these are mere boys, incapable of the treachery for which they stand accused. I ask you only to consider the unseasonably late snows. When you add to that unmistakable evidence such as the testimony of the arms purchase, the presence of a secret area in O'Brien's home, and the march upon the Tower of London, I believe that you have no choice but to render your verdict "guilty".'

He stalked to his seat, satisfaction writ large upon his face at the ugly tenor of the crowd. Jane shuddered anew at what lay in store for them all. Mr Leighton rose to address the judge. 'If it pleases your lordships, I would like to begin by calling Sir David Vincent.'

'So be it.'

Exhaling slowly, Vincent wiped his palms on his trousers as he stood. Jane pressed her hand against his arm to encourage him. He compressed his lips in his small private smile, bowing his head as he passed her.

In answer to the request that he state his name and occupation, Vincent replied, 'I am Sir David Vincent. I am a glamourist who was employed by Lord Stratton, Mr O'Brien's father, to create a glamural in their ballroom, with my wife, Lady Vincent.' He paused, wetting his lips. His gaze darted to where Lord Verbury sat, then away as if burned. 'We are both agents of the Crown, as the Prince Regent, himself, testifies in this letter.'

He handed it to the defence, who seemed more than a little relieved that the paper really existed. Again, the courtroom murmured in astonishment. Mrs Ellsworth's voice carried clearly over the top of the rest. 'There! I told you he was an honourable man! An agent of the Crown!'

Looking it over, the defence passed it, in turn, to the judge, who then read it to the jury, confirming that Vincent and Jane were trusted confidants of the Crown and cleared of any charges against them.

Mr Leighton turned to the jury. 'You have heard that Sir David is trusted by the Crown, but this prosecution seeks to sully Sir David's character. They have brought up some subjects that would under normal circumstances be let alone.'

The Solicitor General stood. 'Objection, sir. This is an argument, not a question.'

The judge nodded. 'Quite right. Please confine yourself to questioning the witnesses, Mr Leighton.'

The barrister bowed. 'Pardon, your honour. Since the purpose of this trial is to consider Mr O'Brien's guilt or innocence, Sir David's testimony is an important part of this. I merely wanted to set the stage for the jury so that they understood the context in which I asked Sir David these questions.' He turned back to Vincent. 'Now then, sir. What is your relation to Miss de Clare?'

'I first visited her when I was sixteen. Though I am ashamed to admit it, I continued to patronise her services until I was twenty and left for university.'

'You have not seen her since?'

'No.' Vincent looked at Jane and spoke as if she were the only one in the room. 'Absolutely not.'

The defence consulted the note that Jane sent him and grimaced. 'Sir David, would you oblige me by removing your shirt?'

Clenching his jaw, Vincent stood and removed his jacket. As he did so, the defence again turned to the audience. 'Ladies, I apologise for this indecorous exercise. The more sensitive of you may wish to depart.'

No one moved. Indeed, most of the ladies leaned forward with eager eyes as Vincent's waistcoat and shirt came off.

The defence asked, 'Would you show us your back?'

Vincent turned and showed the mass of scars crossing his back. Some of the wheals were still an angry red tone. It had been a long time since Jane had seen them by the light of day. She had not realised, until this moment, that Vincent had developed the habit of dressing with his back away from her.

Mr Leighton appeared stricken by the severity of Vincent's scarring, but he composed himself quickly and leaned in. 'The mole that Miss de Clare said you possessed was . . . where? The right shoulder, I believe.' He pointed to the skin there, where only a corner of brown showed through the scars, and spoke to the jury. 'It is barely visible. I find it interesting that Miss de Clare did not mention the scars he bears. Would they not merit some comment?'

Looking away from her husband, Jane watched the jury. All of them were awake now, staring fixedly at Vincent's back. For the first time she saw doubt and some sympathy in their faces. Mr Leighton continued to study Vincent. 'Will you tell the jury how you acquired these?'

'I was flogged by French soldiers while in Binche prior to the Battle of Quatre Bras.' He still faced the wall, but his voice was strong as the court glamourist magnified the sound.

'How long did this go on?'

Every time he inhaled to speak, the scars stretched and shifted. 'Nearly a fortnight.'

'And why?'

Vincent looked over his shoulder, pursing his lips. 'I was in possession of a state secret, which the Duke of Wellington asked me not to disclose.'

'Did you disclose it?'

'No.'

'Thank you. You may resume your clothing.' Before moving on to other questions, he waited for Vincent to pull on his clothes, though her husband left his cravat undone. 'You marched with the coldmongers, did you not?'

'I did.' Vincent faced the front with admirable calm. The set of his shoulders betrayed his tension to Jane, but she thought that others would attribute his perfect posture to good breeding. Lord Verbury might be on the verge of reaping that which he had sown.

'And why did you choose to do that, rather than advising the government of the danger that the prosecution asserts was present?'

'First, the march was composed largely of boys under eighteen, so there seemed little danger from the marchers. Second, I assisted Mr O'Brien in attempting to stop the march, after recognising that the coldmongers had been deceived as part of a bid to displace Lord Eldon from the Lord Chancellor position. The coldmongers were used, but not by Mr O'Brien.'

If Jane thought that the courtroom had been disordered before, this new recital overturned that.

'And so you believe Mr O'Brien to be innocent?'

'Yes. Completely. I believe that Mr Devenny duped him into holding a march, and has contrived the entire event.'

'As part of a conspiracy? By whom?'

She could not hear Vincent's small whine of protest, but she could see it as he held his breath, lips pressed close together. The muscles in his jaw stood out. Wetting his lips, Vincent blew out his breath in a long stream. He swallowed and looked to the gallery. 'The Earl of Verbury.' His face had become quite pale. 'He is widely known to seek the Lord Chancellor seat, and turned Mr Devenny to his own purposes.'

'I have no further questions. Sir David, I thank you for your service to England during the war.'

Jane wanted to jump to her feet with applause, but barely managed to restrain herself.

In part because she was quite certain that Lord Verbury had additional plans involving her husband and Mr O'Brien. Likely her as well.

As the defence yielded the floor, the prosecution swept up, surveying Vincent with something like disdain. 'You seem to be stating that Mr O'Brien is not guilty of conspiring against the Crown because someone else is conspiring to make him appear to be conspiring. A complicated knot. Have you proof of this vast conspiracy?'

'You have had two witnesses who had little to say that was true. The defence, I believe, has discredited Miss de Clare's testimony. We may continue then by discussing Mr Devenny's assertion that the coldmongers are capable of altering the weather. This is decidedly false. It is unequivocally impossible.'

'You are a glamourist. We have Mr Devenny's testimony that this is an ability that coldmongers hide. Might not a glamourist also have a stake in this secret?'

'To what purpose? The ability to make rain would be invaluable in a drought, yet no one does. No one makes ice in the summer. It cannot be done.' Speaking about glamour relaxed Vincent some, and his little sneer of disdain became apparent as if he were thinking – which he probably was – that only a fool would believe such patent absurdity.

'Would you really have the jury believe that snow in May is

natural? What can account for it, or the snow still on the hills in June, if not the coldmongers?'

'Sometimes the weather is simply bad. One does not always need to look for a supernatural explanation. Nature does quite enough on its own. Volcanoes, for instance.' Vincent shrugged. 'The ash they expel can cause cooling.'

'I do not know if you are aware of this, but there are no volcanoes in Britain.' The prosecution offered his own sneer, as if saying that only a fool would believe Vincent. Jane wanted to shake the man. The weather was simply bad fortune, yet the prosecution made it out to be man's fault. 'And yet you also assisted Mr O'Brien in creating a secret area in the musicians' loft – an area that we have already heard testified was intended to allow an assassin to fire, unobserved, on the Prince Regent. One might suppose by this that you have an interest in proving Mr O'Brien's innocence, since your own case is tied directly to his.'

'If I were presently being charged with anything, that might be true.' Vincent bowed his head. 'I am not, however, as the Prince Regent's letter makes clear. The area in Mr O'Brien's musicians' loft is intended to allow musicians to tune without requiring them to leave the gallery. Nothing more.'

'Yes. Testimony from an irreproachable character.' The prosecution referred to his notes. 'And you are also Lord Verbury's son, are you not?'

Vincent's gaze narrowed and he nodded, slowly. 'Although his lordship disowned me when I pursued a career in glamour.'

The prosecution merely smiled at that. Jane suddenly remembered Lord Verbury's own version, which he had presented to Admiral Brightmore. Had she told Vincent about that? She knew, however, with dread certainty, that Lord Verbury would have witnesses prepared to swear that he doted on his son.

'You have reason, then, to dislike your father.' The prosecution turned to the jury. 'Is it any wonder the Earl cast him off, however unwillingly, so that this . . . man did not sweep the rest of his family into his depravity? Even now he continues his contemptible behaviour, in the guise of being an "agent to the Crown" and testifying on behalf of a known conspirator. Oh yes, a man of irreproachable character.' He gestured to Miss de Clare. 'Even if her more recent testimony is in question, you do not deny that you visited her in your youth.'

'My father took me to her. As a birthday present. I was sixteen.'

'In fact, your father was *forced* to take you to a prostitute because, given your interest in the womanly art of glamour, he naturally thought you an effeminate.' He paused and then looked at Jane. 'You have no children, still.'

Jane clenched her jaw, seeing what he was trying to do. By assassinating Vincent's character, he would render all of his testimony suspect.

'My wife miscarried while we were on the Continent, carrying out the Crown's business at the Battle of Quatre Bras.'

'Yes . . . your *wife*, who dresses like a man, as she did the night of the Coldmongers' Uprising. A model of femininity. Anyone need only look at her to see exactly how "feminine" she is.'

'That is quite enough.' Vincent had flushed with anger and his voice was dangerously low. To Jane, his fury was apparent, but she was not sure if another would see it so, or see his heightened colour as a sign of embarrassment. 'You may condemn my character all you like, but you may not speak so of my wife.'

'As you say, that is enough, Sir David,' the prosecution drawled. 'No further questions.'

Vincent stood for a moment longer in the witness stand, as though he wanted to continue to speak. Jaw clenching, he stepped down and returned to the box. Vincent sat next to Jane with an audible sigh. He reached for her hand and clenched it. Through her grasp, she tried to submit all the love and approbation she felt for him. The heat of his palm gave some indication of the duress he had been under. When they were alone, Jane would do all she could to soothe him.

'The court calls Lady Vincent to the stand.'

Vincent pressed her hand as she stood. Jane struggled to draw steady breath as she went to the stand. She had nothing to fear and was already cleared of wrong by the Prince Regent. The defence took his spot and smiled amiably at Jane, as though they were alone in the room. 'I understand that you were instrumental in your husband's escape from Napoleon, so I judge you to be a woman of quick understanding and discernment. Thus I hope you can tell us your opinion of Mr O'Brien's character?'

Jane could feel Mr O'Brien's gaze on her back. She kept her face forward, though she longed to say this directly to him. 'Mr O'Brien is a man of integrity. I believe he was misled by Mr Devenny.' She would have known this all along, if she had not been blinded by her own prejudices.

'In what way was he misled?'

'I overheard Mr Devenny speaking to him and encouraging him to march. It was quite clear that the idea did not originate with Mr O'Brien.' That caused some surprise in the courtroom. Jane continued, 'This is why we at first thought we could stop the march, since it had been intended as an entirely peaceful gathering. Indeed, if you consider disinterested accounts of the coldmongers' passage through London, it consisted entirely of marching and singing. The only incidents of violence I witnessed were committed *against* the coldmongers. They only wished for their concerns to be heard, as is the right of every British citizen.'

'Can you tell the jury where and when you overheard this?'

'In the ballroom at Stratton House, the afternoon prior to the march. Mr Devenny had come expressly to speak to Mr O'Brien about it.' She then repeated their conversation for the jury to the best of her recollection.

'And they were comfortable having this discussion with you present?'

'I was hidden by glamour, and Mr O'Brien had reason to believe that my husband and I were not in the building.'

From there Mr Leighton asked her simple questions to establish the course of events and her own motives for participation. In spite of his genial manner, Jane was shaking by the time he yielded the floor to the prosecution. Jane eyed the Solicitor General with disquiet. She had no doubts that Lord Verbury – who had clearly prompted the prosecution, if not outright purchased him – would do everything in his power to degrade her and destroy her reputation.

The prosecution's first question did not disappoint her. 'I wonder if you could explain to the jury why a "lady" such as yourself wore trousers to the march.'

'I first wore them out of necessity—'

'Ah—*first* out of necessity, and then you found that men's clothing suited you better?'

'No. My husband—'

'Your husband prefers you in masculine dress.'

Jane blushed, remembering that Vincent did, in fact, like her in trousers. 'No. Perhaps *you* prefer ladies attired thus?'

The courtroom tittered. The prosecution frowned. 'Please, only answer the questions asked.'

Oh, they were going to play this game, were they? Fortunately, she had recent practice in verbal sparring through the offices of Lord Verbury. Jane stared at him with a placid expression and waited. 'By all means, ask me a question.'

The door at the back of the courtroom opened and Melody slipped in, but paused when she saw Jane on the witness stand. Jane could not tell by her countenance if her errand for Vincent had succeeded. She relaxed somewhat as Melody gave a folded paper to one of the ushers, who in turn passed it to the defence.

Watching this exchange, Jane almost missed the prosecution's question. Clearing her throat, she answered, 'I recognised Mr Devenny because I had seen him on several other occasions and noted his livery as that of Lord Verbury's daughter.'

'I find it interesting that you describe Mr O'Brien as a man of integrity with one breath, and with the next speak of overhearing a plot, which you did not report.'

'At the time we still thought it possible to stop the march peaceably, while Mr Devenny thought that firing on children was more appropriate.'

'Please, madam. And yet, not only did the march proceed, but you joined it. In men's dress.'

'We suspected that Lord Verbury had arranged for the march to be fired upon, so—'

'This is the second time you have attempted to clear your associate's name by implicating your husband's father. Have you any proof of Lord Verbury's involvement?'

Jane faltered. Beyond a certainty of his character, did they have any tangible proof? 'His desire to displace Lord Eldon is well known.'

'As is your husband's dislike of his father. Neither of you can offer any proof of this supposed conspiracy beyond your own testimony, which is hardly impartial. Have you not, in fact, deceived the Crown and are you not thoroughly involved in this plot and seek only to save your own skin?' He swept away, not even troubling to let her answer the speech that he had thinly veiled as a question.

'No.'

After an awkward moment, the judge said, 'You may step down.'

Jane's knees shook as she walked down the steps of the witness stand. Standing at the bar, Mr O'Brien's face had softened with such gratitude that Jane had to look away in embarrassment. She should have discovered his good character earlier. As she returned to the witness box, Jane kept her head up with difficulty as spectators openly stared at her lower region as though imagining her in trousers. Jane reached her seat and sank into it. Vincent slipped his hand into hers as she sighed with relief.

The defence rose, holding the paper that Melody had given him, and addressed the jury. 'I have another witness for your consideration.'

Jane squeezed Vincent's hand. She had hoped that Lady Penelope was not so much her father's creature as to wish anyone dead. After her testimony that Lord Verbury had recommended engaging John Devenny, surely the jury would be able to see how suspect his testimony was.

The defence looked to the back of the room. 'The court calls Lady Verbury.'

Vincent gasped as though he had been struck. As one, he and Jane turned to look to the door of the room. Melody had been sent to speak to Lady Penelope. His mother's presence was entirely unlooked for. And yet, a heavily veiled woman entered the room, walking to the stand without looking to the left or right. Jane glanced over her shoulder at Lord Verbury, who sat, positively rigid. A vein stood out on his forehead, pulsing with rage as his wife took her oath with the same placid voice, which she offered in every conversation.

Jane turned back to the front as the defence began his questions. Lady Verbury had removed her veils and was staring at a spot on the far wall. She stated, quite calmly, that she was the wife of Lord Verbury and the mother of Sir David Vincent. Through all of this, Vincent stared at her with his mouth slightly agape.

It shocked Jane that a woman who lived in such fear would arrive to testify against her husband. This certainly answered the question of whether his mother had said that she loved Vincent as an instrument of his father or of her own accord.

After Lady Verbury established who she was for the jury, the defence asked, 'And you have testimony you wish to provide the court?'

'I do.' From her cloak, she withdrew a parcel of letters and an account book. The papers rattled against one another with the trembling of her hands. Turning the letters over, she passed them to the defence. 'The Earl of Verbury paid John Devenny to create a disturbance that he could use to discredit Lord Eldon. Due to his fastidious nature, I believe you will find that to be well documented here. There is also a payment, above his usual, to Miss de Clare, who I believe is also his creature.'

Exclamations filled the room. Audience members shouted

their surprise. A woman began sobbing and laughing in the gallery. The judge pounded his gavel, crying for order, but it was some minutes before anyone was quiet enough to continue. Lady Verbury sat with the same fixed composure, staring at the same spot on the wall with the same placid smile.

The defence turned to the judge and handed him the papers. 'I trust, in light of what we have heard today, and the papers I herewith present to the court, that the jury will find my client innocent of charges against him, as well as those who marched with him.'

The judge frowned over the papers. 'These do look . . . good heavens.' He shook his head. 'What possessed you to bring these out today, madam?'

Lady Verbury's smile did not falter. Jane began to recognise that this was the face she wore when distressed. 'My husband has long been very particular about how our household is run, including the raising of our children. I often did not approve, but learned early in our marriage that disagreement was . . . not tolerated.' Her smile faded and she looked down for the first time, turning towards Vincent. 'I have never protected my children from him. I find, today, that there are limits. I regret that I did not reach those sooner, but . . . until his actions endangered the life of my youngest son, I did not have the courage to come forth.'

'Well . . .' The judge shook his head again. 'Does the prosecution have any questions for the witness?'

Looking shaken for the first time, the prosecution stood and glanced back to the gallery. His face paled further.

Lord Verbury's seat was empty.

# TWENTY-SIX

# A Murmur of Alliance

With the disappearance of his patron, the prosecution faltered and granted that the Crown may have been misled in the testimony of their key witnesses. He spent some time looking at the papers Lady Verbury brought, then declined his opportunity to cross-examine her.

The defence turned to the jury. 'I had planned to present you with more witnesses, and to allow you to hear from Mr O'Brien himself, but in the light of Lady Verbury's testimony, I will not waste your time in tedious reconstruction of details. Allow me to only recall for you these items. From Sir David Vincent, we have the testimony of a gentleman – a war hero, if I may be so bold – who was cruelly beaten by the French, yet held his tongue. You are being asked by the prosecution to believe that his character is unsteady – that such a man, who clearly loves his country enough to undergo the most reprehensible torture, could then return to his country and conspire to overthrow it. I submit to you instead that his testimony is irreproachable. Sir David's statements alone should be enough to clear the name of the accused. We have, however, other witnesses who can also testify to Mr O'Brien's innocence.

'Lady Verbury, who is not required to testify against her

husband, was so appalled by his actions that she came of her own accord to speak against him. But you need not rely on her testimony alone, because she brings with her divers papers in Lord Verbury's own hand, which delineate his plan in great detail. These pages include payments to Mr Devenny and Miss de Clare.

'The character assassination that the prosecution has attempted is decidedly false. Mr O'Brien should not be on trial here. Indeed, none of the coldmongers should. The charges against Mr O'Brien and the coldmongers are so clearly fabricated that your only course is to return a vote of "not guilty".'

The judge continued through the forms and summed up the arguments for the jury, but even before they clustered for deliberation, it was clear what verdict he wished them to return. After only eight minutes, the jury delivered a resounding 'not guilty'.

The courtroom burst into shouts of good cheer, making it clear how many friends and supporters Mr O'Brien had. That worthy gentleman succumbed to tears of relief, which no one begrudged him. Lady Stratton ran down from the spectators' gallery. She embraced her son, sobbing and laughing at the same time.

The coldmongers leaped about with the exuberance that only the very young can show. They ran forward and lifted Mr O'Brien into the air, raising another cheer from the gallery.

Jane leaned into Vincent, embracing him. He was shaking violently. She looked at him in alarm.

'They are going to kill him,' he whispered at the floor.

'No.' Lady Verbury took a seat next to them, clearly understanding which 'him' Vincent meant. 'Your father will be on a ship to his West Indies estates by the time they organise enough to seek his arrest.'

Vincent stared at her. His mouth opened but no words came. Jane gave voice to what she thought he must be trying to ask. 'How did you come to be here?'

'Miss Ellsworth . . .' Lady Verbury looked down, frowning. Jane had never seen her with anything but a placid smile. The frown suited her. Lady Verbury sighed and continued. 'She came to ask Penelope to testify while I was visiting. When my daughter refused to participate—when she laughed . . .' Lady Verbury stopped and pressed her fingers to the bridge of her nose. 'I have made many mistakes, but my path was never clearer than in that moment. She thought it was a game.'

Vincent reached across Jane and took his mother's hand. 'Thank you.'

'Jane! Sir David! Oh! I am so relieved.' Mrs Ellsworth flung herself down the aisle with Mr Ellsworth close behind. 'I knew they were lying, but—' She stopped, recognising with whom they sat.

Lady Verbury smiled at Jane – a genuine smile with a hint of fear behind it, not the placid mask she had worn before. 'Would you do me the honour of introducing me to your parents?'

Jane did, and gladly. Mrs Ellsworth was a little overcome to be introduced to an actual Countess, which kept her from being too exuberant. Mr Ellsworth gravely thanked her for her assistance in the trial.

She waved that away. 'The credit belongs to your daughter, Miss Ellsworth.'

At that, Mr Ellsworth frowned, looking about. 'Where *is* Melody? She has been absent a great deal these past few days.'

Jane turned and spotted her sister. She stood with Mr O'Brien, embracing him in the full view of the public. His parents stood next to them, beaming. An answering smile spread across Jane's own face. 'I believe . . . I believe that Melody is engaged.'

When two young people are in love and well matched, it would be foolish parents indeed who stood in the way of their marriage. Mr Ellsworth had already come to London determined to give his permission to Mr O'Brien to address Melody, and nothing he saw of the young man's character made him less inclined to see the pairing with anything other than delight.

Mrs Ellsworth, when she realised that Melody would have a London wedding, with all the consequence that marrying the heir to a Baron could bring, fell with equal delight into planning the wedding. Two weddings, to be exact, for the law required Melody and Alastar to be wed by an Anglican priest before they could proceed to the Roman Catholic ceremony. By necessity, they were to be married by Special Licence, which would give the happy couple the ability to wed in the family's chapel. Mrs Ellsworth could not have been more pleased by having a Special Licence, as it was favoured by the most fashionable set. She and Melody went to all the best dressmakers and – with Lady Verbury's assistance – procured a trousseau that would not have shamed Princess Charlotte.

As for Jane and Vincent, they returned to the Strattons' employment, but this time to ornament their chapel. When it came down to it, Vincent would indeed perform glamour for a wedding, if asked with sufficient sweetness by his wife. The activity was welcome to them both, and not simply for the pleasure of helping prepare for a joyous occasion. The distraction came at a time when they both sorely needed it.

Vincent had slept poorly since the trial. More than once, Jane had woken to find him shuddering in the throes of a nightmare. She rubbed his back to awake him, feeling his nightshirt slide over his scars. Jane curled up against him, pulling him close to her.

His breathing eased and Vincent intertwined his fingers in hers. 'I am sorry I woke you.'

She kissed his neck, tasting the salt on his skin. 'I wish I could do something for you.'

'Oh, Muse . . .' He lifted her hand to his lips and kissed the tips of her fingers. 'You do.'

'The same nightmare?'

She heard, more than saw, his head slide across the pillow in a nod. 'He should be in Antigua by now.'

As Lady Verbury predicted, the Earl had taken ship to visit his estates in the West Indies. John Devenny sat in prison awaiting trial for treason, abandoned by the Earl. He professed, loudly, that Lord Verbury had told him that he was working for the good of the Crown. Vincent's eldest brother was working with legal counsel to preserve the family seat in the event that the Earl should be found guilty of treason. Jane dreaded that trial when it came about.

She slipped her hand free of Vincent's and rubbed his brow, trying to ease the lines that creased it. He grunted in satisfaction and nestled closer. 'That feels good.'

'I surmised as much by your grunt.'

'I did not grunt.'

'Yes, you did.'

Vincent rolled onto his back. 'I do not grunt.'

Laughing, Jane kissed his cheek. 'My dear, when you are pleased, you grunt like a bear, and when you are upset, you whine.'

'No!'

Jane found a spot most likely to provoke a response and caressed him there. Vincent grunted with pleasure and then laughed. He swept her into his arms, still laughing, and pulled her on top of him. She giggled as well, covering his face in kisses between chuckles.

He made his small satisfied noise again, and his laughter redoubled. 'Oh, lord. I do.'

'I told you.'

They spent some time with Jane proving this assertion in a variety of ways, and Vincent being forced to acknowledge that it was true. This release of laughter and high spirits proved better at restoring his steadiness of mind than any fold of glamour could.

When they fell back among the pillows at last, Vincent wrapped Jane in his arms. Her head rested on his shoulder and she traced a finger among the fine hairs on his chest.

He kissed her on the forehead. 'And I whine? Truly?'

She nodded. 'You hold your breath first. It is only when you need to say something you do not wish to say.'

'But a whine?'

'It is a small one. Like this.' She imitated the high little keen and provoked a new round of laughter from Vincent.

'No, no. I do not believe for an instant that I make so silly a sound.' He kissed her cheek. 'You shall have to prove it.'

'By making you say something you do not wish to say?' Jane let her hand drift lower. 'That sounds unpleasant.'

'But you have made me curious.' He barely silenced a grunt

by turning it into a moan. 'Since your first claim is clearly true, I want to hear this whine.'

Jane stopped moving and rested her hand on his chest again. There was one question that had disturbed her, but she had not been able to bring herself to ask. 'When you first came to Long Parkmead . . . did Melody remind you of Miss de Clare?'

Vincent held his breath and a little whine of protest escaped him. Jane nudged him in the ribs. 'There. Do you hear it?'

He gave a half-laugh. 'I do.' Pulling her closer still, Vincent rolled onto his side and buried his face in her neck. 'I—yes, she did.'

Jane held him, running her hands over his back, tracing the lines drawn there and knowing that other scars went deeper still. A bead of moisture dropped onto her neck and rolled down her skin. Jane kissed Vincent's forehead. His breath hitched and caught as he struggled with his sensibilities in her embrace.

Voice hoarse and hot against her skin, he whispered, 'But you do not. You are unique and wonderful and—and a thousand other hackneyed things. You are my Muse.'

Jane could hardly breathe for the force of her emotions. 'And you are mine.'

The result of that moment of distress was that the Vincents spent that night, and others, proving the strength of their love to each other. They repeated it in their actions, and in the art that they wove as they worked glamour side by side.

No glamural could have had more love displayed in it than the one that they wove for the wedding of Miss Ellsworth and Mr O'Brien. The chapel had been done over in a picturesque motif with a few laurel trees masking the pillars that supported the high ceiling. The ceiling itself was where the chief of their effort went. They made it vanish behind layers of glamour so that, in spite of the continuing rain outside, Melody and Alastar would be married under an unclouded blue sky.

At the back of the chapel, Melody stood next to Jane, shifting her weight from foot to foot. In a dress of fine white muslin, with a small lace-trimmed cap to match, she was radiant, with such a glow to her complexion that Jane almost felt they had not needed any glamour at all. Almost.

Jane whispered to her sister, 'Do not forget to breathe.'

With no sign of having heard, Melody turned to her. 'Should I take my spectacles off?'

'Will you be able to see him clearly if you do?' Jane stood in front of her to show where the bridegroom would stand. 'He will be about this far.'

Melody pulled the spectacles down her nose and shook her head.

'Then you should wear them.' Jane straightened her sister's primrose silk shawl to show off the embossed white satin flowers. 'You will want to remember this, and the day will be enough of a haze as it is.'

'La! Jane . . . I am so nervous.' She peered towards the front of the chapel. 'Is he there? He is. Oh—oh, he is so handsome. Are you certain I should wear the spectacles? Perhaps I should take them off.'

'He wears them as well. Do you love him any less because of that?'

Melody coloured and her cheeks curved into a deep smile. She shook her head. 'He is all that I could wish for.'

Jane's eyes pricked with tears, which made her grateful for the handkerchief she had tucked in her sleeve.

The Catholic service was strange to Jane, but she found that, aside from an abundance of Latin, the wedding was very much like other weddings. She felt a greater desire to weep than at others, but that could be attributed to seeing her sister marry a man that she truly esteemed. The small band of true friends who witnessed the ceremony were equally confident that their wishes and hopes would be fully answered in the perfect happiness of the union.

Jane and Vincent had been married in a small private ceremony. This one had all the pomp that Jane's mother had regretted theirs as wanting. Mrs Ellsworth would have had even more parade and spectacle were she allowed, but the taste of the artists conquered that tendency.

From time to time, Jane looked across to Vincent, whom Mr O'Brien had invited to stand up with him. She met Vincent's eye as the ceremony came to a close and they both pulled a slip-knot, releasing a flight of peacocks and white doves overhead.

Vincent winked at Jane. His fingers moved at his side, and a single word sounded in her ear alone, carried by glamour. 'Muse.'

In spite of her earlier fears, Jane was deeply satisfied to see her sister happily married and with a muse of her own.

# Author's Afterword

I should first acknowledge my husband, Rob, upon whom certain aspects of Vincent are very heavily modelled. He is quite literally my Muse for this character. He is also endlessly patient as this is the second book in this series that I finished in the midst of a cross-country move, this time from Portland to Chicago. I am working on the fourth book, *Valour and Vanity*, at the moment and am happy to report that we are not currently moving.

As with any book, there are people who helped this story be what it is. Mark Pallis, the BBC historical consultant for *Garrow's Law*, vetted my legal scenes. British law and American law are vastly different, and even more so when you hark back to 1816. He was amazing and there are copies of his notes on my website, along with the original scene, if you are interested in that sort of geekery.

Paul Cornell helped me translate William from the Dick Van Dyke dialect into something appropriate for a Londoner.

Laura Plett, an English Country dance caller, helped me sort out the dance movements for the Almack's scene. She also answered my questions about the waltz, which was different in the Regency than in our modern era.

Mark Beswick, archive information officer at the Met Office

National Meteorological Archive in the United Kingdom, got me a scan of meteorological records for 1816 in London. To the best of my knowledge, the days that I have it snowing are days when it actually snowed.

John Scalzi helped me sort out how to handle the fact that my readers all thought the bad weather was caused by magic instead of a volcano.

Mary Anne Mohanraj offered excellent advice on my handling of Miss Godwin.

The Multnomah County Library reference librarians continue to be an invaluable resource for all the myriad things that I cannot find on my own. Librarians rule the world.

Jodi Eichelberger helped me with adapting the hymn "Twas in the Winter Cold' to "Twas in the Summer Warm'. The original hymn was written in 1873, so I could not use it, but desperately wanted to.

As always, thanks to the ladies of the Oregon Regency Society (ORS), who continue to provide inspiration and support as I work on these books. Part of the trial scene was written at an ORS retreat in costume and with an actual quill. While the way my writing rhythms changed were fascinating, I was very happy to return to my computer. In particular, I need to thank Stephanie Johansen, Charlotte Cunningham, Nora Azvedo, Agnes Gawne, Lauren Marks and Angel Bruce.

Of course, without my editor, Liz Gorinsky, this book would be messier and not as interesting. She does a wonderful job of helping me craft story. Likewise, my agent, Jennifer Jackson, does more than just sell books and manage contracts, she also helps me sort out where I want the story to go while I'm still in the planning stages. Michael Curry, for whom Major Curry is named, is one of my first readers and provides invaluable advice.

I also have a host of alpha readers, who get the raw draft of the story and tell me how it is playing. Thanks to: Karin Abel, Hanna Brady, Sharat Buddhavarapu, Laura Christensen, John Devenny (yes, that's where the name comes from), Peter Ellis, Grant Gardner, Randall Haverinen, Brent Longstaff, Maggie, Donna McLaughlin, Ian Miller, Nina Niskanen, Kurt Pankau, Putergeekguy, Julia Rios, Dallan Simper, Leonard Suskin and Natalie Wolanski. I also had a number of people who listened to me read the whole darn thing out loud. In particular I want to thank Annalee Flower Horne, Fric Hayoz, John DeLong and Peter Ellis, who not only listened, but provided useful feedback.

And I should close with thanks to Miss Austen, from whom I stole three sentences and the essential character arc of *Emma*.

# A Note on History

1816 was known, historically, as 'The Year Without a Summer'. In 1815, the volcano Tambora blew up in the East Indies. This was the largest volcanic explosion in recorded history. That said, very little about this explosion was known in London in 1816. I cheat a little in the book, because its connection to the weather was not understood until 1819. The blanket of ash that it kicked out was so large that 1816 was cooler than usual, to the point that Washington, D.C., had snow in July. There was widespread famine because of crop failure, combined with the return of all the soldiers from the Napoleonic wars, which increased unemployment.

This was at a time of great social upheaval, as the industrial revolution was beginning. The Luddites were a real movement that began to protest the introduction of automated looms. Prior to this, cloth was woven by individuals at home, for a factory. The introduction of the looms reduced the demand for this labour. It also meant that workers were now employed outside the home, which suddenly caused a need for childcare. For this and other reasons, the looms were seen as a disruption of lifestyle and weavers began a series of riots. They were eventually stopped when seventeen of the protesters were put on trial in 1813 and the key members were hanged.

I based the coldmongers' situation on the Luddites and also on the Cato Street Conspiracy. Some of the language of the trial came directly from the Cato Street trial, and you can read the full transcript in the Old Bailey archives. One of the things that I found interesting while reading these was that there were a number of men of colour involved in the conspiracy and that in 1820 the correct term was 'men of colour'. I think of that as a modern construction. It is also easy to forget that London was a cosmopolitan city and had people of every colour in it. The media tends to depict the Regency as entirely populated by white people, and it was not.

At the time, however, the notion of 'white' excluded not only people of Anglo-African or Anglo-Indian descents but also Irish. Ireland had only recently merged with England, in 1800, to create the United Kingdom of Great Britain and Ireland. The parliaments were merged but there was a provision designed to keep Catholics from taking their seats. The Test Acts had been around since the 1600s and required members of the House of Parliament to take an oath declaring against some of the central tenets of Catholic faith. The oath read, 'I, N, do declare that I do believe that there is not any transubstantiation in the sacrament of the Lord's Supper, or in the elements of the bread and wine, at or after the consecration thereof by any person whatsoever.'

On a more pleasant note: most of the dresses that I referred to are taken from fashion plates from the period and I link to them on my website. The dress with the grey and coffee French knots is one that I made for 'research' purposes. Ahem. So much research was required for this book that I have two new dresses, and a bonnet with blue ostrich feathers.

That said, there are things that I got wrong. If you spot an error, please email me at anachronisms@maryrobinettekowal.com.

# Glamour Glossary

GLAMOUR. This basically means magic. According to the Oxford English Dictionary (OED), the original meaning was 'Magic, enchantment, spell' or 'A magical or fictitious beauty attaching to any person or object; a delusive or alluring charm'. It was strongly associated with fairies in early England. In this alternate history of the Regency, glamour is a magic that can be worked by either men or women. It allows them to create illusions of light, scent and sound. Glamour requires physical energy in much the same way running up a hill does.

GLAMURAL. A mural that is created using magic.

GLAMOURIST. A person who works with glamour.

*BOUCLÉ TORSADÉE.* This is a twisted loop of glamour that is designed to carry sound or vision depending on the frequency of the spirals. In principles it is loosely related to the Archimedes' screw. In the 1740s it was employed to create speaking tubes in some wealthy homes and those tubes took on the name of the glamour used to create them.

CHASTAIN DAMASK. A technique that allows a glamourist to create two different images in one location. The effect would be similar to our holographic cards that show first one image, then anothers depending on the angle at which it is viewed. Invented by M. Chastain in 1814, he originally called this technique a 'jacquard' after the new looms invented by M. Jacquard in 1801. The technique was renamed by Mrs Vincent as a Chastain Damask in honour of its creator.

ETHER. Where the magic comes from. Early physicists believed that the world was broken into elements with ether being the highest element. Although this theory is discredited now, the original definition meant: 'A substance of great elasticity and subtlety, formerly believed to permeate the whole of planetary and stellar space, not only filling the interplanetary spaces, but also the interstices between the particles of air and other matter on the earth; the medium through which the waves of light are propagated. Formerly also thought to be the medium through which radio waves and electromagnetic radiations generally are propagated' (OED). Today you'll more commonly see it as the root of 'ethereal', and its meaning is similar.

FOLDS. The bits of magic pulled out of the ether. Because this is a woman's art, the metaphors to describe it reflect other womanly arts, such as the textiles.

LOINTAINE VISION. French for 'distance seeing'. It is a tube of glamour that allows one to see things at a distance. The threads must be constantly managed or the image becomes static.

OMBRÉ. A fold of glamour that shades from one colour to another over its length. This technique was later emulated in textile by dip-dying.

NŒUD MARIN. A robust knot used for tying glamour threads. This was originally used by sailors for joining two lines, but adapted by glamourists for similar purposes. In English, this is known as a Carrick Bend.

*PETITE RÉPÉTITION.* French for 'small repetition'. This is a way of having a fold of glamour repeat itself in what we would now call a fractal pattern. These occur in nature in the patterns of fern fronds and pinecones.

*SPHÈRE OBSCURCIE.* French for 'invisible bubble'. It is literally a bubble of magic to make the person inside it invisible.